Sacrificial Lambs

CHUCK HANSEN

Conclaire Press

ALSO BY CHUCK HANSEN

Nose-Sucker Thingees, Weeds Whacking Back & Cats in the Bathtub:
Does Life Get Any Better?

A Dad's Work is Never Clear:
Tales of Love, Marriage, Parenting and Ice Cream. Lots of Ice Cream.

Build Your Castles in the Air: Thoreau's Inspiring Advice for Success
in Business (and Life) in the 21st Century

Thank you Stacy

ONE

The church sanctuary exploded in panic.

Worshipers, screaming and pushing, drove for the doors like runners at Pamplona, carrying along in the crush anyone too young, slow or infirm to keep up. Babies cried, children called for their parents, and the elderly fought to hold on against the current. A local news cameraman and his gear knocked over in the rushing wave of freaked out humanity, and he fought to get himself and his equipment out in one piece. The house of worship vomited its contents through every doorway, out onto the sidewalk and into the parking lot.

As the crowd roared past, Tom Smith yanked 18-month-old Billy down between himself and his wife Amy, and they leaned together over their child, trying to protect him from the chaos.

After what seemed like an hour but in reality had been three minutes, the clamor of the evacuation subsided to a low roar, filtering in through the doors at the rear and front corners of the church. Tom tilted his head to get a peek at the nearly empty sanctuary.

Coats, hats and even shoes were strewn about pews and aisles like tornado debris. Here and there an elderly worshiper huddled in pitiful fear, unable to rise and retreat and abandoned by their fellow congregants. The rest of the church was deserted.

"*What in God's name was that?*" thundered a preacher from the front of the church.

Amy and Tom looked at each other, then at their sweet, frightened little boy. Just minutes earlier, his cherubic face had taken on a bizarre, otherworldly countenance, and his words had driven several hundred people into a frenzied, terrified stampede for the exits.

What in God's name had happened?

Tom and Amy had no answer.

BANG! Tom was plunged suddenly into a full-blown mid-life crisis, complete with stark, gut-wrenching, cold-sweat-producing mental wrestling matches with the concept of death.

Struggling to distract himself from the terror, Tom had dived headlong into the material world, upgrading their beat up old sedan to a slippery white minivan, pouring hundreds of dollars into new electronic toys for the house, substituting work in the yard for working on his family relationships, and generally fully vesting himself in earthly treasures which would one day be overrun by moths, rust and crabgrass.

The result had been a growing spiritual, and then emotional, gulf between Amy and Tom. But neither Tom nor Amy were willing to give up that easily, and both were working hard to keep things together.

So as the family minivan rounded the last curve before church, and the steeple of St. Thomas's rose over the tree line, Tom couldn't take it anymore. The idea of another sixty or ninety minutes of silence, without resolving this thing, was unbearable.

Yanking the wheel to the right, he pulled the car onto the gravel shoulder of the road. Tires screeched behind them as a line of late worshipers swerved around the erratic vehicle.

Amy looked at him, still angry, but knowing what was coming. After eight years of marriage, their pattern of arguing was well-established. Amy brooded. Tom exploded. Amy would keep brooding, and Tom would invariably re-address the issue, once he had cooled off. He could not leave a problem on the table.

"Amy, I'm sorry," he began, his voice sincere. "I am sorry. I know church is important to you, and I have no right to run it down. I'm sorry."

Amy's face softened. Reflections of the morning sun rose in her eyes as tears began to well. She didn't cry, though. "Tom, I know it's been hard, and I don't like that any more than you do. But… I'm just…"

"Neither one of us has it figured out," Tom cut in. "We're both trying, at least. But there is no excuse for what I did this morning, and I'm sorry."

The look in Amy's eyes told him that, while this wouldn't be a wonderful morning, they were on their way back. There was nothing else to say at the moment that would move them any further forward. Besides, they were late, Tom's head was pounding, and Billy was in the back blowing spit bubbles and repeating his favorite two words: "Big truck." Tom pulled back out onto the road.

were known to everyone in the church except Ol' Fogey himself, who seemed to be out to set some kind of longevity record.

The young reverend's ambitions were not malicious — he would never think of staging a coup or intentionally undermining his boss. Nonetheless, he had a lot of new ideas that were routinely blocked by his more conservative elder, and Waite was clearly looking forward to the day that he could take the helm and lead St. Thomas's into the Twentieth Century.

As the procession stepped awkwardly over the cameraman and his equipment, Tom could see the white-haired, senior reverend looking around his church in vaguely confused astonishment. Reverend Fogherty smiled blankly at the faces in his newly swollen flock, obviously also wondering who all these people were. Still, any visitor to the house of the Lord was welcome, and Cal Ripken-of-the-cloth looked forward to spreading the Good Word.

The various players in today's ceremony took their places, and soon the unsuspecting congregation was caught like doomed dinosaurs in the tar pit of an Ol' Fogey-led service.

As the service ground on, Tom noticed that Billy had become a bit subdued. Typically the youngster was a holy terror during church, squirming in his father's hands, dropping to the floor and even crawling under the pews. Tom had learned the hard way that nothing brings a church service to life like an 80-year-old woman who has suddenly realized there is a little person poking around under her dress.

As he did every week, the good Reverend Fogherty approached the pulpit microphone while still wearing his clip-on mic. The screech of the feedback jolted the church out of its trance. Young Reverend Waite's eyes were locked on his shoes as he clenched his holy jaw. Befuddled, Reverend Fogherty stepped away, then realized his mistake, turned off the clip-on mic, and stepped back up to the pulpit. Tom had seen the same thing happen every week for the last year.

Jim Blake reduced the angle of slump in his chair. The cameraman aimed his tripod-mounted camera at the pulpit to capture this historic moment. And Reverend Fogherty began.

"My sons, my daughters, uh... my sons' and daughters' children, whether they are sons or daughters themselves of those, my sons and, uh, daughters... Um, my children... I don't mean *my* children, of course... I don't have any children... what I mean is God's children... In a very real sense, we are all God's children, in the sense that he is the Father, and we, all of us, in the world, we are the children... Yes, um, that's it. We are the world. We are the children..."

Ol' Fogey didn't weave sermons as much as tangle them like old fishing line. Members of the congregation exchanged glances as Reverend Fogherty wandered further and further from any discernible point.

"I am often reminded of a time, um, when..." Reverend Fogherty paused, looking down at his notes. His face creased with mild confusion. "I seem to have forgotten...," he murmured.

Sitting in the background, lean, fit and under-employed, Reverend Waite had a stranglehold on his Bible. Unlike the young reverend, however, many of the rest of those in attendance seemed to have resigned themselves to waiting this one out, and some were moving into head-bobbing stage.

Tom's own family was not immune. While Billy quietly looked around the church, Amy was... looking down in prayer? Asleep? Hard to tell. Tom felt the "Ol' Fogey fog" rolling into his own brain. He wiggled his toes to stay awake, and tried to find something to think about that was exciting enough to keep his interest, yet not so inappropriate in church that he'd wind up in Hell...

Just as the sermon was settling on the room like a wet quilt, Billy abruptly and painfully jammed both heels into Tom's thighs, and stood straight up in his arms. Tom leaned out and around Billy to look into the toddler's wide-eyed — but composed — face, and was struck that his little boy looked very different all of a sudden.

Then, turning away from his dad, Billy let rip an ear-splitting, teeth-rattling, guttural belch lasting well over five seconds.

"OOOOOOOOOOOHH WWWAAAAAAAAAAAAAAAAA!!!!!!!!!!!!!"

Tom was so shocked he nearly dropped the boy. Amy *did* drop her copy of the church bulletin, as did several attendees nearby. Reverend Fogherty's sermon also had been dropped, dead in its tracks, like a charging bull sloth. When Tom looked up, the eyes of the entire church were on him and his son. But before Tom could even inhale in preparation for an explanation, Billy provided one for him.

"I AM THE LORD GOD!" Billy bellowed in a low, booming voice.

The cameraman crouching in the aisle fell sideways to the floor, away from Billy and Tom. Ahead, five hundred quizzical looks changed to five hundred frightened faces. Tom heard a soft cry to his left. It was Amy, panic-stricken and staring at the contorted face of her beloved Billy.

Shocked silence ensued. Tom sensed a movement to his right, and realized the cameraman, having regained his composure, had swung the camera around and was now focused at point-blank range on Billy.

Reverend Fogherty, perched on the pulpit at the front of the church, tried to take charge.

"S-s-see here, young man," the reverend began.

"I AM THE LORD GOD," Billy repeated in the same loud, rumbling voice, his cherubic face twisted unnaturally. "I SET IN MOTION THE UNIVERSE AND THE WORLD FOR YOU, AND CREATED YOU, OUT OF LOVE FOR YOU, MY CHILDREN. I ASK ONLY THAT YOU LOVE EACH OTHER AS I LOVE YOU."

Billy fell silent. The words echoed in the hushed hall. The only other sound came from the cameraman, fluidly manipulating the controls of his instrument.

Billy's contorted face relaxed, his eyes fluttered, and the toddler slumped back into his father's arms. A second or two later, Billy's head popped up, and he was a child again. The thunderstruck crowd remained transfixed on his round, smiling face.

Looking at the silent congregation, Billy was puzzled, but delighted, to be the center of attention for hundreds of people. He seized the opportunity.

"BIG TRUCK!" he yelled in his high-pitched voice — and the crowd reacted as if the kid had announced he was wired to a bomb. The room exploded in panic, and hundreds of freaked out faithful stampeded for the exits.

FIVE

"*What in God's name was that?*" thundered Reverend Waite from the front of the church as the chaos of the mass exodus subsided.

Amy and Tom looked at each other. Neither had an answer. Reverend Waite charged down the aisle toward them. Reverend Fogherty followed, falling behind his young associate.

"Just what exactly was that?" demanded Reverend Waite again. "What just happened?"

Billy huddled deep in his mother's arms, clearly frightened. Tom still didn't have an answer, but he leapt to his feet to protect his family from the inquisition.

"Do you think we have any idea?!" Tom shouted. "Back off, you're scaring my son!"

Reverend Waite caught himself short, realizing the boy's father was right. He took a step back and a deep breath.

Amy dropped to one knee between the pews, face-to-face with Billy. Tears rolled from her eyes. Tom could see his wife struggling to maintain composure as she whispered to her baby.

"Billy, honey, are you OK?"

Billy looked into his mommy's eyes with a tear-streaked but reassured face, providing his answer non-verbally. He can't even talk, for Christ's sake, Tom thought. He knows three damn words!

Tom noticed his hands were trembling, and a wave of nausea swept through his gut.

Reverend Fogherty had crept up, and before anyone realized his presence, spoke.

"It was the voice of God. It was the voice of the Father," Reverend Fogherty said, almost as an apology, as he looked at the worn carpet of the aisle. The reverend seemed sad. "It was the Lord, speaking through this child."

Tom whirled toward Amy to gauge her reaction to this theory. In response, she captured both parents' thoughts.

"That's ridiculous! God did not come down and speak through my son!"

Reverend Fogherty's expression was lost, his head moving side to side, as if the debate were still going on within him. But when he spoke, he sounded even more certain. "It sounds incredible, I agree. But we all heard it. This little boy does not know more than a handful of words. What came from Billy was not of Billy. God has spoken through him. God chose him, chose this place, to speak to us."

Tom was struck by the old preacher's tone. If God just decided to make an appearance at Ol' Fogey's church, why did he look so depressed?

Reverend Waite was leaning back against the end of a pew now, eyes to the ceiling. Something was going on in the young man's head as well, Tom could see.

"Oh, sweet Jesus," muttered Amy. Her shoulders slumped, Amy's five-and-a-half-foot frame looked like it couldn't carry the weight of this sudden situation.

All were lost in thought — even Billy, it seemed — and the sanctuary was still.

A distant, shrieking siren cracked the silence. One of the faithful must have called the police, thinking that Beelzebub was holed up in the church, holding the reverends and the two immobilized senior citizens hostage. There was no telling what kind of mob scene or SWAT raid might come next.

"We gotta get the hell out of here," said Tom, breaking from reflection. "Fogey, is there way out through the other end of the church, behind the altar, maybe?"

"Yes," said the reverend, startled at being called "Fogey."

"Amy, take Billy out that way. I'll get the van and pick you up."

A nod from his wife sent Tom bolting for the main exit and out into the bright, frigid day. The scene in the parking lot stopped him cold. In front of the church, dozens of people lay prostrate on the grass and the chilly asphalt, either injured from the rush for the exits or overcome by fear and excitement. Clusters of churchgoers buzzed about what they'd just witnessed, gesturing and shouting or talking into phones. Off to one side, Tom saw Jim Blake facing a camera with a microphone in his hand.

Just as Tom thought someone in the crowd might spot him, two fire trucks, an ambulance and several police cars came rocketing into the parking lot through several entrances, sirens screaming.

Thankful for the diversion, Tom bounded down the concrete stairs and toward his car, dodging and juking his way through the excited crowd, hoping to make it to the minivan before anyone noticed him.

As he reached for the door handle, shouts sounded behind him. He'd been spotted. Without looking back, he jumped into the vehicle, fired it up, and hit the gas. Tires shrieked as he spun the van around and headed for the rear of the church. Tom's head was also spinning.

"What the hell just happened?" was all he could think as he sped to his family's rescue. "What the hell just happened?"

SIX

Carter Ray Jones was just finishing his morning workout in front of the television when GNBNC's familiar breaking news theme music sang out from the speakers mounted around the room. The network was cutting into Jones's regular Sunday lunchtime show, the GNBNC *Weekly Business Preview*.

"Ya' always got to stay ahead of the competition," his daddy used to say, and Carter Ray had followed that advice throughout his long and successful career. *The Weekly Business Preview* helped him stay ahead in the stock market, since most investors weren't paying attention to the markets on Sundays.

But for Carter Ray, Sunday was also his primary day of business. In fact, he'd already worked a full day by the time he'd entered his expansive home gym that morning.

As the overblown "breaking news" graphics package spun and sparkled its way to its conclusion and the theme song moved toward its kettle-drum crescendo, Carter Ray slumped onto a stool at the bar and watched.

The network cut to the anchor desk — empty. Then, from the left side of the screen, a tanned and composed, but slightly aged, male model slid into the chair and inserted his ear piece. The Sunday anchor on GNBNC clearly had been caught unprepared, thinking he had another ten minutes of *Weekly Business Review* to do whatever it was anchors did to get ready to read a teleprompter.

There was a brief flash of white teeth, and the anchor assumed a more serious expression, befitting the situation.

"This is Chip Stone at the GNBNC News Vortex in Atlanta. Let's giddyap!"

Really? Carter Ray snorted. *Let's giddyap??*

"We are getting breaking news at this hour from Richmond, Virginia. A religious service there, at St. Tobias Church in a suburb north of Richmond, has been the scene of some sort of disturbance."

Carter Ray recognized the news reader. Stone had been the host of one of those syndicated trash talk shows for some time, but had hit the skids when he'd been arrested for solicitation. Seems one of the "prostitutes" that he'd booked for a show on "Hookers with Hearts of Gold and Buns of Steel" had turned out to be an undercover cop.

After taping the episode, Stone had suggested a little consensual adult activity. And before he knew it, his chiseled features were splashed across Internet sites, tabloids and television screens worldwide, but not the way he'd always intended. It was his mug shot, and he became a laughing stock.

Now, according to the show business Web sites, Stone was engineering a comeback, striving for respectability again. The GNBNC weekend anchor position was a significant milestone on this long road back.

As the recovering anchor spoke, the image on the screen switched to a blotchy red representation of Richmond inset into an outline of Virginia (minus the Eastern Shore, as usual). A star on the northern outskirts of Richmond marked the disturbance site.

"We have on the phone a reporter from WSSS-TV in Richmond, a Mr. Jack Blake, who happened to be at the service when this disturbance occurred. Jack, are you there?"

On screen, the name "Jack Blake, WSSS-TV" was superimposed under the star on the map. A quavering voice crackled over a bad connection. "Y-, yes, Chip. Ah, it's Jim, not Jack, Chip."

"Jack," continued Chip, "can you tell us what has occurred there at St. Tobias Church?"

"Um, it's Jim, Chip. Jim Blake."

"Right. Good. Can you tell us what happened… uh, Jim?"

"Ah, yes, Chip," Blake replied. "During this morning's service at St. Thomas's Church here in the Lakeside area of Richmond, a child in the congregation apparently was seized in some fashion by a supernatural spirit of some sort. I wouldn't have belie--"

Chip broke in, the tightening lines on his perfect face revealing irritation. "I'm sorry, Jack. I thought I just heard you say that a child was taken over by a spirit or ghost or something. Can you please correct that for us?"

"No correction, Chip," said Jim. "It's Jim, by the way, not Jack."

"Yes, right, okay, Jim, whatever," said the aggravated anchor. Obviously, GNBNC was the victim of a prank that now was being broadcast to all corners of the globe, and Stone appeared horrified that his reputation-salvage operation might be bumped off track by this developing debacle.

"No, I was right there in the church, Chip, and I saw it myself," insisted Blake, scrambling to save his national news debut. "The kid — he couldn't have been two years old — this kid started talking as good as you or me, and he was saying that he was God, and that he'd created the world because he loved us, and..."

"All right," Chip cut in again, determined to end this spectacle. "I think we'd better go to a break before..."

"I've got video, Chip!" Blake shouted. "We've just sent you video! You should have it right now!"

Chip Stone opened his mouth to respond, then sat quietly for a moment.

Back in his spectacular Nashville mansion overlooking the Cumberland River, Carter Ray Jones, a show business veteran, knew someone was talking to Stone at that moment through his ear piece.

Jones was riveted. Certainly, he enjoyed seeing the media screw it up — after the way they'd treated him a few years back, Jones had no love for the national news organizations. But as enjoyable as the fumbling was to watch, this story also seemed to be heading right down Carter Ray's aisle from a business standpoint.

After his workout, though, the big man was hot and somewhat uncomfortable. He stood up from the stool and moved around to the fun side of the bar to pour himself a giant gin and tonic, and then took a seat in the recliner a few feet away, facing the television.

As Carter Ray relaxed, the handsome face on the screen gave a quick nod, and spoke up.

"I'm told we do indeed have some footage of the disturbance at St. Tobias Church in Richmond," Stone said. "We're going to run that video now."

A few more seconds of Chip's tense face followed, and then the network abruptly cut to video of what appeared to be an elderly preacher in a time-worn church. He seemed confused, rambling on about children, or his children, or...

What the hell is this guy talking about? Jones wondered. A second later, he didn't care.

"OOOOOOOOOOOHH WWWAAAAAAAAAAAAAAAAA!!!!!!!!!!!!"

Whatever *that* was, it must have happened right next to the camera, because the volume overwhelmed the mic and caused distortion. Whatever it was also brought the old minister's sermon to an abrupt end — every head in the picture turned to the rear of the church, left of the camera. Some kids began to giggle.

"I AM THE LORD GOD!" someone shouted off-camera. Immediately following this outburst, the picture frame spun sideways, and there was a loud thud. For a split second, the camera, still sideways and pointing up the aisle from the floor, showed the visible congregation's collective expression turn to terror. Now Jones was really curious.

The camera swung back up and around to the left, coming to rest on a man just a couple feet away, holding a little boy. The boy was standing in the man's lap, and the man had a nasty bump on his forehead, over his right eye. Jones couldn't quite read the expression on the man's face, but every other face down the pew to the man's left was locked on the kid, and each wore the same look of shock and fright.

As for the boy himself — well... he was standing in the man's lap, and he seemed to be the right size for a little boy, but the look in his eyes seemed... different... deeper... something...

"See here young man," came a thin, shaky voice from off-camera.

"I AM THE LORD GOD," the little boy proclaimed in an unnaturally low, loud voice.

"*GOD ALMIGHTY!*" shouted Carter Ray, his legs pin-wheeling and his drink spilling as he tried to pull himself up and out of his recliner.

The little boy continued.

"I SET IN MOTION THE UNIVERSE AND THE WORLD FOR YOU, AND CREATED YOU, OUT OF LOVE FOR YOU, MY CHILDREN. I ASK ONLY THAT YOU LOVE EACH OTHER AS I LOVE YOU."

"God almighty!!" Carter Ray repeated. *"God almighty!!"*

As Jones watched, the boy seemed to waver, then fell backwards into the man's arms.

Then the kid opened his eyes and sat up. Now he was a little boy again. Looking around, he began to smile, paused, and then shouted out, in a squeaky but loud little kid's voice: "BIG TRUCK!!"

The room detonated behind the kid. The screen was filled with screaming people running toward the back of the church. The camera was jolted, then tilted sharply left, and the picture went black.

"God almighty," Jones said to himself one more time.

Just then the door on the far end of the workout room burst open.

"Reverend Jones! Did you see that?" shouted a well-groomed, attractive young woman as she ran in.

"Cindy, pack a bag. We're going to Richmond."

As the click-click of his assistant's high heels faded down the hallway, Reverend Jones considered the implications of what he'd seen. If this was a hoax, then there was profit to be made for the Lord in the old Capital of the Confederacy. And if it wasn't a hoax… well…

Jones recalled the joke where a cardinal runs excitedly into the Vatican to inform the Pope that Jesus was, at that moment, entering the Holy City's front gate. "What should we do?" cries the cardinal.

"Look busy!" shouts the Pope.

"Time to look busy, I suppose," the famous reverend said to himself as he switched off the television.

SEVEN

"Vvvvvvvvvrrrrrrrooooooooooommmmmmmmmmm!!!"

Billy never was allowed to drive his truck on the kitchen table. For some reason today, his parents didn't seem to mind. They were sitting on the other side of the round table, talking about something.

Billy didn't much care what they were talking about — he was just happy to get the opportunity to drive his Big Truck on the table.

"Vvvroooom, vrrroooomm, VVVRRRRRROOOOOOMMMMMMM!!!"

Amy watched her son play with the toy on the small kitchen table. All around Billy were mixed reminders of the family's modest financial stature: faded wood paneling on the walls of their nearly 50-year-old house clashing with brand new ceramic tile on the floor; here and there a water stain or a crack in the walls or ceiling, contradicted by a gleaming new granite countertop. And, of course, on that countertop, two maxed-out credit card bills.

Also all around Billy, however, were the unmistakable tell-tales of a loving family: photos on the refrigerator; crayon "art" hanging from the walls; colorful plastic cups in the cupboard on which Amy had carefully painted Billy's name and little woodland creatures; and, a well-used cookie jar.

Tom watched his son play and wondered if he had any idea or memory of what had happened.

"*Vvvrrrrrrrrooooooooooommmmmmmmmmm!!!*" Billy shouted in his high-pitched voice.

"He *seems* OK," Tom ventured.

"But how could he be OK?"

Tom found the simple counter-argument difficult to refute.

"I have no idea."

"Maybe we need to bring him to the hospital."

"Yeah, that's probably the right thing to do," Tom replied, just as the doorbell rang.

Tom took another look at Billy before walking through the living room to the front door. Without a thought or pause, he opened the door wide. Something big flashed forward and a large, heavy object hit him in the chest and sent him soaring. Tom crashed backward into a cabinet. Heirlooms and wedding gifts smashed into one another, shattering to slivers.

"I MUST SEE THE CHILD!" the man yelled.

Jumping to his feet, Tom saw a man, about six feet tall, with wild hair and wilder eyes, scrambling to a standing position in the middle of the living room.

The intruder's demented look triggered primitive alarms in Tom's gut, and he lunged for the man. Grabbing the trespasser by the midsection, Tom anchored his feet into the carpet and pulled the attacker toward the front door. The wiry, surprisingly strong man flailed and thrashed to shake loose, still shouting.

"I must see the child! I must see the child!!"

"Tom!" screamed Amy from the kitchen door.

"Amy, get out!" Tom yelled, struggling to gain footing and arrest the man's sudden progress toward the kitchen. "Go out the back!"

"Tom!" Amy yelled again, not sure what to do to help her husband.

"GET OUT!!"

"The child! Is he here?" cried the man, head swiveling between Tom and Amy. "I must see him!!"

"I'm calling the police!" Amy screamed, holding the receiver of the old-fashioned wall phone in one hand. Frantic, she tried to punch the numbers 911, but in her panic, mis-dialed.

In the background, Tom heard Billy wailing, frightened by the noise and his mother's reaction.

Meanwhile, Amy's threat to call the police seemed to add fuel to the man's fire, and with a burst of strength he powered himself to within just a few feet of Amy. Tom's grip betrayed him, and he slid down the man's torso, struggling to hold on.

The man's legs pumped like locomotive pistons, and Tom took several hard kicks to the head and jaw as he lost his grip and fell to the floor.

The wild man was almost upon Amy before she could react. Just as the man reached for her face, Tom caught one of the man's legs and knocked him off balance. As the intruder fell forward, Amy smashed the phone receiver down on the intruder's forehead, gouging a fleshy trench clear to the bridge of his nose. Blood spurted from the wound as he fell. Flailing, he snagged the phone cord and pulled hard, ripping it from the phone.

This was enough for Amy. She gave him a vicious kick in the face, then her head disappeared around the door frame.

Tom heard, with relief, chaos from the kitchen as Amy grabbed Billy and crashed through the dining room toward the back door.

The wild man recovered and scrambled on hands and knees toward the kitchen, trying to catch up with Amy and Billy.

Tom had been a district champion on his high school wrestling team, and he let his instincts take over. He drove forward, landing on the back of the attacker, and the force of the lunge smashed the man forward into the floor. Still driving with his legs, Tom rammed his hands into the base of the intruder's skull, and then straightened his arms. As he pushed hard with his legs, Tom rocked upward, his full weight pressing down on the man's head. With a neat pivot move, Tom vaulted off the back of the man's head and neck, landing in a crouching position in front of him.

With Tom positioned just inside the kitchen door, between the man and the rear rooms of the house where Amy and Billy had disappeared, the attacker finally focused fully on the family's father. The man's eyes left no doubt that one of the two combatants would wind up dead or close to it before this fight was over. Although he didn't stop to reflect on it, Tom experienced a surge of adrenaline, and a hardening of his determination that the man would not reach his family.

The man rushed toward the kitchen doorway. Almost instantly, Tom dropped his shoulder, planted his rubber-soled shoes against the new ceramic tile and thrust upward, lifting the man off his feet, and redirecting his forward momentum sideways.

Momentarily, Tom had the attacker high in the air, nearly balanced on his shoulders. Then the two men crashed down on top of the small, round kitchen table, which instantly collapsed. Tom scrambled to a ready crouch. The intruder, sitting on the destroyed tabletop, looked around, shocked at his sudden repositioning. Then he reached behind his back, rooting around the crushed table underneath him, and pulled out Billy's treasured dump truck, now twisted into uselessness. The man examined the toy for a moment, then looked up at Tom with a homicidal smile before leaping to his feet and charging back into the battle.

Just before impact, Tom dropped low and grabbed the man's shirt collar, yanking the attacker's head and upper body downward while dodging the main thrust like a bullfighter. With skull-splitting impact, the man's forehead slammed into the corner of the granite kitchen counter. The attacker folded against the cabinet, then slid to the floor, his forehead leaving a trail of dark blood.

The unconscious man spread out and across the kitchen floor like cooling lava. A blood-red cross — the result of the bludgeoning from Amy and the impact with the countertop — welled up from the flushed and split skin in the center of his forehead. His eyes, although open, did not appear to be registering at all. Tom could see the man breathing, and he hoped, almost out loud, that he was not dying.

But there was no time for regrets — a brief honk from the family van sent him dashing for the front door. On the way through the yard, Tom passed two more strangers sitting in the grass, adorned in multicolored robes. He didn't stop to ask their business. In a few strides he was in the van, and Amy peeled out down Crystaldale Drive.

Tom turned to look at his house fading into in the aging neighborhood — the home where he had grown up and planned to raise his family. As the house grew smaller, three more cars pulled up, and more strangers invaded his front yard. His hands began to shake from the post-fight adrenaline overload, but he did not notice. A profound sadness overwhelmed him as he watched his home disappear.

EIGHT

Governor Rolfe descended the stairs of St. Paul's Church into the cold afternoon air and a throng of admiring worshipers and media. Cradled in the rising Republican star's left hand was The Good Book. In keeping with the governor's custom, the right hand was always empty, so as not to miss a chance to firmly shake a voter's hand.

Just before reaching the mob of fellow church attendees, the middle-aged but youthful governor cast a modest glance at the ground, managing to appear humble while simultaneously performing a quick appearance check. Coat, fine. Blouse, fine. Skirt, fine. Panty hose, fine. Shoes, fine. Looking fine, as usual.

Among Governor Mary Rolfe's very attractive features — for Virginia's voters and national party leaders alike — were her very attractive features. A striking beauty, 44-year-old Rolfe was tall, with honey blonde hair, penetrating green eyes and an outstanding figure. But those who stopped at her physical appearance when taking stock of Mary Rolfe were sitting ducks for her more formidable weapons — a dagger-sharp mind, consummate political instincts and the ability to nearly always say the right thing at the right time.

At the moment, her instincts told her the reporters at the base of the stairs were more agitated than usual this morning. The pack appeared swollen, and included faces she didn't recognize.

Maybe Sunday morning replacements? A bunch of weekend writers ready to commit seven days' worth of errors in a single story?

She angled toward the pastor to ensure the session got off on the right foot.

"Governor, it's wonderful to see you here today," gushed the Reverend O'Donnell as Rolfe reached the steps just above street level. The reverend's church sat immediately outside the Virginia Capitol grounds, and many governors had attended this church over the years. Still, Rev. O'Donnell was especially fond of this governor.

"It was a beautiful service as usual, reverend," replied the governor. "I only wish I were half as eloquent as you are on the pulpit."

Reverend O'Donnell blushed. "I can't claim credit. It is the Lord's word, and I am but His simple servant, through whom He speaks."

The reporters surged forward, interrupting the exchange. An unfamiliar face shoved a microphone at Rolfe and blurted a most unexpected question.

"Governor, GNBNC is reporting that God has spoken through a child this morning here in Richmond, at St. Tobias Church. What's your reaction?"

Despite her composed appearance, Rolfe was taken aback that a reporter would ask such a ridiculous question, but... he had said the magic acronym of GNBNC, which, in addition to being a respectable news organization, was a politician's best medium for reaching the nation and the power brokers on both sides of the aisle in D.C. Several television cameras focused on Rolfe; a well-phrased answer that included "GNBNC" would probably make it onto the global news network.

But how to answer a question more suited for a tabloid news show? Rolfe had made it her business to visit nearly every church in the commonwealth during her campaigns, and she knew there was no "St. Tobias" in Virginia. But to point that out would be to call into question the accuracy of GNBNC — a touchy subject since the network had been forced to retract several stories over the past year — and would certainly damage her prospects for future network appearances.

Three-tenths of a second had elapsed since the question was asked.

If she didn't answer within a half a second, she would appear to have been taken by surprise. A quick stall was in order.

"That sounds more like a question for Reverend O'Donnell," Rolfe said with a smile. By diverting the reporter with a bit of understated humor, she bought herself a second or two. Plus, now she could gauge the seriousness of the issue by whether other reporters followed up with questions on the same topic. A quick sweep of the pack told reporters she was ready for the next question. A regular Capitol beat reporter from the Richmond daily paper spoke up, to Rolfe's initial relief.

"Governor, a video news report running on GNBNC shows a toddler speaking in a deep voice, using very sophisticated language, and claiming to be God," the reporter began, and the governor knew then that this was a real issue, if not a real event.

"Some people who were there are convinced that God chose this child to speak to the world. What is your reaction?"

Real or not, the issue and the commonwealth she served were now on the *Global* News Broadcasting Network Company. This had the makings of a significant news story, regardless of its veracity, and Rolfe knew it was an opportunity to enhance her national profile. She just needed to avoid coming down on the wrong side of the issue.

"My staff is studying this issue carefully as we speak," she announced, to the surprise of her staff hovering in the background. "At 3:00 p.m. today, my office will release a statement on this issue. Thank you."

Governor Rolfe turned from the reporters with a polite but firm smile and strode up the sidewalk toward the Governor's Mansion on the far side of Thomas Jefferson's resplendent Capitol Building. Her staff scurried to catch up. First to reach her was Scott Butler, her chief of staff.

"For chrissakes, Scott, do I have to learn everything from the media?"

"Sorry, governor."

Rolfe took no mind.

"Get me some information on this kid. I want to know what GNBNC is saying, what actually happened, and who the hell the kid is. We either have to be the first to debunk it or the first to jump on board. This is going to be a five-day story at least."

Butler nodded and tore off for his office on the third floor of the Capitol Building. Rolfe continued across the Capitol parking lot, headed for the pale-yellow, Georgian-style governor's mansion nestled in the corner of the Capitol grounds. Her mind raced. This could be the event that catapulted her into the national consciousness — something she desperately needed if her career plans were to come to fruition. But if she mishandled it, she could become a national laughingstock rather than a national leader. She refused to be the Second Coming of Governor Moonbeam (his most recent tenure as California's governor notwithstanding).

Rolfe had always kept a keen eye out for an opportunity to break onto the national radar screen, and at some point she might even have unconsciously prayed for it. But despite her public and political persona as a woman of deep faith, she was a believer-of-convenience, putting her stock in personal action and ambition rather than divine intervention. And in keeping with her core beliefs, she intended to seize this opportunity with both hands, whether divinely provided or not, and choke the shit out of it.

NINE

The emergency room doctor paused outside the examining room. Minutes earlier, he'd been prepared to call social services to deal with the parents of his patient. They'd arrived 45 minutes earlier, screeching up to the emergency room doors with the most unlikely story he'd heard in 23 years of medicine: their toddler had spoken in a deep bass voice and proclaimed himself God during a church service.

The initial examination had shown the boy had an irritated throat, but that could be the result of a morning of screaming. He seemed like a happy tike, and showed no signs of godliness or other supernatural characteristics.

The doctor had determined it was best to get the kid away from the unstable parents before a tragedy occurred in their mini-cult. After excusing himself from the examining room, he had walked a straight line to the on-call physician's office. Just as he dialed social services, he'd noticed the waiting room television, tuned to GNBNC, as usual.

The image on the tube froze the doctor mid-dial. There was the same boy, wearing an odd expression and mouthing what looked to be a long combination of words.

The doctor couldn't hear the audio, but the reactions from those in the waiting room told the story — something not-right was coming out of that boy's mouth. The child slumped into his dad's arms, then seemed to wake up and look around, as if coming out of a trance.

One more quick movement of the boy's mouth, and pandemonium broke loose in the church. The screen cut back to the anchor, and the doctor slammed down the phone. He hurried around to the registration desk where a stunned nurse sat transfixed by the screen.

"What'd that kid on television just say?" the doctor demanded.

"He… he said he was God, and that he wants us to love one another."

Now, outside the examining room door, the doctor wondered what to say, what to think, what to do. He stepped inside. Billy sat quietly in his father's arms, playing with a toy car. His parents waited for the doctor to speak.

"Folks, I'm not sure what to tell you," the doctor began. "I've never seen a case like this, and I've never heard of one either. About the best I can say is we should watch him carefully. He looks healthy to me — no red flags of any kind, other than what you described, for which I think the term 'red flag' is something of an understatement. I'd like to check him in for a couple days, to watch for signs of distress: inconsolable crying, high fever, loss of appetite or a change in personality — apart from the most recent change, of course."

"So you believe us?" Amy asked. "Do you think the preacher was right about God and all?"

The doctor paused.

"I'll level with you," he said. "Usually, when a parent comes in complaining that their child is God, it is a reasonably good sign that something's wrong with this picture. But when I saw you on TV --"

"TV?" Tom said.

"WSSS," said Amy in sudden realization.

"Aw, hell, that's right!" Tom scowled. "That explains the maniac at our house, and the others who were showing up! We're gonna have to deal with every busybody and idiot in Richmond!"

"Um, it wasn't WSSS," said the doctor. "It was national. GNBNC."

"GNB…?" Amy and Tom went wide-eyed.

"This is a news story made in heaven," Tom said, alarmed. "We can't stay here, and we can't go home. We've got to get completely out of sight."

"I strongly recommend that you allow us to observe Billy, at least overnight," the doctor urged.

"Doc, we can't," Amy said, stride for stride with Tom's reasoning. "We've got to hide until this blows over. People would look for us here."

"We can't risk it," Tom agreed. "Every trash reporter, con-man, crazy person and crook in Virginia — in the world — is going to be banging down our door."

TEN

The bookish-looking young man in the suit knocked again, getting no response. He snuck a glance at the growing crowd of adults and kids milling around on the front yard of the apparently empty home, on the street and in other front yards. Most were talking or texting or recording the scene on their cell phones.

So far no media, but a few odd-looking guys sat in various spots on the grass, including one fruit loop on some sort of blanket. In front of the guy sat a pot and a hand-lettered sign with a wayward attempt at the word *Armageddon* and a request for cash. The other onlookers gave this bird a wide berth.

Along the curb, two gray and dark blue Virginia State Police cars with lights flashing (one of which the young man had arrived in), drew children like moths. A steady stream of auto traffic inched past the house, with carloads of passengers pressed against the windows like monorail riders at Lion Country Safari. And, despite it being Sunday, two service vehicles — a plumber's van and a lawn service van — parked nearby.

Meanwhile the millers-about, focused mostly on him. One group had inched closer, and after what appeared to be a short conference, one woman broke away and approached.

"Where are they?" the envoy demanded.

"Who?" the door-knocker replied, with zero believability.

The inquisitor shot a skeptical look. "Are you with the police?"

The young man glanced involuntarily at the police cars, where he noted with relief and alarm that the state troopers were getting out of their cars. The last thing he wanted was a confrontation between the crowd and law enforcement in front of all these cell phones and with the media due any moment.

He revealing his identity would be a mistake. Despite his youth — he was the youngest-ever assistant deputy press secretary to the governor of Virginia — he was no idiot.

"Me? I'm…" he then pointed to the right and yelled at the top of his lungs, "— HEY, WHAT'S THAT OVER THERE?!" As heads turned, he leapt off the stoop, catching his foot on a bush and bouncing hard across the green grass. Leaping to his feet — a flailing blur of black wing-tips, khaki slacks, white pressed shirt and grass stains — the assistant deputy press secretary to the governor of Virginia ran like a 13-year-old nerd around the side of the crowd.

Seeing their young charge charging toward them, the troopers scrambled into their cruisers. Even as they flipped on their triple-digit-decibel sirens, the worldly-wise press aide dove into the back of one car screaming *"GO GO GO!"*

Children and adults lunged for safety as tires screeched and smoke billowed from the rear wheel wells of the two powerful autos. Fishtailing wildly, they roared up Crystaldale Drive. Half-a-dozen cell phones recorded the departure.

A member of the dazed crowd finally cleared his throat and spoke. "That dork must work for a politician." Nods all around.

Seconds later, one of the service vans pulled out onto Crystaldale Drive and sped off in the direction of the fleeing police vehicles. A moment later, the second van followed.

The occupants of the police cruisers did not notice the vans trailing them. The young press aide sat up and inspected his appearance.

"That went all right, don't you think?" he chirped.

The career law enforcement officer did not respond, but instead directed a cold stare at the aide through the rear view mirror. After a couple awkward seconds, the press aide cleared his voice for maximum importance.

"Better check in with the governor."

The trooper rolled his eyes.

A speakerphone rang in a conference room on the third floor of the Capitol, interrupting a raging debate. On the walls of the room hung hundreds of photos of Governor Rolfe and her staff doing the people's business, meeting with world and business leaders, listening with serious expressions to constituents, speaking with inspired eyes to unseen audiences, and cutting up at staff get-togethers.

Several of the photo subjects were at that moment sitting or pacing around the conference room table: Scott Butler, the governor's chief of staff; Marc Byrd, the governor's top political advisor; Steve Armstrong, the legislative and policy director; and, the press secretary, Jimmy "Stonewall" Jackson — a nickname he'd earned from a frustrated Capitol beat reporter at a press conference after the umpteenth non-answer: "Look, there stands Jackson, like a stone wall!" (Richmond is very hip, Civil War-wise.)

Butler punched the pickup button before the second ring.

"We just left the Smith house," came the hyperventilating voice of the press aide over the speaker, sounding a bit like a space mission in trouble. "They're not there. Nobody's seen them since they left for church this morning."

"Any media there?"

"Negative, not yet, but a bunch of people are hanging around the front yard, taking pictures."

"What'd you learn?"

"The family's got one kid: the miracle boy, Billy. Two years old. Mom's name is Amy or Tracy or something, and the dad is Tom. He works somewhere in Richmond. The mom stays at home, I think."

Faces fell into hands around the table. The young reverend at the church had been more helpful, although he had thought he was talking to the *Washington Post* at the time.

"Did you attract any attention?"

Rocketing down a residential street in the police cruiser, sirens screaming, the press aide glanced at the trooper's eyes in the rear view mirror. "Nope."

"All right. Get back here."

Inside each service van, men smiled and tapped keys on laptops. Digital recording devices flashed. A man in each van picked up secure telephones.

"Dog Pound?" began one. "This is Big Dog…"

"La guarida, este es el gato grande…" began the other.

ELEVEN

In the third floor Capitol conference room, Butler looked up from the speakerphone. "Comments?"

The other three men all began shouting at once.

"WHOA WHOA!" yelled Butler. "The governor will be here in five minutes and we have to have a recommendation! Stonewall?"

"This is a damned dangerous story!" the ever-cautious PR guy responded. "We don't know the deal on this family. They could be cult-types or con artists. Hell, the damn dad may have killed the whole bunch of 'em by now. We can't come out on their side till we know more."

The bravado and raw language was typical. Without noticing it, the governor's (mostly male) staff had taken on an ultra-macho persona over time, as if to compensate for having a woman as a boss, or more likely to compensate for their low-paid, anonymous, behind-the-scenes status in a society that admired celebrity first, wealth second, and real power last. The staff itself had never really noticed this aspect of their organizational culture, but meeting attendees from the outside invariably came away shaken.

Butler looked over at the policy and legislative boss. "Twist?"

Another nickname bestowed by the press. Armstrong had been known as "Stretch" in college, in a reference to some '70s-era action toy, but his skill at "persuading" legislators of both parties to see things the governor's way had earned him the new moniker.

"I'm worried about the church and state thing," Twist said. "We can't endorse a fricking religion — it's constitutionally suspect from a federal and a state standpoint."

"Technically," Butler, said, unable to resist… "Both the U.S. Constitution and the Virginia Constitution specifically prohibit the *legislature* from passing laws authorizing or respecting an establishment of religion. Neither document mentions the chief executive. I think we're in the clear."

"Good," shot back Twist. "You can field the first call from the assholes at the ACLU."

"Marc?" continued Butler.

"Constitutional sensitivity notwithstanding," said the always circumspect political director, with an eye toward Armstrong, "This is a killer issue for us. If we can find a way to endorse the message, if not the messenger, we can strengthen our hand with the religious conservatives. Their support is critical in the presidential nominating process."

As if on cue, the door to the conference room burst open and in strode their leggy boss.

"I've got two things for you to think about, boys," announced Governor Mary Rolfe. "Kiss the baby and the Madonna — and I ain't talking about the slutty geriatric singer!"

TWELVE

Unlike her top people, Governor Rolfe had noticed her staff's tendency toward chest-beating bombast. After ten minutes to themselves, Rolfe knew they would have spent the last nine minutes arguing, and that the testosterone would be washing across the floor like a storm surge before a hurricane. So she'd opened strong, to remind the boys who was boss. This fluency in human behavior had helped Mary Rolfe effortlessly ascend through Virginia's good ol' boy political establishment and into the office of governor.

Mary Virginia Rolfe's training for her career in politics began early, at the knee of her mother, Katherine Virginia Rolfe, a willful, beauty queen-turned-trial lawyer. Mary's father, John Simon Rolfe, had been a bit player in the family. He possessed none of the heroic characteristics of his namesake, John Rolfe of Jamestown, a trader and tobacco farmer who survived shipwreck, heartbreak and three wives (one Pocahontas) en route to establishing himself as a Virginia legend.

Katherine Virginia Rolfe and her daughter may have come by their historic surname via marriage, but in the Rolfe family, the daring and audacious chromosomes ran exclusively through the female lineage.

Mary Virginia learned early that the domination and manipulation of men was a key skill by which she could advance in this world — not out of feminist principle, but out of necessity, especially given the patriarchal power structure of the United States in the late 1970s and early 1980s. And, while Mary easily could have surpassed her mother in the beauty pageant world, both mother and daughter knew that ownership of a tiara would be an anachronistic and even counterproductive line on her resume.

Instead, the practice of law seemed to be the best course through which Mary could achieve self-actualization in this world. She excelled, graduating at the top of her law class at the University of Virginia, and then rising to partner with astonishing speed at Richmond's Childress-King/Belfield+Barthol, one of the largest law firms in the Southeast.

After maxing out in the legal profession, she looked around for her next field of conquest, and settled on the political world — the 21st Century-equivalent of the beauty contest.

Rolfe again leapt to the head of her class — initially through the ranks of Virginia's General Assembly as a delegate, and then as a state senator. Two years ago, she'd come from the back of a large pack of Republican gubernatorial wannabes to capture the party nod in a knock-down, drag-out nominating convention. Senator Rolfe's main themes had been a pro-life stance, a strong law-and-order initiative and disciplined fiscal restraints in state government.

With those, she'd neatly tied up the votes of the social conservatives, the tough-on-crime types, and the Tea Party-wing of the GOP.

Having secured the party's nomination, though, she adroitly moved to the center for the general election.

Law-and-order rhetoric gave way to aggressive insistence on stopping crime before it started through interventions with high-risk kids, and her vigorous participation in volunteer programs bolstered her image as a tough-love candidate.

The promise to slash state budgets became a vow to introduce modern business management techniques into state bureaucracy. As part of this plank, Rolfe had enlisted the dynamic CEO of a Fortune 25 company in Virginia to head up a blue-ribbon task force that would be formed the day she was inaugurated.

Rolfe's expert maneuvering resulted in the biggest election victory in Virginia history, as she pulled support from every band of the political spectrum.

Most political observers and many voters agreed that the Governor's Mansion was but one stop in Mary Virginia Rolfe's meteoric career, and that her final destination could very well lie 100 miles up Interstate 95.

As Rolfe explained her "Kiss the baby and Madonna" strategy to her staff — to claim for herself the mantle of motherhood by stepping in to protect this innocent child from societal predators and possibly from scheming parents — she had to agree: Washington, D.C. was getting closer all the time.

THIRTEEN

"I want to talk to them," said Chip Stone during a commercial break. "Lou, I need to go to Richmond." He was talking through his microphone to his managing editor, who was following the story from the control room one floor below.

"Out of the question," came the brusque reply through Stone's earpiece. "You're a copy reader. We need you reading copy."

"*I — AM — A — JOURNALIST!*" erupted Stone, indignation spewing like shrapnel. On the set, it looked like he was shouting at invisible spirits. The crew didn't flinch. Hyper-inflated egos with hair-trigger tempers were nothing new behind the anchor desk.

"Oh really, Mr. Murrow?" the editor shot back. "Is that what you grave robbers call yourselves these days?"

The editor was referring to another of Stone's infamous debacles. Several years ago, Stone became convinced that Abraham Lincoln had kept a black mistress, based on the writings of a lone historian of thin qualification. According to the historian, it was Lincoln's secret dalliance with a daughter of Africa that motivated the Emancipation Proclamation, rather than political genius, Machiavellian calculation or basic beliefs in human rights.

Stone theorized that Lincoln might have spilled some of his "DNA" (in the parlance of today's political reporting) on his alleged mistress's clothing. To be first and biggest with the story, Stone planned to harvest this DNA from the woman's garments and prove his case. After failing to convince her descendants to part with the few remaining artifacts they had of their beloved great-great-great-grandmother, he tried to secure the clothing in which she had been buried — without permission.

To his dismay, an anonymous tip to a competing news host led to an ambush at the cemetery, along with an embarrassing, live graveside interview.

Yet another stain from the past that Stone labored daily to overcome. Still, Stone knew that this baby-speaking-in-tongues event was exactly the kind of story that could redeem him.

"By the way," the editor added. "What with the 'Let's giddy-up' nonsense?"

"It's my catch-phrase!" Stone said, indignant.

"You don't get a catch-phrase! Walter Cronkite gets a catch-phrase! You get a part-time chair to sit your sorry ass in!"

"Chris Cuomo has a catch-phrase!" Stone retorted.

"Chris Cuomo has a *name* and that's *all* he's got! Chris Cuomo's *ego* has a catch-phrase!" the editor shot back. "He's no Cronkite and neither are you!"

Stone had let himself be taken off-track.

"Look, dammit, I broke the story and I'm staying on it!" he shouted, back on message.

"You *broke* the story? You answered the friggin' phone, you pompous idiot! You didn't catch this fish — it jumped into your boat! Now keep your copy-reading ass in that chair and do your job!"

Stone could see the floor director motioning that they were about to come out of commercial. He had one more card to play, and it was all or nothing.

The floor director counted down. "Five, four, three," then switched to hand signals for two and one. As the floor director pointed at the anchor, Stone snatched the earpiece out of his ear and stuffed it down the back of his shirt collar. The red light above the camera lens lit up, and he was back on the air, live, before the entire world.

"Welcome back to GNBNC," Stone intoned in his best copy-reading voice. "This is Chip Stone at the anchor desk at GNBNC's News Vortex in Atlanta. We're keepin' on keepin' on!"

The editor threw his coffee cup against the wall.

OK, that one sucks, Stone thought. Then he pressed on.

"We are following a breaking story out of Richmond, Virginia this afternoon that has caught the attention of the world. A small child has been filmed in a church by local station WSXS, apparently speaking as God to the congregation. GNBNC has been bringing you that video since the story broke just hours ago."

Stone's shift was almost over, and he could see Preena Squall (a former *weathergirl,* for chrissakes) standing behind the camera, waiting for her shift at the anchor desk. Now or never.

"Beginning tomorrow morning," he continued, "I will be reporting to you from Richmond on this important story." His earpiece instantly vibrated like a dentist's drill against the back of his neck.

"GNBNC will provide complete and accurate coverage of 'The Miracle at St. Tobias's,'" he said, using the moniker concocted by the Crisis Marketing Team, and ignoring the barrage of anger bouncing off his neck. "Stay with GNBNC for all the latest breaking news on 'The Miracle at St. Tobias's,' throughout the day today, tonight, tomorrow, and for the foreseeable future."

The floor director signaled a cut to commercial. Stone ripped the audio equipment off and dashed for the door. He knew his burly managing editor was bounding up the stairs at that moment in hot pursuit. If Stone had to fight this out, he would do it on the friendly turf of his office, not in the News Vortex, where his dressing down would be witnessed by others and maybe caught on video.

Quick-stepping, he reached his office, sat down and composed himself. Seconds later, the editor crashed through the door.

"STONE WHAT THE HELL IS WRONG WITH YOU? Now you're *definitely* not going — to Richmond or anywhere else at this network! I'm gonna run your ass out of here on a rail! I'm gonna fire you so hard your ears'll bleed! You'll never get another national gig!"

Concerned faces peered in around the door. Stone had not succeeded in keeping the scolding private. Time to go on the attack.

"Lou, I know you've been in this business a long time, and that kind of experience counts for something. But you cut your teeth in a different world, a different news environment —"

Stone let his voice rise as he projected feigned anger and genuine self-righteousness. "But Lou, this could be the biggest story of the decade — maybe the *millennium*!" ["Hyperbole is GREAT!" was one of Stone's mottos.] "And *DAMMIT, I am not going to let GNBNC fumble this story just because some people are stuck in the Twentieth Century!*"

A crowd had gathered just outside the door. The editor's features darkened and the veins in his neck popped to the surface as the big man leaned over Stone's desk. He crashed his meaty fist onto the desk like a wrecking ball, bouncing celebrity photos and mementos to the floor. Stone jumped, despite himself. From deep inside the old editor came an ominous rumbling.

"You punk. You little piece of crap. You wouldn't know a respectable news operation if it grabbed you by the throat."

Stone's Adam's apple bobbed involuntarily. Sweat trickled down the side of his tanned face and his manicured hands trembled. This was not going well. As the old lion leaned farther toward Stone, the desk slid across the floor, pushing the anchor toward the wall until he was pinned between desk and chair.

A forearm worthy of a longshoreman rose toward Stone, and just as the editor seemed ready to strangle him, Stone's young secretary interrupted.

"Chip, um, Mr. Stone, I mean," said the young woman, who was not just his secretary, but his biggest fan, among other things. "Um, Mr. Munroe is on line three for you."

Jack Munroe was the founder of GNBNC, a world-renowned maverick and a liberal icon. Chip wasn't sure whether this turn of events would be an improvement, but another one of his mottoes, roughly articulated, was "Do anything to avoid getting punched, unless you're on-camera, and even then try to fake it." He fumbled for the phone.

"Stone, is that you?" demanded the unmistakable voice of Jack "Attack" Munroe. "Are you in the middle of something?"

"Yes sir, it's me," Chip said, still keeping a wary eye on Lou. "Lou and I were just having a meeting."

"Good! Put me on speakerphone!"

Stone did, and what came next shocked both men.

"Stone, great idea to announce on air that you're going to Richmond! This Christ-child story is huge, and we've got to show our viewers that we are on the case! Jesus, do you realize how many Bible thumpers and Jesus freaks are out there? And they all have TVs! Pack your bags and get going! See ya!" The phone clicked dead.

Lou stood frozen, so Stone wasted no time. He extracted himself limb by limb from behind the desk, he grabbed his things and headed for the door. "I'll call you when I get there, Lou!"

Chip Stone was on his way to Richmond and, he was sure, on the road back to respectability.

FOURTEEN

Office of the Governor of Virginia

FOR IMMEDIATE RELEASE

Contact: James Jackson
(804) 786-2211

STATEMENT REGARDING INCIDENT
AT ST. THOMAS'S CHURCH:
VIRGINIA GOVERNOR MARY ROLFE APPEALS TO ALL
PARTIES FOR CALM "FOR THE SAKE OF THE CHILD"

RICHMOND, Va. — February 7, 3:05 p.m. — Virginia Governor Mary Rolfe released the following statement today regarding the incident at St. Thomas's Church in Richmond, Va.

"No one can doubt that an extraordinary event occurred today in the Commonwealth of Virginia at St. Thomas's Church. While the facts are not yet clear, one thing is certain: a little boy is now the center of the world's attention, and his life has been changed, possibly forever.

"I understand the fascination that this event generates in all people. Regardless what anyone thinks of the authenticity of this specific event, I myself have found that, in the process of reflecting upon the possibility that God might speak to our world so directly, I have experienced a spiritual stirring of my soul. I am sure many other Virginians, Americans, and world citizens have experienced similar feelings.

"In looking at the news report, however, and at the face of Billy Smith, I have also experienced deep and profound feelings of tenderness for that child and what he will be going through in the wake of this extraordinary event.

"So at this time, while we are still unsure of the ultimate meaning of this morning's occurrence, I appeal to all interested parties — the media, our community leaders, religious leaders, and the great people of this Commonwealth and this nation — to remember that little boy's face when you act, and for the sake of the child, please act circumspectly.

"We may or may not have witnessed a miracle today. But we will certainly witness a tragedy if we allow Billy Smith to be hurt in any way as a result of his involvement in the incident."

# # #

FIFTEEN

The hotel room was bleak, dirty — and anonymous. Tom and Amy didn't want to come here, but after having to fight off — and kill? — the crazy intruder back at home, the decision was a no-brainer.

Before coming to the hotel, the family sneaked one last peek at their house, from a safe distance up Crystaldale Drive. The scene was not encouraging. Three local television stations had parked mobile transmission vans in front of their home and clusters of people were camped on the lawn — complete with tents.

Most of their neighbors were there, probably discussing the greatest bit of gossip that had ever graced a chatty neighborhood. Many had been interviewed by source-hungry reporters, including Jim Blake. Even from a distance, Tom had sensed Blake's excitement.

Turning on the radio, they had heard the local morning Zoo Crew advertising that the Zoo Mobile would broadcast live from the Holy Baby's Home the next morning.

"That settles it," Amy had declared. "We can't go back until this thing dies down."

They'd decided on a nondescript hotel about a mile from their neighborhood. Now they were holed up in this dump with no clothes, no toiletries, and no idea what to do next.

"We need help," Amy said. "That guy at our house — he could have killed us! We should call the police."

Tom thought about that option, and not for the first time. As they sped away from their home earlier that morning, Tom actually dialed 911 on his cell phone to report the attack. But when emergency operator answered, he could not bring himself to report the assault and, in the process, reveal their location. Something in his gut told him not to trust anyone. So he'd hung up and they'd driven to the emergency room. When the operator called back to make sure there was no real emergency, Tom turned off the phone.

Now, he debated whether the police should be brought in.

"I don't know, Amy," he said. "Something… for some reason… it doesn't feel safe to call the police. This whole thing is so weird — you saw the reaction the doctor had this morning. He was going to report us to social services. What if the police take …"

Tom completed the thought with a nod at Billy. Amy understood.

"But we need to figure out what's going on," she insisted. "The doctor said this isn't a medical problem… Maybe Reverend Fogherty could talk it through with us?"

Tom agreed — they needed to talk to *somebody*. So while he snuck out to get some essentials, Amy placed the call.

In the convenience store, Tom heard customers talking about the day's events to each other and on their cell phones. Fortunately no one seemed to recognize him.

Passing by the newspaper rack, he caught a headline about the government spying on citizens via their cell phones, and it occurred to him that his own phone might allow someone to track them down.

Returning to the hotel room, he grabbed Amy's phone and doubled-sealed both phones in Ziploc bags he'd purchased.

"I may be paranoid, but…,"

Amy didn't need her arm twisted. "After what's happened today, paranoia is probably our friend."

Tom left and drove a hundred yards down the road to an abandoned building which, over the years, had housed a series of now-bankrupt businesses, from an independent pizza joint to a one-man CPA firm to a Chinese restaurant. He parked in the cracked asphalt lot, walked around the back of the building and found a sheltered nook set into the masonry, hidden from view. He tucked the phones in the hole and returned to his car.

As an afterthought, he walked over to an ATM next door and withdrew $275. The withdrawal limit was $300, but they didn't have that much in the account.

By the time he walked back in from the fading light of the cold Sunday afternoon, Ol' Fogey and Reverend Waite were sitting on the edge of the sagging, nasty, queen-sized bed while Billy played happily.

Reverend Waite was chattering about the media attention.

"All four networks have contacted us, and GNBNC is sending a reporter to Richmond," he said in short bursts, as if he'd run to the hotel. "I've seen our church on television more times than I can count. It's a shame really, because the building badly needs painting."

Reverend Fogherty seemed oddly subdued, but maybe he appeared that way in contrast to his yippy lieutenant.

"Reverend Fogherty," Tom said, "we're overwhelmed, as you can imagine. In church this morning, you seemed convinced that it was really God who spoke through Billy. Do you still think so?"

Reverend Waite leapt in. "Oh, definitely. There's no other viable explanation. It really is an honor that the Lord chose our church, and your son, of course, to speak to the world."

Tom stared at the young reverend for a long second.

"Reverend Fogherty, what do you think?" Amy asked.

"Well, yes, I suppose I do still believe it was God who spoke through your child." His words stooped and shuffled out.

"Don't you see? This is a wonderful event," Waite broke in. "This is the Lord God speaking to the world from our city, from our church! This is His Living Word! It's a chance to reach many more people with the word of God, a chance for St. Thomas's to blossom."

"What I can't understand," Fogherty said, seeming to talk to himself, "is why He chose us. Why did He feel the need to interrupt *my* sermon? Was I not getting the job done? Was I that far off? Couldn't He have just… passed me a note?" His voice faded off, and the room stayed silent.

"Reverend," Amy finally said, "I am sure it had nothing to do with God's opinion of your sermon."

"I agree," said Reverend Waite. "God chose us *because* of you. He saw the need to expand the flock, to upgrade the facilities, to improve the situation. It had nothing to do with your sermon."

Tom was glad that Fogherty was so lost in thought at the moment, or he might have caught what Waite just said. Clearly these men of God were still just men. Their interpretations were colored by issues most important to them. Neither seemed focused on Billy.

"Well, thank you both for coming," Tom said. "You've been a great help."

Fogherty mumbled a thank you, still looking at the floor, while Waite remained ebullient.

"Call if you need anything," Waite offered. "Will we see you next Sunday? Oh, we have a Wednesday night service as well. I'm sure Billy would enjoy it."

Out the door, out the door. "Thank you Reverend," Tom said. "You two take care."

He closed the door behind them.

"Next?" Amy grimaced.

"Why don't we chill for a little while, collect ourselves, maybe get some rest. By tomorrow, maybe things will have calmed down a bit and we can go back home."

He clicked on GNBNC, ready to settle in. Mercifully, they weren't greeted with the "Miracle at St. Tobias's" theme song. Instead, a story was wrapping up on the New Hampshire primary, coming a week from Tuesday, in preparation for the presidential election in November. The incumbent Democrat had no opposition for the nomination, so the fight was centered on the Right. But thanks to one candidate's aggressive fundraising over the past three years, the GOP primary wasn't much of a fight either, with a single front runner — a sitting Senator from Arizona — and a bunch of also-rans.

The next story was about Nicholas Walters, a multi-billionaire in trouble with the Securities and Exchange Commission. Seemed Mr. Walters had used his significant market shares in multiple industries — oil, chemicals, cattle —

to crush his competition and create monopolies. Now everyone from the government to environmental groups to animal rights activists were after him. Even his own family didn't like him. The most hated man in America. Somehow the story cheered Tom up a little.

Tom took stock of his family's current situation. Amy and Tom had married in their mid-twenties, and until this morning, being a parent of a spirited little boy had been the most pressing issue on his plate.

Billy had been unplanned. As Tom and Amy had approached 30, they hadn't yet conceived, and just when they'd finally decided they were too old to deal with an infant anyway, the blue plus sign changed their lives.

Of course, having a son turned out to be the most unexpected, wonderful occurrence in Tom's life, early mid-life crisis notwithstanding. Now, this wonderful late surprise had delivered a surprise of his own.

Tom headed to the bathroom to splash some cold water on his face. It had been a hell of a day. Cupping the water in his hands, he bent over and immersed his face, felt the cool sensation washing over him, allowed himself to exhale and relax a bit.

He gathered more water in his hands and brought it slowly to his eyes, ran his wet fingers smoothly across his forehead and down the sides of his face. As he did, he got a strange feeling that something was … what? Missing? Different? He looked at himself in the mirror. Nothing...

In the reflection, he saw Amy sitting on the bed as Billy played next to her. She had opened the drawer of the night stand. Inside it, he could see one corner of Gideon's Bible. Amy was staring at the Good Book. *That might be exactly what she needs.*

She reached toward it, hesitated, then pushed the drawer closed, leaving the Bible inside.

SIXTEEN

It was nearly ten o'clock on Sunday night by the time Reverend Jones's rented limousine approached the throng in front of the small brick tri-level on Crystaldale Drive. The home sat in the geographic center of the modest neighborhood with the grand name of West End Manor. Populating the neighborhood were a hundred houses just like it, along with a couple hundred others of a limited variety.

In suburban-archeological terms, the neighborhood belonged to the great expansion of the early 1960s, when America's already-roaring economy was beginning to scream. Companies were expanding into areas outside the northeast, spreading Yankees like kudzu into Dixie soil. Across the country, thousands of neighborhoods like West End Manor grew out of cornfields and horse pastures on the outskirts of major and mid-sized cities.

Small by today's standards, the homes in West End Manor must have looked like mansions back in the 60s, especially to the New York and New Jersey immigrants. In his business travels, Jones had seen plenty of northern suburban neighborhoods, stained by decades of industrial air emissions, with tiny squares of grass and just enough room between houses to fit a chain link fence.

By contrast, the ranchers, bi- and tri-level homes in West End Manor boasted a third of an acre of land each, three and sometimes four bedrooms, wide streets and clean air. As northerners poured in, neighborhoods like this were soon overrun with kids, an infestation that lasted through the early 80s. Then the life left the streets, as the kids struck out from home to start college or their lives.

It was at this point that most neighborhoods from that great expansion went one of two ways. As the houses in the area became more affordable, the empty nesters either held on and began living mortgage-free and a little bit higher on the hog, or they sold out to bargain-hunters. The former scenario often led to higher property values, an influx of young professionals and their families and a quiet revitalization of the neighborhood. The latter scenario sometimes led to rental neighborhoods, cars on blocks in the driveways, overgrown backyards and a steady decline of the community.

This, thought Jones, was clearly a case of the former. Youngish parents clustered with retirees on the street, as kids of every age shouted and laughed and chased each other and gawked at the television news vans and staffs.

Jones studied the media turnout for this suburban circus. Four news vans had staked out positions, raising their transmission towers and forming an impromptu, squared-off court with WSSS-TV as the affiliate for GNBNC. The local reporter who broke the story, Jim Blake, was in the midst of a standup report in front of the house. The other reporters would get a dose of the Reverend Jones Charm, but Jim Blake would be Jones's primary target.

The other national networks were important, of course. Each national network had established a respectable cable news channel, which operated separately from entertainment side of the network. The problem was that the networks' all-news channels still drew only a fraction of the parent networks' viewers, and the news channels' viewers were split along political and cultural lines. None really hit a solid cross-section of the country.

So when the huge stories broke, as they did every 1.8 months, according to Jones's media consultants, the national entertainment networks were torn between relegating all coverage of the event to their weaker and polemic news channels or breaking into their normal, ratings-heavy network schedule. The decision *always* came down to ratings — would the crisis/air disaster/mass murder/celebrity arrest/political debacle *du jour* draw more eyeballs than the regular line-up of shows?

Tonight was typical. The networks were struggling to determine whether God speaking through a toddler would out-draw their Sunday night programming: a reality show featuring a double-blind-date between two beautiful twenty-somethings *and* their wrinkly great-grandparents (sponsored by Cialis); a parade of sitcoms in which attractive couples talk about having sex, have sex off-camera, and then talk about having had sex; and, two one-hour dramas about doctors / police officers in gritty urban settings who deal with chronic social ills while showing their assets at least once every 30 minutes.

Meanwhile, GNBNC drew viewers from all points of the cultural, political and socio-economic spectrums, and had no entertainment network to distract from its primary mission of reporting stories like this to within an inch of their lives. Crises *du jour* were GNBNC's primary profit opportunities, and the network seized them like a pit bull on a toy poodle, shaking them lifeless before its network rivals could react.

Therefore, GNBNC was first on any newshound's list. The slower-moving pack of networks could get in line.

Jones instructed the driver to pull up next to Blake, prepping for his next internationally broadcast report. Jones wanted to be on the kid before he knew what hit him.

The butterflies in Jim Blake's stomach had nearly disappeared after his ninth live report on the Godbaby (as the cynical news crews were calling the kid). The crippling nausea that had preceded the butterflies had been mostly relieved in the middle of his second report when, as his technician ran a clip of the Godbaby's performance at St. Thomas's, Blake had leaned over a sewer opening in the curb and vomited. By the time the camera's red light blinked back on, Blake had wiped his chin and recovered nicely. *The mark of a pro*, he thought.

This was more than a big story for Blake — this was his ticket out of Richmond. Nice town, but if he had to be reporting on race-tinged feuds between urban downtown leaders and suburban county leaders, Atlanta would be a preferable locale. Godbaby might just deliver him to the promised land of a larger media market.

A director sitting in Atlanta barked into Blake's ear that they'd be cutting to him in 30 seconds.

Blake once again began his pre-air prep cycle. It had started years ago as a simple appearance check — hair, face, shirt, jacket, pants, shoes (if visible). Over the years, though, the pressures of television and self-confidence issues had compressed the appearance check into an obsessive-compulsive ritual.

Resisting the urge to add the hand motions, Blake quietly voiced the mantra, set to a childhood tune, so low that only his camera man and the network folks in Atlanta could hear him:

"Head… shoulders… knees and toes, knees and toes…

"Head, shoulders, knees and toes, knees and toes…

"Head shoulders knees and toes knees and toes…

"Headshoulderskneesandtoeskneesntoes…

"Headshldsknzzntzzknzzntzz…

"Hdshzzknzzntzzknzz…"

Mid-O.C.D., a black limo pulled up next to him. Through Blake's ear piece, the director shouted ten seconds to air time. At nine seconds, the world-famous Reverend Carter Ray Jones stepped from the limo and into the shot, knocking Blake out of his routine. As Jones flashed that world-famous smile, Blake froze like a possum in headlights. Jones caught Blake's limp hand in a firm grip and introduced himself. In response, Blake's face blanked as he stared over the reverend's left shoulder at the monitor.

"Five seconds!" called Atlanta.

Blake's cameraman, seeing his reporter stuck in a standing coma, made a desperate attempt to jump-start the prep routine.

"HEAD SHOULDERS KNEES AND TOES KNEES AND TOES!!" he screamed.

Jones wasn't sure what to make of the cameraman's anatomy review, but he knew a star-struck reporter when he saw one.

"TWO SECONDS KNEES AND TOES KNEES AND TOES!!" shrieked the cameraman.

Jones mistook the nonsensical words as instructions, raised his leg and stomped on Blake's left foot.

Pain sheared through the panic-induced fog in Blake's brain just as Preena

Squall, the anchorwoman in Atlanta, introduced his next report. Glancing at the monitor, Squall recognized Reverend Carter Ray Jones, and smoothly ad-libbed a segue for Blake.

"Now reporting to us on The Miracle at St. Tobias's is GNBNC's Jim Blake," said the former weathergirl. "Jim, I see you have a guest there, who needs no introduction, of course: the Reverend Carter Ray Jones."

Headshoulderskneesandtoeskneesandtoes, Blake repeated silently one more time. Then he looked to his left where, indeed, the Reverend Carter Ray Jones stood with a calm and expectant smile. Ignoring the complete incongruity of Reverend Jones's presence, Blake took a breath, and recovered.

"That's right, Preena, I am joined here in front of the Godba — in front of the Smith home — by the Reverend Carter Ray Jones, who has apparently come to Richmond in response to what some are calling a miracle."

Turning to his unexpected guest, Blake didn't realize he also was turning over control of the interview with his very first question. It really could have been any question, and any reporter, though. Control of the interview was Jones's first objective.

"Reverend Jones, what brings you to Richmond from Lynchburg?"

"Actually, I'm just in from Nashville, Tennessee, world headquarters of the Jones International Ministry and home of the Christ Almighty Family Theme Park," came Jones's warm reply. "I saw your masterful reporting this morning, Jim, on GNBNC, The Global World News Leader, as you broke this story to an unbelieving world and billions of people."

At the words *billions* and then *people*, Blake's knees buckled slightly.

"Thank you," Blake reflexed to Jones's transparent stroke.

"Yes, well, it was masterful, and of course, it only makes sense that this story first appeared on GNBNC, The Global World News Leader."

In Atlanta, the seasoned director rolled his eyes.

Some of the odder members of the crowd noticed the red light and gathered behind the reporter and the preacher. Several held signs warning about the end of the world or false idols. One sign claimed that the miracle baby was in fact the Antichrist and should be killed immediately.

"And, of course, when I saw your report here on GNBNC, I knew I had to get to Richmond right away," said Jones, indifferent to the growing chaos behind him.

Blake was struck by Jones's familiar but unusual drawl. It was not so much Southern as sophisticated… cosmopolitan, even… all the while remaining a drawl. The conscious, complex affectation had been developed by Jones's media advisors, who believed it would hold his Southern base while improving his appeal to potential church members across the country. (Jones actually hailed from Newark, New Jersey.)

"Have you met with the Smiths yet?" asked Blake, playing into Jones's hand.

"Not yet, though we plan to soon," said Jones. "First I wanted to experience this house that the Lord has blessed, to get a better understanding of the family's lives."

"So you believe it was God who spoke through the child?"

"It's hard to say just from the brief video clip, and without having spoken to the boy myself," Jones hedged before the big pitch. "But, based on my experience with other children in similar circumstances [*a lie — Jones had never seen anything like this before*], it seems God could indeed be using this child as a communication channel to the world. And, as with any other communication device — a radio, for example — the quality of the reception depends on how well the receiver is tuned. I see my job as providing that expert tuning — enhancing this boy's gift so that the world can get the strongest and clearest signal possible from God."

"Well, we are certainly pleased to have the chance to talk to you before you begin that process. Thank you for coming on with us." Blake turned to the camera. "Reporting live from the home of the miracle baby in Richmond, this is Jim Blake. Back to you, Preena, in Atlanta."

In a dark, moldy, smelly, cramped hotel room a mile away, Tom turned off the television and sat in silence at the end of the bed. The sound of his family's peaceful breathing surrounded him. His only comfort was that Amy had not seen the news report. Two issues disturbed him. First, and most frightening, was the kook with the sign calling Billy the Antichrist and demanding he be killed. Hiding out was now the only option — but how long could they last?

The second issue was the arrival of Reverend Carter Ray Jones, and his obvious intention of getting mixed up in this already mixed-up situation. As difficult a time as Tom had with religion in general, he harbored particular ill will toward slimy televangelists like Jones, who preyed on the spiritually vulnerable. Some preachers used television, radio and the Internet to do good work, but Jones's ilk was a horse's ass of a different color. His periodic pronouncements that all people in various groups would burn in Hell due to their religious beliefs/culture/sexual orientation/country of origin/television viewing habits/lack of sending in donations didn't increase the preacher's credibility in Tom's mind.

Well, I'll burn in Hell before I let him near Billy. He turned off the light.

SEVENTEEN

The sun broke into view over the barren, leafless tree line at 7:10 a.m. Rather than a leisurely ascent behind drifting clouds, this morning the sun seemed to leap fully into the sky in an instant, a white hot klieg light at maximum brightness, intent on making use of every second of the winter-shortened day.

Yet the sun was running behind, as a half-dozen concrete arteries into the nation's capital were already clogged with one million cars, containing 1.005 million commuters, all struggling to reach their places of employment and cursing whatever government entity was responsible for the scandalous lack of pavement in the Washington, D.C./Maryland/Northern Virginia area.

And even these early-morning warriors were running behind. In the basement of a glass and metal building on the outskirts of a suburb on the outskirts of D.C., a smart young woman already four hours into her workday was putting the finishing touches on a report. After a final scan, she clicked "Send," dispatching the encrypted electronic bulletin to a satellite positioned 23,000 miles above. The sun might look with favor upon America for sixteen hours or so a day but spy satellites in geo-synchronous orbits never abandoned their watchful posts.

In another basement room, this time in a gleaming white mansion in the center of the car-clogged city, a serious man opened the incoming bulletin on his laptop and quickly condensed the information into a brief slide presentation. Leaning over the younger man's shoulder, an equally serious but older man absorbed the report's details.

In the background, eight senior intelligence officials sat around a table, reading other reports.

Five minutes later, the silence was interrupted by the click of a knob, and the suction noise of the secure room's door opening.

"Good morning, Mr. President," said the older man, standing up straight.

"Mornin'" replied the president as the ten men and women in the room stood as one. The president, absorbed in scanning the morning news summary prepared by his press office, barely noticed them. As he worked his way toward the head of the long, shining black table in the middle of the room, his security detail took up positions at the door.

One by one, the senior intelligence officials found their seats, and the man at the laptop completed the presentation with a couple more keystrokes.

His boss, the older, serious man, opened the meeting.

"Mr. President, as I'm sure you've seen, yesterday in Richmond, Virginia, an unusual and unexplained incident occurred in a local church. I'd like to replay the initial report that triggered this situation."

The room darkened slightly, and a wall-sized digital screen flickered with images of the first GNBNC report.

The report finished, the lights came up as the officials in the room exchanged raised eyebrows, without elaboration. Glances and looks flew around the room like mental hot potatoes, as each person, in deadly silence, tried to maneuver someone else into feeling he or she had to be the first to offer an opinion. If, in the give and take of the pre-discussion mental wrestling, a victim could be identified by the larger group and several gazes could be brought to bear on that one person, he or she might succumb to the pressure and jump.

The president witnessed this phenomenon daily. Often his advisers reminded him of a flock of penguins. All of the penguins want to dive from the ice floe into the water, but no one wants to be first, in case a leopard seal or killer whale awaits in the cold, murky depths beneath the surface. So they crowd and bump and push and shove toward the edge of the ice until one penguin loses his footing and falls in. Then the rest of the flock watches intently to see if the unfortunate first is torn to pieces. If not, the rest leap happily in behind him.

Who will be first to jump — or get pushed? the president wondered.

After the usual pause, during which no penguins got wet, the serious man resumed his presentation. As he spoke, a series of images appeared on the large screen.

"We believe the video is genuine, and that some sort of event did in fact occur…"

A picture of the Smiths flashed up, three times larger than life.

"The Smiths have no history of criminal, suspect or even notable activity. We do not know their whereabouts, although we believe they are in the Richmond area. Last night, a covert FBI team entered their home to gather more information. They found an unconscious man in the kitchen. He'd been beaten rather severely. On his forehead were two wounds that formed the shape of a cross…"

The screen showed an image of a disheveled man, his forehead marred by the cross of blood. He was sitting upright with a vacant look, not entirely unlike Nick Nolte's mug shot.

"…We're analyzing the wound to determine if it's ritualistic in nature, and the man is in custody. He may be an accomplice in the incident; however, interrogation has not yet produced usable information. He remains about as coherent as he looks in this picture.

"Based on evidence in the house, our crime scene investigators think he was an intruder, and that the struggle occurred between him and one or more members of the family.

"We have put these two ministers from the church under surveillance…"

The men of God appeared on screen, then four additional, more familiar faces were added in the corners.

"No other players seem to be involved directly, although several prominent figures, such as Virginia Governor Rolfe, Carter Ray Jones and high-profile media figures are attaching themselves to the incident…"

The screen flashed an ugly photo of the child, face distorted by whatever possessed him, splashed across the front page of a London newspaper.

"So far, the media are giving the issue wall-to-wall coverage and, of course, the GNBNC video has gone viral. Several European tabloids included it in their print editions this morning…"

Three more newspaper front pages appeared, one from each of the New York City tabloids, and all sensationalized. The *New York News* featured two images of Billy's distorted face — one with a halo and the other with horns, and the screaming headline, "Angel… or Devil???"

The room contemplated the images for a long moment, then the older, serious man added dryly, "The New York tabloids have covered the story in their usual deliberative manner…"

The room, led by the president, broke into laughter. The president was very familiar with the reporting style of the New York media, particularly when it came to matters of religion, or more frequently for the president, matters of morality.

After the laughter subsided, the president looked at the older man, "What's your next step?"

"Once we find the family, we will take them into custody under the auspices of protecting them. Then we can perform an assessment of the child."

Turning to another figure at the table, the president inquired, "Willy, what have your boys at Langley come up with?"

The president didn't really expect an opinion from his Central Intelligence Agency director. The man had spent a career climbing the limbs of the organizational tree without ever going out on one. He'd survived by clinging to the trunk — the original tree-hugger — and he wasn't about to change now. A penguin of the first order.

Willy glanced down, unconsciously, before speaking, as if checking the distance between himself and the edge of the ice floe.

"We have determined there was no activity prior to this event that would suggest the involvement of another nation or off-shore group. We have detected some jumps in activity in countries with religion-centered governments or traditions, such as Israel and most of the larger Islamic states. We have detected very little activity at the Vatican, but our sources say the issue is being monitored closely. Some of the more extreme religion-based international terror groups appear to have increased their chatter, but it's too early to say if the issue is prompting any new terror initiatives."

The head of the FBI jumped in. "Likewise, we've seen additional movement by the Neo-Nazi organizations — especially those that claim divine favoritism for their cause. But we don't expect action from these groups."

"Homeland Security?" the president asked, glancing over to a woman at the table.

"Given that none of our usual suspects appear to be gearing up for terror attacks, we recommend taking no action, and *not* issuing an Elevated Alert. At the same time, we have sent a recommendation that local governments consider a slight up-tick in diligence."

"I agree," the president said. Still irritated by his staff of penguins, he turned and gazed at his CIA director, stretching out the uncomfortable moment, waiting to see if the bureaucrat would add an actual opinion. For his part, Willy dug his toes deeper into the ice floe and held his ground silently.

Finally, the president moved on, letting the advisor off the hook. "Jim, what does the NSA think of all this?"

The penguins turned as one toward the oldest man in the room. The National Security Agency was the most potent intelligence gathering unit of the bunch, having vastly expanded its electronic eavesdropping, data collection and surveillance in recent years. This value was only magnified by the inexorable insinuation of electronic technology into the world's daily life.

The NSA director paused before answering. "Mr. President, the National Security Agency has not found evidence that this was a real event. Following the broadcast, we detected a significant rise in secured communications traffic in the capitals of most major countries — allies and potential adversaries alike. The most significant jumps occurred in totalitarian states that have been wrestling with religion-based dissident activity, such as China, Russia, Cuba, Venezuela and Indonesia.

"Among our allies, the traffic was notable but not alarming. The German chancellor placed five calls: three to his mistress and two to the head of intelligence services. In the UK, the prime minister made four calls: three to members of his cabinet — and one to the German chancellor's mistress."

Any discomfort in the room about the level of intrusion of the NSA snooping was apparently suppressed by the penguins' desire not to rock the floe.

"Regarding the event itself, there were no radio transmissions, no microwave transmissions, no significant energy releases — nothing that our land- or space-based equipment could detect. No miracles have occurred, no water turned into wine, no manna falling from Heaven, no burning bushes."

The skeptical vibe of the comments washed across the room. "In the absence of anything to support the extraordinary explanations of that report, we must return to more ordinary possibilities — a father trying to use his son for publicity, a trick by a local reporter going for an Emmy, even a preacher looking to create a domestic pilgrimage Mecca. We're back to the old saying: when you hear hoof-beats, think horses, not zebras."

The president nodded. As convincing as the video was, the NSA director was right. This was Virginia, not the Holy Land, and miracles didn't happen here. It was a horse, not a zebra, and probably a fake horse at that.

"Well, absent any evidence other than this video" — the penguins already nodding vigorously in agreement, before they'd even heard the president's conclusion — "I agree with Jim on this…"

"Before we go with Jim's interpretation," said the director of the FBI, "I have one more point to make."

The roomful of advisors looked at the FBI director with shock that he would interrupt the revealing of their conclusion. The FBI man didn't appear to care; in fact, he seemed to be enjoying the moment.

"Guthrie," he said to the young man by his side, "please bring up the second video."

"There's a second video?" the president asked.

The NSA director stared daggers at the FBI director. *Just what fresh hell was this?*

The young man worked with rapid movements on the laptop, and a frozen image of the boy and his father appeared — from a different angle than the news report video.

"A congregant took this video with her cell phone and sent it to the FBI," the director said.

The FBI director basked in his victory over the NSA and the CIA momentarily, then told Guthrie to play the video.

The video flickered into motion on the wall screen, then froze again. There was the boy, mouth open, and his father holding him.

"This is just as the kid begins his proclamation. Look at the father's forehead."

Chairs tipped as everyone leaned forward. Visible in the frame was a large, ugly bump on the right side of the man's forehead, with an even uglier crust of dried blood across a gash that topped the bump. The whole unsightly mess was surrounded by a dark bruise.

The president, unimpressed, looked over at the director.

"Now watch," said the FBI director, and motioned to his assistant to set the video into slow forward motion. As the boy's distorted face mouthed the now familiar words, the father looked even more distraught.

"Stop there," the director commanded. "Look at the bump on the father's head now."

Everyone strained to study the image. The bump looked a little different. Something about the lighting, or the angle of the camera — or something — had made the bump, gash and bruise shrink.

The president rose to his feet slowly.

"*Now* watch," said the director. The video crept forward. All eyes were on the father's head.

"Good God!!" yelled the president simultaneously with other exclamations from around the table as the bump, bruise, and gash disappeared. The blood, too. All of it — gone, as if that part of the video had played in reverse.

And for the president, and the entire room, the doubt disappeared with it. Picking up a phone on the polished table, the president pushed a button.

"Sarah, get the political team together."

EIGHTEEN

The sun streaming in through the crack in the heavy curtains did not wake Tom and Amy. They were already lying awake, after restless nights.

Tom got up and peeked through the window. The parking lot was silent, but more cars had appeared overnight — most with North Carolina or Maryland license plates.

Amy sat up in bed and stroked Billy's hair.

"I dreamed I was alone and afraid on a dark road through the mountains. I was hurt and scared and there was no one to help me."

The meaning of the dream was painfully obvious, but Amy seemed so exhausted that she could not grasp it.

"Maybe we should go back to Reverend Fogherty today," he suggested.

Amy shook her head. "What's he going to tell us? That God chose our son to tell him that his sermons suck?"

The uncharacteristic cynicism took Tom by surprise. "Hey," he said with a gentle smile, "that's my line."

His reply slid by Amy unnoticed. "If it was God talking through Billy, why would He make everything so hard on us, and on Billy? Why would He put us in a position where people think we're crazy, where we can't even go home?"

Tom opened his mouth to answer, but no words came out. Spiritual reassurances had never been his forte. Amy didn't wait for it, anyway.

"You saw the signs those people were carrying. Those crazy nuts might be *in* our house by now. Even if we did go home, another maniac might try to hurt us. If this is an example of God's love and wisdom, it's bullshit!"

"Sweetie," Tom said, sitting next to her, "everything will be all right. God won't let something bad happen to us."

The angry expression on Amy's face took Tom aback, so he tried a different tack.

"I don't know what's going on, but I promise you everything will be all right. I'll straighten it all out today. I promise."

Reassurance flickered across Amy's face. *At least she still has some faith in me,* Tom thought. *I can't let her down.*

Amy headed to the bathroom and turned on the shower. Unsure how he would keep this promise, Tom flipped on the TV and turned on WSSS. But he could not escape the Miracle at St. Tobias's. Jim Blake's radiant face filled the screen.

"…so what began as a quiet celebration of a preacher's anniversary has turned into an event of international proportions," Blake was bubbling. "At noon today, we'll be holding a special town hall meeting, live from our downtown studios, to talk about the importance of the Miracle Baby. Our guests will include Reverend Carter Ray Jones, Reverend Waite from St. Tobias's Church, and local community leaders. I hope you'll join us."

Tom switched off the television, disgusted. The damn media and that slimy evangelist would milk this thing for all it's worth. And what the hell was Waite thinking? He wasn't even the preacher at the service!

As Tom stewed on the involvement of these jerks, an idea began to form. All of these bastards would be in one place at one time… he could catch them before the show… chew 'em out good… maybe that would make them think twice about what they were doing to his family. He could end this circus once and for all.

NINETEEN

As the political team assembled, the intelligence team dispersed. Only the National Security Agency director stayed behind, and now he sat across a luxurious mahogany desk from the president in the Oval Office.

"Jim, this ain't a hoax," the president said to the old spy.

"Nope."

"It ain't exactly good news, either," the president added.

"Nope," agreed the advisor.

"It would be helpful if we knew where this family is. Isn't this why we have all those electronic eavesdropping programs?"

"Well, not technically, no," smiled the NSA director, referencing the fact that Congress had intended to authorize the NSA to snoop *outside* the country, and on *terrorists*, not innocent American citizens. "But that hasn't stopped us before."

What the old intelligence pro did not tell the president — nor had he shared with any of his intelligence colleagues — was that on Sunday his boys had identified a suspicious 911 call from a cell phone near where the family lived. The NSA had used the identifying data to track the cell phone to where it was hidden at a small strip mall not far from the family's home, and they'd detected a withdrawal of cash from the couple's bank account. The ATM camera confirmed it was Tom Smith who made the withdrawal, and traffic cameras showed the family's van leaving the bank parking lot. Due to a gap in traffic cameras, the agency lost the van after that, but the NSA was zeroing in on the Smiths.

During the meeting earlier in the morning, the director had stifled a snort at the FBI's belief that the call they'd picked up from the house phone was intended to be a call to information. *They were dialing 911, not 411, you idiots*, he had wanted to say during the presentation. *They'd misdialed in their panic.*

But the NSA director had declined to speak up then, and despite being sandbagged by the FBI about the father's head wound, he continued to play his cards close to his vest now, in keeping with his custom. Better to stay quiet and see where things led — very possibly to the family itself.

Under-promise and over-deliver — that was the key to managing up.

"We will give it our best shot, Mr. President."

TWENTY

Reverend Fogherty slammed his Bible down.

"I'll be d--," he shouted, then stopped short.

"I'll be darned if you're going to turn this church into some kind of three-ring circus!"

"But Reverend Fogherty," said Reverend Waite, "This is a blessing, a miraculous event. And, if you hadn't noticed, it already is a circus. What would you call what's going on outside in the parking lot *right now*?"

"I saw," Fogherty grumbled. About a hundred — well, pilgrims one might call them — had set up on the grounds. They'd spent the morning praying and staging goofy demonstrations for the television cameras.

"God spoke to the world from our church," Waite said. "He must've chosen our church for a reason!"

Waite gestured around them.

"The worn carpets, the old lighting fixtures, paint peeling off the walls. God gave us the opportunity to fix all this and bring more faithful into our flock." Waite's eyes went wide, even a touch manic. "We could even start a televised service. We could become larger than we've ever been — larger than any church in the area!"

"This isn't the Olympics!" said Fogherty. "We're not competing against other churches!"

"Of course not. But if we continue on our current path, our church will disappear in a matter of years. Don't be the son who buries the coins given to him by his father, Reverend. We are obligated to prosper and to build on what the Lord gives us."

Fogherty regarded his young colleague "Please don't…"

"I'm going on the show, Reverend," said Waite. "I refuse to waste this gift."

TWENTY-ONE

At 11:30 a.m., Jim Blake was in a panic. Sitting in the make-up chair of WSSS, he was 30 minutes away from the broadcast that would finally get him out of this rut and bring him to the heights he deserved. It was a pressure-filled moment.

"*Headshoulderskneesandtoeskneesandtoes, headshoulderskneesandtoeskneesandtoes…*"

The make-up artist rolled her eyes as the odd little newsman mouthed some sort of song to himself over and over.

So intent was Jim on his hyper-obsessive compulsive routine, and so intent was the make-up artist on ignoring the completely nuts small-town reporter (while masking the flock of crows' feet perched around his eyes) that neither noticed when Chip Stone slipped into the room. He tapped Blake on the shoulder and scared the crap out of the panicked newsman.

"*Headshoulderskneesandt---AAAAAHHHHHHHH!!*"

"*Eeeeeeeeeeekkkkkkkkkkkk!!*" shrieked the make-up artist, throwing her instruments in every direction.

"*What?*" yelled Stone.

"*AAAAAHHHHHHH!!!!!!!!!!*"

"*Eeeeekkkkkkkkkkk!!!!!!!!!!!!!!!*"

"*What?! WHOA!*"

The moment of chaos was followed by a few seconds of nervous laughter as each regained composure.

As the make-up artist worked to undo the damage she'd just inflicted, Stone explained his presence to the awe-struck Jim.

"Jeff," Chip began.

"It's Jim," said Jim.

"Right," said Chip, admiring his tan in the mirror. "Big Man, I think you've done an excellent job on this story."

Blake's face flushed and his chest swelled as Chip continued. "This town hall meeting — it was your idea?"

"Well, yes, it was…," answered Blake innocently.

"Well, you've done just an excellent job. Top notch. You've provided that critical local presence that's so important to our viewers. And I hope you've been satisfied with the national coverage I've been giving our story."

"Uh, sure," said Blake, missing the key possessive pronoun.

"Good. As the show progresses today, give me the high sign if you think I get off-track at any point," Stone said.

"Sure," Blake said, still star-struck and being star-mugged, assuming the program producer had added Stone to the guest line-up.

"Great," concluded Stone. "Honey, can you touch me up bit?"

TWENTY-TWO

In a nearby make-up room, Reverend Waite fidgeted while a make-up guy powdered his face. Waite was more accustomed to serving than being served, especially like this, especially by a man.

As Waite struggled not to regard the flamboyant make-up artist as a caricature, a large, cologne-soaked, jewel-encrusted caricature of a holy man dropped into the chair next to him.

"Well, hello there, compadre," boomed the familiar voice of the Reverend Carter Ray Jones. "Let me be the first to congratulate you on the excellent work you are doing for the Lord. How's about a little touch-up here, Judy."

Waite frowned. Who is Judy?

A contemptuous expression, missed by both preachers, flashed across the make-up man's face.

"Reverend Carter Ray Jones, at your service," Jones said, thrusting out a ring-laden right hand. "Pleased to meet another man of the cloth, particularly one involved in this historic event."

Waite tried to return the pleasantries, but Jones trampled Waite's words.

"Now, son," Jones plowed on, "I can only imagine what kind of pressure and confusion you've been experiencing since this whole thing blew open. You must feel like you're at nut-house central these days."

"It has been chaotic, yes," said Waite, trying to be respectful, despite everything he'd heard about, or from, the televangelist.

Jones leaned in Waite's direction and dropped his voice. Waite felt dizzy as he tried to maintain eye contact. Jones placed a hand on Waite's forearm.

"Just between us Christians, how is your church these days? I noticed you may not have had the time — or maybe the resources? — to keep the house of the Lord in top condition. Things OK there?"

Waite's reaction to the insulting insinuation was mitigated by the hypnotic effect Jones was having on him. "We're doing OK."

"Listen brother. I know what it's like. I know how it is to bust your backside doing the work of the Lord when you don't even have two shekels to rub together, much less the thousands of dollars it takes to keep a ministry ship-shape. It wears on you — the walls need painting, the pews start to splinter, the television cameras are blown out by lightning." He chuckled. "Well, I guess you can't even *afford* that problem yet, can you? All the while the flock shrinks. The kids move away, the old faithful die off, and the in-betweens head over to that new place with the gajillion-dollar capital budget and the fancy red brick architecture. It is a real challenge."

My Lord, Waite wondered. *How does he know?*

"Fact of the matter is," Jones continued, "organized religion was not organized with the modern world in mind. We got 17th Century financial and organizational structures trying to make it in the 21st Century world. Like trying to win the Toyota Owners 400 with a '78 Tercel."

The NASCAR reference was lost on Waite, despite the fact that the Toyota Owners 400 was run at Richmond International Raceway.

"If you don't mind me asking," said Waite, "what are you getting at?"

"Scale, son. It's all about scale. Hell, look at the amusement park industry. My Christ Almighty Family Theme Park has a devil of a time competing against those sons-of-guns down at Disney. Why? Scale. They buy stuffed mice and dogs and dwarfs by the truckload, and they get a price to match. At Christ Almighty, we gotta pay top dollar for our Jesus dolls. Don't even get me started on the disciple dolls. Sure, we move a lot of John, Paul, Mark and Luke — and Judas, of course — but how many folks you think want to toss a ring on a nail to win one of the other guys? Still, we gotta have 'em, or there's hell to pay."

Waite was so stunned he didn't notice the televangelist slipping into his good-ol'-boy drawl — his go-to dialect for closing a sale.

"Tell you the truth, padre," Jones continued in confessional tones, "if I knew then what I know now, I never would've opened Christ Almighty. One park just ain't enough scale. Just to get to break-even, we'll need to open another coupla-three parks. I tell you, the Pope has the right idea with Vatican City. Walled in, no rides, no liability insurance, no teenaged employees with their hands in the till and who knows where else all the time — just a self-contained facility, all about atmosphere. Like Colonial Williamsburg.

"We should've gone for 'Olde Bethlehem' or 'Olde Jerusalem,'" Jones continued, making exaggerated air quotes. "We mighta' lost the kids, sure, but we would've made it back in lower costs and scalability. Lot easier to build another stable and manger with a petting zoo than keep up in the roller coaster arms race these days, I'll tell you that."

Waite sat, bewildered. Jones angled for the kill.

"My theme park doesn't have scale, but you know what does? The Jones International Ministry. In addition to the global headquarters and the operational facility there in Nashville, we've taken a stake in several dozen churches around the world. Catholic, Protestant, Episcopalian, Southern Baptist, it don't matter. We even have a handful of synagogues in the fold. We're majority or minority partners in facilities in the biggest cities in the States, Europe, Central and South America, and now we're looking at Eastern Europe. We'll wait for a consumer base with disposable income there. Eventually, naturally, we'll move on China and Russia, but there will need to be some changes in those governments before we risk capital.

"With all these locations comes scale. We have national and international supplier contracts for paint, carpet, robes, communion chips, candles, stained glass — you name it.

"I saw the video, son, and your facility needs this stuff. Don't get me wrong, I know it ain't easy. But we can help. Get you paint at 60% of what you'd pay — same for everything you'd need to make the place shine.

"All we gotta do is fold St. Thomas's into the organization. We'd buy a stake in the church — say, 51% of the total value of your operation, including buildings and grounds, assets, the weekly offering take plus some amount of goodwill. That's an immediate cash infusion, padre, probably to the tune of a couple hundred grand. That, plus lower supply costs, and soon your church looks like the Sistine Chapel.

"Of course, as a 51% owner, we get a cut of your weekly offerings, and plow most of that back into local operations.

"One other thing," he added, as if an afterthought. "We supplement the salaries of our ministers, of course. Working in the service of the Lord makes it tough to build a retirement portfolio, eh? We men and women of the cloth are scandalously underpaid. To attract the best and the brightest — people like you — we pay along the lines of the private sector.

"So what do you say, brother? Will you join us in our crusade for God?"

Then Jones clammed up. The salesman knew that the first person to talk after the pitch was the loser.

Except when the first person was the pimply-faced gopher for a local talk show.

"Ten minutes to airtime!" he announced at the door. "We need you on the set."

Waite rose slowly and sidestepped toward the door, eyeing the big televangelist as if he were a hooded cobra.

"We'll talk later," said Jones with a wink and an overly friendly pat on the shoulder.

Waite nodded, suppressing an urge to brush his jacket where Jones had touched him, and headed for the set, with Jones trailing close behind.

TWENTY-THREE

Tom maneuvered through traffic on Broad Street, working his way toward the red and white television tower, a 843-foot lighthouse on the outskirts of Richmond proper. For decades, the tower had stood sentinel on the western edge of the city, visible on a clear day from West End Manor, ten miles away.

Tom remembered the stir in the late '60s when a man, distraught over a family dispute, had climbed the tower in a half-hearted attempt to kill himself. Firefighters scaled the tower in pursuit and, after several tense hours above the steaming pavement, had talked him down.

For years, Tom and his friends referred to the soaring structure as "the tower that the man climbed up." Its height had given WSSS-TV tremendous reach, extending 100+ miles in any direction. In today's age of cable and satellites, the tower was an anachronism existing on the edge of consciousness of a suburban city, barely noticed by citizens. It was stippled with microwave dishes and tiny antennae, reduced from a beacon of modern communication to scaffolding for a more compact and electronic age.

Ironically, inside the studio under the tower, a program would be broadcast this afternoon that would reach more people than even existed on entire planet when the station was launched in the 1950s. WSSS-TV, through its affiliation with GNBNC, would broadcast to billions the story of a child who was either a divine messenger, the Antichrist or a fraud, depending on whom you asked.

If anyone asked Tom, he knew the answer. Billy was simply a child caught up in some weird phenomenon. He was not a vehicle for anyone's ambitions, or a platform for someone's agenda, and not the Second Coming or a threat to the world. But the chance he'd perish in the feeding frenzy of self-interested sharks, parasites and sons-of-bitches was very real — unless someone stopped this madness. Tom intended to do just that.

It was 11:45 a.m. when he pulled up to the station. Hundreds of people spilled off the sidewalk and poured in from nearby side streets and alleys. Outside the squat brown WSSS-TV building, a line of people three-wide stretched to the corner and around to Broad Street.

A harried guard at the gate motioned for Tom to stop his van.

"You got business here today, sir?"

"I'm here for the show!" he yelled back.

"You gotta find parking on the street," the guard replied.

"No, you don't understand," Tom shouted. "*I'm* here for the *show*," he repeated, thinking his word emphasis would convey his real meaning.

"Park elsewhere!" yelled the guard, in uncoded language.

Tom motioned the guard over to the van. Under his breath, he said, "I'm the kid's dad." With a smile, he added, "I'm *here*… for the *show*."

"You're also the fifth guy to say he's the kid's dad, including one in a toga and another in a paper hat. Park elsewhere."

Conversation over.

Tom backed the van through the throng and found a spot two blocks away. He kept his head down, trying not to be noticed. The last thing he needed was to be recognized before he could get in.

A few people gave him puzzled looks. Did they recognize him? Did they realize they were in the presence of the miracle baby's father? Then, with a shock, he realized the stake his ego had taken in this matter.

Don't be an idiot! he chastised himself. *This isn't about you, and Billy isn't some freak miracle baby.*

It was amazing how strong and insidious the ego could be, injecting itself with high self-regard into the most inappropriate situations. Tom was a daydreamer, always had been, and sometimes he indulged in daydreams in which he courageously stepped in front of a bus to save a child, or charged into a burning house to save an infant. But to his dismay, his heroic daydreams always involved potential harm or death for others.

Don't be a frickin' idiot! was his typical reaction to this realization. *How sick is that?*

As he walked, wrestling with his ego, a large, black SUV accelerated toward the station. Tom managed to step right into its path as it turned into the station lot. The driver slammed on the brakes, and the SUV screeched to a halt inches short of Tom.

Tom steadied himself with a hand on the hood, glaring at the windshield, but its dark tint prevented him from seeing two men inside drawing pistols. He also didn't notice two additional armed men rapidly approaching from behind.

In a flash, the front doors of the SUV popped open and guns filled the v-shaped space between the windshield and doorframes. Simultaneously two men took up firing positions three feet from where he stood.

In the din of the moment, Tom was only dimly conscious of the screams of the crowd.

TWENTY-FOUR

"FREEZE!! Put your hands on your head!! PUT YOUR HANDS ON YOUR HEAD!!"

Tom obeyed.

"On the ground!! NOW!!"

Tom laid face down on the cold sidewalk. A knee landed painfully in the center of his back, and sharp gravel cut into his chest. The owner of the bony knee wrenched Tom's arm behind him, and slapped handcuffs on Tom's wrists.

"What the hell is going on?" Tom yelled.

Before anyone could answer, someone yelled out, "Hey, that's the kid's dad! He was in the video! He's the dad!"

Cries of recognition rose up and the mob pressed inward to get a better look. The space around the "crime scene" shrank, and the armed men looked around with concern.

"That's him!"

"WHERE'S THE DEVIL CHILD?" someone screamed, and then several of the Armageddon-minded joined in.

"Father of the devil!"

"Antichrist!"

"Satan!"

Just as quickly, the hope-focused contingent spoke up.

"He is NOT a devil child!"

"Let the kid alone!"

"It's God speaking to us!"

The crowd pressed farther in as the verbal battle escalated.

"Get him!"

"This is the father of the Devil!"

Then a shout from the edge of the crowd: "KILL HIM!" The crowd surged forward at the cry, to within three feet of the prostrate Tom and his captors.

That was enough for the armed men in the SUV. One grabbed a shotgun and vaulted to the hood of the SUV. At the same time, the driver leaned on the horn, setting off shrieks and screams from the crowd. With great flourish, the man on the hood pumped a shell into the shotgun and held the weapon high.

As the crowd fell back, he lowered the shotgun to shoulder level and swept it in an angry arc above the mob.

Suddenly, a piercing voice cut through the rising tension of the moment.

"ENOUGH!" shouted Governor Mary Rolfe, emerging from the back seat and towering above the crowd. She had one foot on the bench seat, one foot on the open door's armrest, and her fashionable skirt hiked up above her knees.

"THAT… IS… ENOUGH!"

The crowd fell silent, and the man with the shotgun slowly raised the barrel of his weapon.

Glaring, Rolfe climbed down to the sidewalk, smoothed out her skirt, and strode toward Tom.

"Put him in the back seat," she ordered. Then she turned to the crowd.

"Ladies and gentlemen," she began. "I am no more sure of what is going on with this child than you are. But I will be *damned* if we are going to allow our Commonwealth to sink into fear-driven riots! Whatever the truth, *no one* is killing *anyone!*"

She turned to a state trooper. "Get more men down here!"

"And *you* people," she shouted, turning back to the crowd. "*Straighten up!*"

With that, the governor of Virginia climbed back into the SUV, next to the handcuffed father of the Godbaby, slammed the door, and motioned the driver into the parking lot. After all, she was here for the show.

TWENTY-FIVE

Inside the SUV, the governor sat quietly, twitching slightly and making odd little noises in her throat. A few barely audible words squeaked out under her breath, and then she was still.

After a moment, she turned to Tom.

"Hi, I'm Mary Rolfe," she said, as if nothing had just happened.

Tom had often envisioned himself meeting famous people, and even had an occasional fantasy about meeting this particular famous person. In none of his daydreams, however, had he met them while cuffed in the back of an armored government vehicle after a near-lynching while held at gunpoint immediately after nearly being run over by the previously mentioned armored government vehicle. Also, never while being known as the father of a boy considered to be the Devil or the Second Coming of Christ.

Therefore, he found himself with no imagined precedent for the subsequent conversation.

"Uh, nice to meet you," he stammered, instinctively moving to shake hands, but finding himself short-sheeted.

Rolfe smiled pleasantly, even pleasingly. "Sorry about the confusion back there," she said with breathtaking understatement. "When my E.P.U. — that's the executive protection unit — saw you step in front of the truck and put your hands on the hood, they reacted, well, forcefully. They also hit the emergency signal that brought the two state troopers running."

Raised to be deferential to women, celebrities and high-ranking officials, Tom had no choice regarding what to say next.

"It's OK. No problem." *I damn near pissed in my pants, though.*

"This issue with your son has a lot of people on edge," she sympathetically. "My security team is concerned that if I get involved, I might become vulnerable to attack from extremists."

Tom sat in quiet understanding.

Rolfe held his gaze.

"What on earth are you doing here anyway?"

"I…," He paused, this being the first time he'd spoken his plans out loud. "My family is being harassed and attacked, and I think it is the media's fault for blowing this whole thing out of proportion. I want to tell Chip Stone to lay-off."

"Or else what? You'll beat him up?"

Tom hesitated. Maybe he hadn't thought this plan all the way through.

"Because GNBNC would *love it* if you punched Stone," said the governor. "And the network won't pull back just because the kid's dad doesn't like it."

Of course they wouldn't — it would just add fuel to the fire. He sat without a word, face reddening in embarrassment.

Rolfe gave him a kind smile.

"What if *I* told Chip Stone to lay off? What if I said it on air? Do you think that would help?"

Tom's optimism soared. Surely the network would call off the investigation if a powerful government official asked them to.

"That would be amazing," Tom stammered. "That might work."

"It might not, but I can try."

"Thank you, governor."

"It is my pleasure," the governor replied.

Tom had no idea what to do or say. "Big truck," he managed.

The governor continued smiling.

"A truck this big ought to have bow-thrusters on it," Tom stammered on, shooting for humor. "Does Captain Stubing know you've got his boat?"

The governor shifted a bit in her seat. She seemed closer. "Now, what else can I do for you?"

Blood rushed to Tom's face at the governor's sudden proximity. Afraid to say anything, he just sat there.

The governor broke the silence. "I would think you're concerned about your family's safety."

"Yes," replied Tom. Inside his chest, guilt mixed with rising concern for Amy and Billy back in the hotel room.

The governor placed a slim, graceful hand on Tom's shoulder, and her brilliant green eyes locked on Tom's. "I can only imagine what you are going through," she said, leaning closer.

Tom could smell her perfume. His breathing quickened.

Rolfe shifted her rear end, her elbow brushing Tom's rib cage as she held eye contact.

"You know, my protection detail is pretty effective, as you just saw."

Tom couldn't help but agree. His back still hurt where the trooper's knee had come down, and his wrists were aching from the handcuffs.

"It might not be a bad idea to assign a few of the guys to protect your family from the whackos," she continued.

Something didn't seem right. The governor seemed genuine enough, but a flashing red light in the back of his mind warned him not to ally so closely with any of the players who had jumped in to "save" Billy and his family.

Still, he remembered the crazy eyes of the man who attacked them in their home. And the governor *had* just offered to intervene on his behalf with Stone. Maybe it wasn't a bad idea to have armed men protecting Amy and Billy.

Rolfe moved in, figuratively and literally, until her face was six inches from Tom's. "I can have your family under armed guard within the hour. Just tell me where they are."

Tom was overwhelmed. "We're…"

Suddenly, the door to the SUV popped open like the vacuum-sealed hatch on a spacecraft, and light flooded the interior. With a *whoosh*, the sexual tension and expectancy of the moment escaped into the cold afternoon air.

A balding man in short sleeves and a clip-on tie poked in his head. "Welcome!" sang the general manager of WSSS-TV to the grimacing governor.

Then his eyes darted over to the handcuffed man sitting oddly close to the governor.

"Who's the perp?"

TWENTY-SIX

A block of six sizable high-definition video screens dominated the wall of the room where the president and his closest political advisors sat this morning. On the screen was a multi-colored United States map. Officially, the map was intended to help the president monitor and direct the response to natural disasters.

An astute observer, however, would find it interesting, and perhaps even inappropriate, that the screens more often displayed one or more of the 434 congressional districts in the nation. The color-coded districts could be sub-divided based on party affiliation, demographic make-up, average/mean/median per capita income, major industries or agricultural output, union membership, per capita political contributions, voting patterns over the past 50 federal elections, and other non-natural disaster-related characteristics.

From time to time, the room *was* used to monitor natural disasters, but mostly it served up political disasters — which this president specialized in creating.

The president's superlative political instincts, combined with his avarice, ambition, ego and sexual appetite, had helped him craft a swerving, sometimes effective, sometimes comedic administration record. From one Sunday to the next, his cabinet secretaries and political spokespeople populated the morning news shows alternately basking in the glory of breathtaking political victories and scrambling to explain breathtaking indiscretions on the part of the president, his wife, friends, relatives or associates.

White House staffers joked that this was great work if you could get it over with.

The president cruised to victory three years earlier, but the next election loomed ten months out, and the GOP candidate this time would likely be Moneybags from the West. The president faced a real challenge. Thus the war room disguised as a Federal Emergency Management Administration (FEMA) command center, located steps from the Oval Office and staffed around the clock, it seemed, by political operatives from his first campaign.

Gathered in the room were ten smart and ruthless twenty- and thirty-something men and women, dedicated to their leader and ready to do whatever it took to win. The president loved this band of merciless "warriors for justice" — his justice. These kids didn't fight for the Democratic Party. The weak-willed "leaders" on the Hill disgusted them. They fought for their president, and the ideals for which he stood, and if they had to deliver a few bribes, break a few laws or destroy a few lives to accomplish their mission, so be it.

Lately they'd been dealing with a rash of corrupt friends, relatives and former business associates. Some were pure criminals, and some were idiots in over their heads. But all represented threats to the operatives' man, his political viability and the causes for which he fought. So each was distanced and then dismantled and destroyed on the national stage through smear campaigns featuring lies, rumors, innuendo and, often, the truth.

The political team didn't just take out wayward allies and friends who's poor judgment sullied the president. Similar hit jobs had been carried out against over-zealous Republicans who had questioned the propriety of president's associations. After a sound thrashing in the headlines, on the evening news and on myriad political talk shows, these yapping amateurs folded their tents and retreated with their sthrishattered reputations and shell-shocked families.

After each win, these political assassins gathered at their favorite Mexican restaurant on the Hill, celebrating their swath of destruction with margaritas and tequila shots.

The president looked at his storm troopers with satisfaction, then glanced at his watch. It was 11:30 a.m. GNBNC planned to broadcast a special town hall on the issue at noon, and the Virginia governor might take part. Her presence would move this issue further into the political realm, so the assembled group would be watching.

"OK folks, let's focus," called out the president.

The young Turks quieted and fell into seats around a big conference table.

"By now you've all seen the two videos of this kid," he said. "I can't explain it, and my intelligence penguins are afraid to come to a conclusion, but something odd is definitely going on. That kid's father went from freak show to normal in ten seconds on the second video. Now, I'm no doctor, but that ain't how it usually works."

Cool smiles circled the table. This group was too hip to laugh at every joke the president made.

"We've got to get ahead of this. What are the polls saying?"

A skinny guy with fashionable glasses rose, remote in hand. "Mr. President, here's what we have so far…"

The wall map disappeared and a PowerPoint presentation took its place.

"The GNBNC/Washington Post overnight polls asked Americans whether they thought the kid's act was real or fake. A surprising majority, 72%, thought the incident really happened. Twenty-one percent said it was a hoax, and 7% had no opinion."

"Seven percent, huh?. Probably my intelligence advisors."

The group smiled.

"The interesting break is how that 72% views the event," continued the presenter after an appropriate pause for no laughter. "Thirty-eight percent think the kid was channeling God. The other 34% think he's some kind of Antichrist.

"Our own polling lines up pretty well with the media result. We sliced our numbers for party affiliation. For Democrats, 20% think the kid is on God's team, 17% think the kid is working for Satan, 45% think it's a hoax, and 18% have no opinion. For independents, 13% think the kid is channeling God, 21% think the kid is connected to the devil, and 65% think it's a hoax. A lot of those folks think it's a government-orchestrated hoax, and a disturbingly high percentage mentioned Area 51. Only 1% of independents have no opinion.

"Finally, of Republicans, 21% think the kid is channeling God, 10% think it's a hoax, 3% have no opinion, and a whopping 66% think the kid is connected to the devil."

"OK," said the president. "Let's run through some scenarios. Say the kid is the real thing, and that he's working for God — what does that mean for us?"

An attractive blonde with a talent for interpreting the mood of the country and a future on the political gab shows spoke up. "If the general population becomes convinced he's on God's team, then we can expect a surge in spirituality in the country. Coming with that would be rising sentiments for a mingling of church and state, faith-based initiatives, and possibly a sea change in the abortion debate toward anti-choice."

Heads nodded in agreement.

"OK, that's not good. And what if he's proven to be working for the devil?"

"In that case, we'll see an even more dramatic shift toward spirituality, as a defense effort against evil or the apocalypse. We'd also see an accompanying militant bent, bringing with it right-wing extremists and conspiracy theorists, as well as the moderates in the mushy middle, all lining up behind the most logical banner to follow: that of the religious right."

Again heads nodded in grim agreement.

"OK, that's *really* not good," said the president. "And if he's shown to be a hoax?"

"That depends on who's behind the hoax. If the boy's family, then the country and media will lynch the parents and the boy becomes a national foster child. There is opportunity in that scenario for a more active government role in child-rearing, but otherwise, things go back to normal pretty quickly.

"If the government is implicated in the hoax, however, then the populace will turn against the party in power — against you, Mr. President. Finally, if religious or political extremists are behind the hoax, then the country's sentiments shift toward a more active government role in opposing dangerous elements in our society, and toward protecting children. The GOP could be tainted by their direct or indirect association with these groups, and we will be positioned much better for the election and for implementing a more proactive, progressive agenda.

"The kid and his family will be destroyed, of course. As will whoever is perceived to be behind the hoax. But the last scenario has by far the best possible outcome for us."

"I know which one I like," deadpanned the president. "How do we make it happen?"

TWENTY-SEVEN

Tom's sneakers squeaked as he made his way through the backstage area of WSSS-TV. The governor led him around like a sorority date, clutching his arm, steering him through the borderline chaos of a television production, and in a low voice passing along bits of her planned strategy for the broadcast.

The room was packed with spectators, crew, security and participants. About 250 people were seated in the shallow, half-bowl-shaped audience section of the studio, and dozens more lined the back wall.

"Five minutes folks!" yelled a young woman dressed in black, with short hair, multiple piercings and a headset. "Guests, we need you to take your seats, please!"

Four chairs arranged in an arc spanned the stage.

"Why don't you stand back here, out of view of the cameras?" whispered the governor to Tom. "If you need anything, I'll be right there," she added pointing to a chair on the stage.

Tom nodded. As he surveyed the scene, he heard a woman softly say, "Going to ruin his life, too?" But when he looked around, the only woman within range was the governor.

Great, now I'm hearing things, he said to himself.

"Governor?"

"Yes Tom?"

Tom paused, struggling for words.

"Thank you," he finally said.

She leaned in, way in, until Tom could feel her warm breath on his neck.

"My pleasure, Tom," she whispered, and he shuddered involuntarily as the her lips brushed his ear.

Rolfe pulled back, and after a quick wink walked toward the chairs on the stage. Tom's knees wobbled and he leaned onto the back of a folding chair for support.

Rolfe took her seat at the end of the row. To her right sat a rumpled man with gray hair, a fuzzy gray mustache, thick glasses, and a worn, brown sports jacket. He looked like a stereotypical professor and, as it turned out, he *was* a professor, of modern theology, from a nearby state college.

At the other end sat Reverend Waite, looking lost in thought, and between him and the professor sat Reverend Jones. He was leaning over and whispering something to Waite, who appeared to be avoiding eye contact.

Tom recalled Jones's statement that he intended to help "tune" Billy to get the best reception of God's message.

A chill swept over Tom as he thought about the danger his family was in, from the crazies on his lawn to the vultures like Jones and the media. The thought focused Tom's mind, and he felt a calmness as he scanned the room with more skeptical eyes.

In the audience, Tom saw dozens of people with fanatical looks in their eyes. They shouted to each other, shouted at each other, and shouted at the seated panel.

Mingled with the zealots were hopeful-looking people, many holding rosaries or Bibles. Several were on their knees, praying and rocking. When one caught Tom's eye, he looked away.

In the rear of the room stood a dozen or so men and women in business-casual slacks, shirts and sport jackets, with hard faces and alert eyes. They took in the scene with no apparent emotion. Governor Rolfe's executive protection unit, no doubt.

In the wing, off the far side of the stage, stood Jim Blake, the local reporter, and Chip Stone, the blow-dried buffoon from GNBNC. Stone, clearly in command, spoke to the woman with the clipboard. Jim Blake, silent and morose, stood to the side.

As Stone gestured to the woman, Blake stepped forward to make a point, but the GNBNC anchor waved him off, and the woman never even looked Blake's direction. Blake looked down at the floor, took a half-step in one direction, then walked directly to a door marked "EXIT." After a brief look back, he pushed the heavy door open and walked into the bright parking lot, the door slamming behind him. Tom Smith and the rest of the world's television viewers would never see Jim Blake again.

At that moment, the woman with the clipboard strode onto the stage and called out with unexpected volume.

"Thirty seconds to show time, folks!" She clapped, quieting the crowd. "I know a lot of you feel strongly about our topic today, but this is *not* the Jerry Springer show, so no screaming or fist-fights! We have lots of police here today (*gesturing toward the burly cops stationed at all the exits*) and they will arrest anyone who gets out of line. Thank you for your support, and let's have a good show!"

TWENTY-EIGHT

"Hello, and welcome to a very special town hall."

Chip Stone's chiseled features beamed out at the table full of political operatives in the White House political war room.

"We are in Richmond, Virginia, where the eyes of the world have been riveted for past 24 hours."

Stone's words echoed through the halls of Congress on more than 1,100 television sets in 535 offices of elected officials.

"In this quiet southern city, known mostly for its past glory and controversy as the capital of the Confederacy, an event has occurred that is changing how the world views God, mortality, and indeed, even itself."

In a tiny, cluttered office in the rear of St. Thomas's Church, an older, sad man of the cloth nodded at Stone's words.

"Many now expect a religious revolution to sweep the world," Stone was saying, "transforming the globe into single, unified flock and sweeping away the vestiges of 20th Century injustices and oppression."

On another screen, far from Richmond, the image was out of sync with the sound, but that was to be expected during simultaneous translation to Spanish. Cigar smoke formed a low cloud layer in the room. A dictator and his top henchmen leaned forward through the haze to catch every word of the broadcast from America.

"Millions more people tie the child to the Devil, or believe these events signal the end to our world."

A dozen career intelligence officers sat silent as Stone spoke.

"Finally, a sizable portion of our population believes the little boy is merely a puppet, being played for notoriety and riches by his parents."

In a huge red brick home, set like a cherry atop the rounded, snow-covered foothills of the Blue Ridge Mountains outside of Charlottesville, Virginia, an old man and a younger, mountain of a man watched Stone. The old man felt increasingly uneasy about what he was watching.

The screen flickered as Stone turned toward a panel of people, and a second camera followed. Governor Mary Rolfe of Virginia and televangelist Carter Ray Jones were instantly recognizable to most viewers.

"Now, today, GNBNC is hosting a very special and intimate town hall, where we will explore these issues with four important individuals — a theological expert, the top-ranking Virginia government official, a preacher from the church where the miracle occurred, and a world-famous religious leader. We'll also talk to our audience of ordinary citizens and take your calls, today, on a special GNBNC news program."

In a stark, darkened room of an aging hotel, a little boy ignored the images on a beat-up television on the dresser, and instead watched with concern as his mother cried softly at the end of the bed.

TWENTY-NINE

"Quiet please!" shouted the woman with the clipboard. "We're back from commercial in five, four, three…"

She counted off the final two seconds with silent hand motions, then pointed at Chip Stone.

"Welcome back to our special town hall, live from the hometown of the baby who some are calling the Second Coming of Christ.

"We are pleased to have with us for this town hall four very distinguished guests: Virginia Governor Mary Rolfe; the Reverend Michael Waite from St. Thomas's Church, where the incident took place; the Reverend Carter Ray Jones of the Jones International Ministry in Nashville; and Dr. Albert Swanson, professor of modern theology at the University of the Commonwealth of Virginia.

"Dr. Swanson, let me start with you. What do you make of all this? What is the meaning of this event?"

The audience focused on the gray-haired professor, who shifted in his seat and adjusted his Coke-bottle glasses. The room was dead quiet.

"This entire situation is a travesty," began the professor, and both factions in the audience — the true believers and the Armageddon types — exploded in jeers, boos and shouts.

Stone raised his hands in a feeble attempt to quiet the crowd. Professor Swanson raised his voice to be heard above the din.

"The boy is a fake! He has to be! All of you are following a counterfeit deity, and I believe a good number of you know it and don't care!"

The audience rose to their feet, and the roar of disapproval drowned out the professor's voice. Shouted down like a conservative speaker on a college campus, he waved off the audience with a scowl and a shoo-ing motion of his hands and stopped talking.

The studio audience was in full throat. Out of the corner of his eye, Stone saw the floor director signal for commercial break, so he shouted that the show would be right back, and the red light on the camera in front of him blinked off.

The crowd either did not know or did not care that the show was breaking for commercial, and both contingents continued shouting. Two opposing demonstrators in the front row shoved each other and nearly came to blows before the security guards could separate them.

Professor Swanson, not accustomed to being shouted down himself, rose from his seat, yanked off his microphone and stalked from the stage. Both factions roared their approval.

The gallop toward a riot was suddenly checked by several sharp barks from an air horn. A series of longer blasts took the wind out of the audience, quieting them enough for the stage director to be heard.

"All right, you assholes!" she yelled, striding onto the stage, air horn in hand. "Get hold of yourselves! Security, get rid of those two idiots who were fighting!"

As more guards and officers moved in to apprehend the two combatants, the stage director held on with both hands to her momentary command of the crowd. "Listen! You people are going to cut the shit or so help me I'll clear out this whole damn studio! Do you understand me? You may be confused about who is in charge of the world right now, but DO NOT be confused about who is in charge of THIS STUDIO! It is ME and I SWEAR to GOD I will have each and every one of you ARRESTED or thrown OUT of here if you keep this shit up! DO YOU UNDERSTAND ME?!"

Several heads in the chagrined audience nodded reflexively.

"Now, we're back on the air in," she paused, checking her watch, "25 seconds. Don't think I won't go right back to commercial and clear you numskulls out of here if you start up again! Just *try* me!"

The tiny stage director glowered at the audience, then checked her watch and put her headset back on.

"We're back in…," she began in a calm voice, looking at Stone, "Five, four, three…" then again switched to hand motions for the last two seconds and pointed at Chip Stone.

THIRTY

Recovering from the chaotic commercial break with all the grace of a national news reader, Stone was already in stride when the camera's red light flickered.

"Welcome back to Richmond, Virginia, where we and a spirited audience are hearing from four…, uh, that is, *three* prominent players in the drama surrounding the child who *may have* spoken for God." He turned to the panel. "Governor Rolfe, what do you make of all this?"

Rolfe swept her green eyes around the room, leaving every audience member feeling as if the governor had just made direct eye contact.

"Naturally I am hesitant to become too involved in an issue of religion," began Rolfe, "My caution comes from the separation of church and state mandated by both the U.S. Constitution and the Virginia Constitution.

"However, as it is my privilege to be the civic leader of this commonwealth, my domain must extend to societal issues as well, and certainly this issue impacts our society as much as any political or governmental issue."

One of the few clear-headed audience members screwed up her face, as if wondering, *Did the governor just say anything?*

"In that context, I feel it is important that I am involved in this issue. As such, I've reached out to Tom Smith, the father of young Billy Smith, and expressed to him the concern and interest with which I view this issue."

Tom listened, still somewhat in shock at the fact that he was sitting backstage watching the governor of Virginia mention his name on a nationally, probably internationally, broadcast television show. It had been a weird day or two, to say the least.

The expressions on the faces of the audience suggested that the governor was imparting some sort of wisdom, but Tom was beginning to hear tones of manipulation, and felt a creeping, growing shame for his earlier star-struck behavior toward Rolfe.

"That's why," continued Rolfe, "it's important for all Virginians — all Americans — to remain calm during this time, so we can best judge our proper reaction and course of action."

Chip Stone gazed at the governor expectantly, then realized with a start that she had finished her statement.

"OK. Thank you, Governor." He turned to Jones. "Reverend Jones, have you ever seen anything like this in your experience?"

"Frankly, Chip, no I haven't. 'Course, I've been involved in any number of miracle situations where someone has been used by God to convey messages to this world. And I've served as, well, the trail guide, I guess you'd call it, for many of these sheep as they navigated the treacherous waters that come with involvement in a miracle.

"One of my most important functions during a time like that is to adjust the recipient's attitude, if you will, toward God and humanity, to ensure that the person is best situated to receive any further messages. I've often likened it to tuning a radio to get the best possible reception. In fact, several members of my staff at the Jones International Ministry have served as channels for God's messages. These folks earn a respectable living working in the Lord's employ and, of course, their glory reflects upon and extends the reach of the Jones International Ministry as well."

Sitting in the chair next to Jones, Reverend Waite heard the underlying message. *The Lord's employ... extending the reach... reflected glory... a respectable living...* Money. Power. Using the work of the Lord — even possibly faking the work of the Lord — to make money, to gain power. This angle of attack troubled Waite to his soul, more profoundly than such crassness and vulgarity normally would. But he couldn't put his finger on why.

"What few people realize though, Chip, is how dangerous it is to be involved in a miracle. Not dangerous *during* the miracle, of course. Our Lord would never harm a servant while communicating to him and through him — heck, if He did, I'd've been hurt several times by now.

"No, the danger comes *after* the miracle, when God is gone and the person is left to fend for themselves as a host of parasites and fortune-seekers descend on him, using any number of underhanded techniques to forward their own agendas at the expense of the child. Or the adult — whichever. That's when it's important to have a shepherd, as it were, who's been there before and can help the recipient of this blessing avoid the pitfalls that come with it, which can even be fatal."

Many in the audience focused on the pontificating salesman, but a few noticed the man of the cloth next to him closing his eyes and grabbing onto his armrests like a skinny kid trying to hold himself in a roller coaster seat.

As Jones droned on, Waite no longer heard. His stomach was churning and his head was spinning and he thought he might be ill — all the result of an unholy revelation. He finally understood the source of his deep disconcertedness about Jones, and the jarring insight knocked him for a loop.

With slow, deliberate breaths, he fought to regain control and balance. He had slammed into a horrifying vision of himself, but there was still time to stop before he was transformed into a miniature version of the spiritual bloodsucker to his left.

He lurched out of his chair and proclaimed, "This is disgusting! And I am disgusted by myself!"

As the surprised audience and guests waited, Waite stared into the distance, as if reading a blinking signal light far away. A look of calm came over his face.

"With all due respect," he continued, glancing at Chip, "Reverend Carter Ray Jones here is a money-grubbing fraud who shamefully robes himself and his sales pitch in God's word."

Jones was stunned to the point of speechlessness — no mean feat.

"What's worse, I have been acting just like Mr. Jones. Since the moment I witnessed the miracle, I've focused on putting butts in pews instead of putting joy and hope into souls. I've looked at it as an opportunity to improve my church, when it's my own spiritual condition that I should be worried about. I am ashamed, and I apologize to my congregation, to our pastor, Reverend Fogherty, to the Smith family and to God. I ask for forgiveness from of all of you."

"I forgive you," whispered Reverend Fogherty to the small television in his cluttered office.

As Waite sat back down, the audience, unprepared for such intimacy and reflection, sat in silence. After a pause, a few, more lucid audience members began to applaud. Others, raised on trashy talk shows, joined in instinctively.

Chip Stone, while missing the actual weight of the moment, did sense that a weighty moment had occurred, and responded with what appeared to be a perfectly affected and solemn expression.

Somewhere in Atlanta, the thick fist of Stone's news editor slammed a table. He knew the pretty boy had no idea *why* he was making that serious face.

At the studio, Tom shot Stone a look of contempt. This fake-tanned, blow-dried, inch-deep dimwit was the personification of the media vultures who'd descended on his family like fresh road kill. Tom fought the urge to stride on-stage and break the jerk's nose.

A low buzz caught Tom's attention. He looked at the audience. Many were heads down… not praying, but… looking at their phones, and sharing their screens with neighbors.

Stone, meanwhile, waited what seemed like an appropriate amount of time, given the apparent gravity of the moment, and then turned to Rolfe.

"Governor, you've heard Reverend Waite and Reverend Jones speak of this event in terms of a miracle. What are your thoughts? Is this child the real deal, or were his father and mother pulling some sick publicity stunt that has spun beyond their control?"

Back at the hotel, Amy sat on the end of the bed, riveted to the television. She knew that Tom was at the studio. Her husband was not one who could sit on a problem without taking action to fix it. With nearly all of the main players involved in their son's situation in one place, there was no way Tom *wasn't* there. But she couldn't fathom Tom's plan, so she watched, a quiet panic brewing in her gut and a roll of toilet paper in her hands. She'd long ago exhausted the contents of the lone box of tissues in the room.

Billy played on the floor, occasionally looking up at his mom, vaguely concerned.

Amy felt anger rising. How could Tom have taken this step without consulting her? But then waves of sadness swept in over the receding anger — sadness at what had become of her family, their marriage, and her blossoming faith.

Backstage at the studio, Tom switched back and forth between the action on stage and the agitated crowd. Many now talked amongst themselves, ignoring the panelists. *Something's going on,* Tom thought. He wished he had his phone so he could check Twitter or a news site.

Without a phone, however, he was forced to focus on the here and now.

Tom shifted his eyes to the governor, who looked like she was keeping a secret. Every minute or so she smoothly uncrossed and crossed her legs, momentarily distracting 48% of the human beings in the room.

She is good, Tom had to admit to himself, then looked away before the governor could catch him looking. He did not want to give Rolfe the satisfaction of thinking Tom had fallen for her trick. He was ashamed for having entertained the idea that her attentions were based on anything but his status as the father of her ticket to power.

She'd promised to stand up for his family against the bullying media and the others using his family for their own gain. Would she do it?

The governor inhaled to speak.

THIRTY-ONE

"Chip, you are about to get an exclusive," Rolfe began, and Stone reflexively felt aroused.

Rolfe took another breath. She was about to place a big bet in this whole confusing mess.

"Not only do I believe the family is the victim in all this," she continued, "but I am personally working with Tom and Amy Smith to help them through this perilous period."

Once again, Carter Ray Jones's mouth fell open. How has she beaten him to the family? Waite also was stunned. But most surprised were Tom, in the studio, and Amy, at the hotel.

The audience, however, was not surprised.

"He's here!" some shouted.

"Who's here?" Stone asked.

Rolfe knew what was happening and rushed to get ahead of it.

"In fact, I met with Mr. Smith just a few minutes ago—"

"The father is here!" More yelling from the crowd.

"What is going on?" asked the befuddled anchor.

Rolfe knew the encounter with Smith in the parking lot had gone viral. The audience ran ahead of the newsmakers.

"Where's Smith?" came the shouts. "The dad is here!"

Earphones buzzed all over the studio as the director in the control booth yelled: "The dad's here! It's all over Twitter! Get a camera on this guy!"

Sneakers squeaked as two men with small cameras ran backstage. Audience members rose from their seats, torn between watching their phones and the live action.

Rolfe raised her voice above the crowd. "Tom Smith is here! He arrived with me. Tom, will you come speak to us?"

Tom was frozen, shocked beyond reaction. He couldn't believe it. The governor had sold him out. *She'd sold him out!*

On a nearby monitor, he suddenly saw himself, looking at himself on a monitor looking at himself on a monitor and on and on, into an ever decreasing hole in the screen. The odd sight shocked him further.

Finally, his view was blocked by a cameraman shoving a lens within inches of his face, and Tom looked into the dark eye and out at the world.

And what the world saw was a man who'd had enough.

With a sweep of his arm, he easily cleared the cameraman from his path and strode into the intense white lights of the stage.

"Here he is," Stone announced, like a circus ringmaster, "live on GNBNC, Tom Smith, father of the miracle child of St. Tobias!"

THIRTY-TWO

"It's *St. Thomas*, you idiot."

"I'm sorry?" Stone said. Although it was far from the first time he'd been called an idiot on the air, it was only one of a couple dozen or so times that he wasn't entirely sure *why* he was being called an idiot.

Looking at his feet, Reverend Waite found himself breaking into a grin.

"The name of the church," said Tom from the center of the stage, his eyes drilling holes into the anchorman's skull, where his brain should be. "You and your GNBNC pals have been using the wrong name all day."

Stone looked dismissive, as if he were too important to feel embarrassed.

"You would know it's St. Thomas's if you were the least bit concerned about accuracy. But you're not here for the facts. You're here for the story, the circus. For the 24/7 event you're trying to create."

Stone, sensing he might get punched, took a step backward, assuming position between a karate stance and a runner's crouch.

"My family is just cannon fodder for you and the breaking news storm troopers, isn't that right, asshole?"

Reverend Waite couldn't help himself. He grinned broadly at the stunned anchorman. In a control booth in Atlanta and a hotel room in Richmond, two more faces broke into smiles.

"ASS-HO!" Billy sang cheerfully from the floor.

"Now, see here, son," cut in Reverend Jones in his best we're-all-jes'-

friends-here drawl. "Mr. Stone don't mean no—"

"Don't start, preacher!" Tom barked, with such force that even Rolfe jumped. "I may not be the most spiritual man, but I know B.S. when I see it, and preacher, you are genuine walking, talking, jewelry-wearing bullshit!"

The crowd shifted in its collective seat, uneasy. Even the most zealous among them hadn't expected to run into someone who appeared to be even more out of his head than they were.

Off to the corner of the set stood the floor director with a big smile on her face. *Now this is great TV*, she thought.

"Tom, please," said Rolfe.

"Governor, you're no different. I know what you're about and I don't like it."

The governor didn't say another word.

"You people have destroyed our lives!" Tom shouted at the panelists.

Tom spun toward Stone to include him in the indictment. Tom's wrestling instincts strained to take over and he took two involuntary, aggressive steps in Stone's direction, prompting scattered shrieks in the audience.

Stone reacted like a squirrel to a Labrador, darting right then left, his slick dress shoes slipping out from under him with each change of direction. Showing a considerable lack of grace, the anchor then skip-ran around the row of panelists, his tail seeming to push his midsection out in front and his arms wind-milling. On the verge of hyperventilating, Stone slid to a halt with his guests between him and Tom.

Tom tried to collect himself but the anger was still too strong.

"We've been forced out of our home, forced out of our lives, forced to live in a crummy little hotel room with no..."

Tom stopped short. There were only three crummy little hotels within five miles of their house, all right next to each other, and his family was in one of them. Google Maps would make it possible for anyone in the world to figure out in minutes where they'd been hiding for the last 18 hours. In the split-second of silence since he'd said the words, Tom realized that he'd just told their enemies exactly where his family was!

Without another word, Tom bolted for an exit on the side of the studio, the same one that Jim Blake had walked through 20 minutes before, and burst out into the parking lot.

I've got to get to them first! was all he could think.

Feet and heart pounding, Tom rushed down the street toward his car. He didn't notice a nondescript service van slide to a halt on the side of the street as he ran by it. He didn't see the man step out of the van, and he didn't hear the rifle discharge behind him. But he did feel the sudden, sharp pain in his hamstring — like a nail-tipped baseball bat slamming into his leg.

The impact and pain caused him to stumble onto the rock-strewn sidewalk, sliding to a bloody halt ten feet later. Automatically he leapt to his feet and kept running, only vaguely aware of the burning sensation in his hamstring.

The man with the rifle leapt back into the van and nodded to the driver. The van yanked a hard U-turn, climbing the curb before straightening out and heading down the road in the opposite direction.

THIRTY-THREE

In an air conditioned office in a compound surrounded by a barbwire-rimmed wall, a pudgy man puffed a cigar and turned toward his security chief.

"The father just told us where the family is," he said in Spanish.

The security chief nodded.

"A South American Pope, even in Rome, is bad enough — we don't need a messiah in our own hemisphere. Kill the family."

The dictator turned back to the television. The news program was in chaos. *Good*, the old man mused. *No one will know what has happened until it is too late.*

* * *

A phone in the basement room of the White House rang. The FBI chief's aide picked it up and jotted on a legal pad. Hanging up, he looked at the table of senior intelligence officials.

"Our friend in Venezuela has ordered a hit on the family," he said. "A Navy EP-3 reconnaissance plane picked up a transmission to agents in or near Richmond."

The NSA director stood up. "I'm going to inform the president."

The rest of the penguins exchanged silent glances.

* * *

The political operatives in the FEMA command center were stunned.

"Holy shit," exclaimed the blonde. "Did he just say what I think he said?"

"And now the world is heading to that crummy hotel to destroy his family," the president said, as yet unaware of how accurate his statement was.

The door opened, and the NSA director strode through and straight to the president, like a man who didn't need permission to approach the world's most powerful leader. He slipped the president a small piece of paper.

The president scanned the note, his face unreadable to those around him.

"Megan," he said, "Could I speak with you for a minute?"

The blonde woman joined the president and the NSA director, away from the table.

"Venezuela put a hit on the family," the president said quietly. The political warrior struggled to hide her amazement.

"What do we do?" the president asked.

The advisor studied both men. "We could try to stop this," she said. An unspoken "but" hung in the air.

The president and his NSA director said nothing. The advisor took the cue and finished her thought.

"But, if no one can reach the family in time…"

She paused, then took another tack. "From a human standpoint, it would be tragic. But from a political standpoint…"

The president nodded. "Thank you," he said to NSA director.

"Very good, Mr. President," the intelligence chief answered, with complete understanding, and left the room.

The president walked back to the table of political operatives. "OK, folks. Let's do some contingency planning."

* * *

"Do we have people in Richmond right now?"

"Yes sir," replied the muscular aide. "We have three men taking small arms practice northwest of the city."

"Can they get to the hotel quickly?"

"Yes sir."

"Get the family."

THIRTY-FOUR

The minivan's wheels left the ground as Tom roared over a bumpy, curved highway ramp leading from the Downtown Expressway onto I-64 West. When rubber met road again, the van skidded, the outside wheels sliding into sand left from the last snow. Tom fought to regain control, narrowly missing the concrete wall, then mashed the gas pedal. He rocketed out of the acceleration lane like a fighter off a carrier catapult, flying at 90 miles per hour toward his family, and not conscious that he was praying aloud.

* * *

In the parking lot of a chain restaurant next to a hotel, a beat up work van stopped next to a blue dumpster. A grim man exited the passenger side holding a Chinese-made grenade launcher. Dropping to one knee, between the dumpster and the van, he hoisted the weapon and peered through the sighting scope.

Thanks to the front desk clerk (and two $100 bills), he knew exactly which room to target.

He swept the building's first floor of windows and doors until he spied the desired number, then braced himself and flipped the safety to "OFF."

* * *

The minivan's tires screamed through the entire 90-degree off-ramp onto Parham Road. Tom hit the gas again, cutting out and across two lanes of traffic into the left turn lane, oblivious to dozens of swerving, honking cars. At the first light, he yanked the wheel, cutting through oncoming traffic, and roared down the road behind the old high school. This was the short-cut he used every day, but he'd never traveled it at 80 mph.

* * *

A car pulled up on the other side of the dumpster. The hit man lowered the grenade launcher and listened as a loud family piled out of the car, the mother shrieking.

"Timmy! Bethany! Get back here right now!!"

"Mo-ommmm!"

"Git over here or I'm gonna tan you good!"

"But…"

"Dammit! Git your asses over here right now!"

Listening, the man wondered how the hell this nation ever achieved super power status. It sure won't stay there.

After 45 painful seconds, the crying and shrieking receded into the chain restaurant. In the distance, a persistent car horn rose above West Broad Street's lunch-time traffic. The assassin ignored the sound and refocused.

* * *

Careening up a side street toward West Broad, Tom prayed the light would stay green, or at least yellow. Neither prayer was answered. He was definitely going to run the light, though. The only question was whether he'd be killed or kill anyone doing it.

Tom leaned on the horn and flashed his lights as he skidded into a high-speed left turn. He escape three lanes of east-bound traffic unscathed, but west-bound traffic filled the intersection before he reached the opposite side of West

Broad Street, and he slammed on the brakes to avoid a little red sports car.

The hotel was 100 yards ahead, just beyond the fast food restaurant. He punched the accelerator and roared into the parking lot.

Tom drove straight for their room, but a car backed out of a space on the left, and he again hit the brakes with both feet to avoid a collision. The oversized Plymouth, and the surprised elderly couple inside, showed no sign of moving, so Tom jumped out of the minivan and ran.

A hundred feet short of the door, a massive fireball knocked Tom flat. From his new vantage point, he saw the cold blue sky, then a mushroom cloud rolling toward the heavens.

Tom jerked his head up. Flames, smoke and falling debris replaced the hotel room.

"No. No. NO! NO!!!"

Tom staggered forward, searching for life.

Supreme loss shattered his heart. Then a white flash and a brief stab of pain behind his ear, and Tom plunged into darkness, lit faintly by swirling, frightening images of his dead family.

THIRTY-FIVE

"Governor, the whole world is talking about Virginia's most famous citizen: Billy Smith."

Mary Rolfe sat, waiting out senator-turned-talking head Alan Schaeffer's monologue. Meanwhile, she tapped her feet to a tune in her head: *Mama's little bitch loves shortenin', shortenin'. Mama's little bitch loves shortenin' bread…*

She bit her cheek to silence the voice.

The town hall had imploded just a few minutes before, and this special edition of "Pork 'n Beans," one of GNBNC's dozens of political talk shows, had been cobbled together by a quick-thinking Atlanta-based producer in less time than an extended commercial break. The co-hosts, Alan "Bean" Schaeffer and op-ed columnist William "Porky" Portuguese, had been preparing for their 3 p.m. show in GNBNC's Washington, D.C. studio.

"What is your take?" Bean Schaeffer finally got to his question.

"Well, Bean," Rolfe said, gazing into the dark, unresponsive eye of a television camera, "I like to think all Virginians are special, but this is a very unusual story."

To those watching, Rolfe appeared to be sitting in a warm, red-walled studio. They could not know that in fact Rolfe was sitting alone on an uncomfortable stool in a cramped, four-foot by six-foot, curtain-walled booth. Just 24 inches from her face, a remote-controlled television camera stared her down, operated from the control room down the hall.

Rolfe heard the program hosts through a small ear piece. With no monitor in the booth, these sounds were her only clues as to what was happening on screen, so she gazed with warmth and affection into the cold aperture, assuming she was *always* on television (not much different than her daily life, really).

Rolfe had known Bean since his days as Congressman Alan "Beanstalk" Schaeffer (R-NV), named for his towering, gangly stature. Folksy and funny, Beanstalk Schaeffer was a prodigious fundraiser for the GOP, and for Rolfe.

When Schaeffer moved up to the Senate, he'd unofficially shortened his nickname to "Bean," as in bean-counter — more dignified by a degree or two. He figured, correctly, the new nickname reinforced his fiscal conservative image while retaining the "Beanstalk" moniker's equity.

After just one term, Bean Schaeffer grabbed the brass ring of television talker (a profession now rivaling lobbying as the next stop for former public servants), and developed a sizable following.

"Pork 'n Beans" competed in a crowded industry. Anyone with a modicum of political experience (for males) or a modicum of political experience and good looks (for females) had a talk show, so it seemed. Even the most popular shows reached only about three million viewers, about one percent of the nation's population. But that audience included decision-makers in D.C. and the 50 state capitals, making political talk shows a sort of internal communications network for the power structure of American politics.

Advertisers didn't care that they reached only a tiny slice of Americans. They were exactly the right Americans for their commercials about corporate philanthropy, missions/visions/values/blah blah, making the things that make things work, global reach, diversity, supply chain management, or some combination of any of these. It was narrow-casting — television by the few, of the few, for the few — but available to the masses. Rifle-shot communications transmitted via a scattershot medium.

"Pork 'n Beans" (like most of its competition) examined current events and superficial governance issues such as budgets (the beans) and pothole politics (the pork, as in pork barrel). The show title's double-meaning was considered high wit in the political broadcasting community.

"Governor," said Portuguese, "I've watched you on several national interviews regarding Billy Smith, and I have yet to see you take a position on what really happened yesterday. It's been a remarkable display of political dexterity, suggesting to me you might have designs on other government-subsidized housing beyond the Virginia Governor's Mansion."

Rolfe flashed a brilliant, modest-yet-knowing, "what? who me?" smile, her automatic response to remarks about her potential for higher office. She said nothing. It was more seemly for others to promote her political future.

"Screw you, fatso," sang a voice in her head. Rolfe curled her toes to distract herself from the voice.

Rolfe did not know Portuguese. But she, like every ambitious politico, faithfully read Porky's syndicated column, sometimes called "the TMZ of the Potomac" (and prior to that, "the Liz Smith of the Potomac," and prior to that, "the Herb Caen of the Potomac"). Porky was part gossip columnist, part political reporter, part liberal icon, but it was his inside political sources that made him a must-read. No one ferreted out potential appointees, forecasted administration firings, or found damaging dirt like Porky.

"We'll return to your career aspirations in a moment," continued Porky, "But first I want to get you on record regarding yesterday's occurrence."

"William," said Rolfe, careful not to use the familiar "Porky" until invited by the Porkster himself, "I am a deeply spiritual person, as you may know."

Porky reflected on the rumors about her volcanic and often cruel temper. *Spirited, perhaps*, he thought.

"I can't speculate about the family, having only met the father briefly this morning," she continued, distancing herself from the suddenly unstable Tom Smith. "But this event has prompted me to reflect on my own faith and my spiritual direction, connecting more deeply with God. I think people across the country are reacting in much the same way."

All lies, of course, but if lying were a problem Rolfe would never have entered her chosen profession.

"Pardon me for jumpin' in here, but I can't help being a little skeptical about this whole God-Speaking-Through-the-Kid scenario," interjected Schaeffer. "For one thing, it's a concern if the modern version of the Three Wise Men is Carter Ray Jones, some hot-headed theology professor and Chip Stone, with all due respect."

Schaeffer knew neither Porky nor Rolfe would bite, so he kept rolling.

"Besides, what if this kid actually *is* a messenger from God. Can he go to public school? Wouldn't his presence, by definition, violate the separation of church and state? Is he in daycare? Every time he dirties a diaper, is the babysitter wiping God's rear end? What about in high school? Who's *not* voting for him for Homecoming King?"

Bean was on a tear.

"God love the believers, but I don't think this was anything more than a hoax by a father greedy for his 15 minutes of fame."

"Bean, make no mistake," interrupted Rolfe. "I've asked the Virginia State Police to thoroughly investigate this incident. If there's even a hint of a hoax or child endangerment, we'll come down hard. Protecting innocent children in our state and our nation is my number one priority."

She'd done it — wrestled the camera away from the rampaging Bean, then come down on both sides of the issue simultaneously without so much as a mental muscle pull.

"I have to hand it to you, Governor," said Portuguese. "I'm not sure which side you're arguing, but I still like what you're saying. I'm not quite sure how you do that."

Rolfe laughed and deflected Porky's troubling inference about her (lack of) personal convictions.

"And I'm not quite sure how to take that, William, but I'll consider it a compliment if you'll consider not repeating it."

The three shared a laugh worthy of the last scene in a sitcom, and the show went to commercial break.

THIRTY-SIX

A voice in Rolfe's ear said this was a four-minute commercial break. She nodded.

"Governor?"

Dan "Stonewall" Jackson, the governor's press secretary, poked his head through a seam in the curtains. "Telephone," he said, holding her cell phone.

"Dan, I'm not sure this is the time," Rolfe snapped, still smiling for the camera and hoping her mic was muted.

"Governor, it's…," Jackson paused, looked at the microphone clipped to the governor's blouse, then mouthed the caller's name with exaggerated motions.

Rolfe furrowed her brow, trying to decipher the name.

…*My…* She was stumped. …*My… monkey-ass…?!*

No clue.

"*What?!*" she stage-whispered.

He tried again, using even more dramatic facial motions. Rolfe squinted, leaning within a foot of his face.

…*buy bonky brass…??*

"Are you OK, Governor?" asked the director in her ear.

"Yes, I'm fine," Rolfe straightened. "Sorry, just talking to one of my staffers."

"*Write it down!!*" Rolfe hissed.

Jackson pulled a business card from is pocket and scribbled.

Mike Montegrande!!

Rolfe grabbed the phone and Jackson's head disappeared.

"Mike, how are you?" Rolfe purred into the phone. In her other ear, the director called out two minutes.

"I'm great, but I can't seem to get on the air these days," replied Montegrande. "Some hot shot from Virginia is hogging all the news shows."

"Well I'm sure I don't know anything about that," Rolfe said in true Southern fashion. Men ate that deferential crap up. And Montegrande was all man.

"I'm really not in a very good position to talk," continued Rolfe.

"Yes, I know," said Montegrande. "I've been watching. You've got Porky wrapped around your little finger."

"Not quite yet," Rolfe replied. "But stay tuned."

Montegrande laughed. "I will, believe me. How much time left?"

"About 90 seconds."

"Great," said Montegrande. "I just wanted to let you know how impressed I've been with you during this entire episode."

"Thank you," Rolfe verbally curtsied.

"I shouldn't be surprised that such an odd issue has come up," said Montegrande. "This has already been an unusual election year."

Rolfe *m-hm*ed.

"The president shut down any primary challengers. But we've raised a lotta money, nailed down endorsements and scared off any serious primary candidates ourselves, so we shouldn't see any real challengers either."

Rolfe liked the sound of that: "We."

Montegrande had impressed Rolfe as he opened a huge fundraising lead for the upcoming Republican primary, collecting $100 million before any rival had reached $10 million. The conservative western governor was rolling into the primaries with only token Tea Party-backed opposition between him and the nomination.

"So the only race left to settle before the general election is my vice-presidential slot," Montegrande said, and then paused to gauge Rolfe's reaction.

Rolfe relaxed, slowing her breathing and even heart rate, a trick she'd taught herself for high-stress situations, such as debates, high-profile interviews and being sounded out for the Vice-Presidency.

After a pause suitable to an objective listener, which she was not, Rolfe tossed off a reply. "Sounds right."

"30 seconds!" the director called out.

"What concerns me is that, if we drag the selection out, the media may focus on Republicans' internal disagreements in the meantime," Montegrande said, impressed by Rolfe's detached response.

Montegrande was right. An extended VP selection process would highlight the many philosophical and ideological rifts within the Republican Party. Typically, the VP pick was announced just before the party's nominating convention in August. In the six long months between now and then, Republicans on all sides of topics such as abortion, spending, Constitutional overreach, size of government, school prayer, education reform, affirmative action, campaign finance reform and a dozen other hot-button issues would use the vice presidential selection process as their stage to make their case — and in the meantime tear the party to pieces and destroy the chances for victory in November.

Of course, the Democratic Party was equally torn on controversial internal issues, but with a single ticket to rally behind, those differences would stay out of public view. The Republicans needed a unified front to avoid an autumn loss.

Montegrande continued, "Some of my advisors say we ought to pick our running mate now — someone who can appeal to, or at least not offend, both sides on all the tough issues. Then we'd start the general campaign six months early, catching the president on his heels."

"15 seconds!" the director called out.

"You probably have about 15 seconds until you're back," said Montegrande, impressing Rolfe with his clock-management skills. "I just wanted to let you know we're rooting for you."

"Thank you, Mike," Rolfe cooed. "I'll do my best, and I'm happy to help your campaign any way I can."

"Thanks, Mary. Your future is getting brighter all the time. Go easy on Porky and Bean."

Rolfe handed the phone to Jackson just as the break ended and replayed Montegrande's words: *Someone who can appeal to, or at least not offend, both sides on all the tough issues.*

That was as close to a description of Rolfe herself as she could imagine.

THIRTY-SEVEN

Abortion, perhaps the toughest of the tough issues, perfectly illustrated Rolfe's talents.

She'd run as a strong pro-life candidate throughout the difficult Republican primary for the gubernatorial nomination. Once securing the nomination, however, she'd evolved her stance for the general election, from pro-life to pro-child, intent on using education to eliminate the need for abortion.

"No one wants to see our little girls getting abortions," she'd say. "But I'm realistic: if we outlaw abortion without changing hearts first, then we'll lose more of our precious little ones to back-alley butchers."

As governor, she'd executed a full-court press for sufficient budget dollars for aggressive education programs in the state's schools. Overwhelmed by her tenacity and high approval ratings, the General Assembly's money committees complied.

She also taped public service announcements in which she spoke convincingly to Virginia's teenagers about the advantages of abstinence. And, in fact, the abortion rate among Virginia teenagers had dropped.

It was a testament to Governor Rolfe's political skills that the moderates on both sides considered her an ally. It was a testament to Rolfe's political expediency that she'd had two secret abortions — one while serving as governor.

While these skills put Rolfe on lists of potential national candidates, she faced the same obstacle that had vexed past ambitious Virginia governors: she was limited to one term by Virginia's Constitution, and that term always expired the year *after* the presidential election.

That left two bad options. She could launch a campaign for president just two years into her term as governor, but Virginia voters typically disapproved of this tactic, and an unpopular governor is hardly a strong presidential candidate. Or she could serve out her term, leave office, then watch her national profile evaporate while she waited for the next opportunity to run for the White House.

Rolfe wrestled with this issue six years ago, when mapping out her new career path in politics. Her conclusion: being plucked from the Governor's Mansion to be the Vice Presidential candidate would give her the shot she wanted plus plausible deniability to Virginia voters.

The first condition necessary for this plan was fulfilled almost four years ago when America elected the current Democratic president — and even better, a corrupt Democrat. Rolfe saw herself — an articulate, appealing, Republican woman of faith — as the perfect antidote to the current resident at 1600 Pennsylvania Avenue.

The second condition she needed was a suitable issue to raise her national profile while solidifying her Virginia base.

Now that issue had presented itself. In just ten months, the next president and vice president of the United States would be elected, and the following year Virginia would hold its gubernatorial election.

Rolfe planned to watch the Virginia governor's race from the Old Executive Office Building in Washington, D.C., as vice president of the United States of America. Eight years later she'd move next door to the White House. The fact that she'd be the first woman elected president was inconsequential to Rolfe — she just wanted to be the president.

There are few times when a person is fully aware she is at a cross-roads in life, Rolfe thought. This was one of those times. Rolfe smiled as Pork and Beans resumed their banter. Her destiny was now in the hands of the one being in the universe she trusted most — herself.

THIRTY-EIGHT

"Welcome back to this special early edition of Pork 'n Beans, with special guest Virginia Governor Mary Rolfe," said Portuguese. "Governor, how have Virginia's citizens reacted to this event?"

Simultaneously, Rolfe heard her cell phone ring again, and then heard the muffled sounds of Jackson answering it. Refusing to be distracted, Rolfe launched into her answer.

"Well, as you would expect, this has created some uncertainty and worry," said Rolfe. "What I've tried to do, though, is…"

"Governor," hissed Stonewall Jackson through a crease in the booth's curtain wall.

Resisting the urge to look to the side — to tell her idiot aide to shut the hell up — Rolfe skipped back onto the balance beam of her answer, missing only a half-step.

"Well, I've tried to reassure folks…"

"GOVERNOR!" Stonewall hissed again.

"I'm sorry, William," Rolfe improvised. "I seem to be having some audio difficulties."

She turned her head left and pretended to fiddle with her ear piece. Jackson's round moon face and his hand holding the telephone poked through the red curtains. Rolfe shot Jackson an evil stare with her left eye, hidden from the camera.

Jackson mouthed a response. Rolfe tried, again in vain, to read his lips.

The skids in Bologna?

"Oh, for Christ's sake!" Rolfe almost said out loud.

"Governor?"

"I'm sorry, Porkster," said Rolfe, realizing too late, in her distraction, she'd not only abandoned Portuguese's formal name without invitation, but used one of the more vulgar of the nickname's various conjugations.

Fortunately, Porkster was also distracted at that moment.

"Governor, we need to go to Preena Squall at the GNBNC News Vortex in Atlanta for a special report. Preena?"

Squall's chirpy-yet-somber voice came through the ear piece. Just as Squall read the bulletin, Jackson whispered the same news (in different words).

"The kid's been blown up."

THIRTY-NINE

Floating.

Warmth.

A white light…

Was he… dead? Was Amy? Billy?…

A warm, wet… something… hit his cheek, rolled along his face and into his ear. Tom opened his eyes, and watched another huge glob of drool fall from his son's smiling, gurgling mouth. Billy shined a little flashlight up Tom's nose.

Amy stood next to the bed, smiling. Tears welled in his eyes. His family was alive. Tom grabbed Amy's hand, pulled her close. Tears gave way to sobs, and for several minutes the couple embraced without words, Billy wriggling and giggling in the middle.

As the emotion subsided, Tom released Amy looked at the room. Dark, rich wood furniture, ornate trim along the walls, and graceful curtains framing the crimson hues of a sunset.

This was a far cry from the hotel room, or their home.

"Where…?" Tom asked, and a starburst of pain exploded in his head. With a bandaged left hand he felt an impressive knot under his scalp.

"Shhh…," Amy whispered. "The doctor said your head will hurt for a day or two. Your hands and arms were pretty scraped up too."

Tom eased back onto the pillow while Billy played on his chest. "I thought you were dead," he whispered.

"I know, sweetie. We're all OK though."

"What happened?"

"Someone tried to kill us."

"Who? How?"

"The 'how' is the easy answer," interrupted a gravelly voice. "By my reckoning, though, the 'who' could be a real horse race."

Tom looked in the direction of the voice. A gray-haired, African-American man stood in the door, unlit cigar in his one hand, glasses in the other, dressed in slacks, a button down shirt and a sweater vest. The wrinkles in his face suggested a lifetime of hard work, and held the ghosts of laughter as well.

"How are you feeling, Mr. Smith?" the man asked as he walked in. Behind him, an NFL linebacker minus the uniform took up a position at the door.

"OK, I guess," Tom answered cautiously.

"My physician tells me you'll be fine with a day or two of rest," the man continued. "Sorry about the nasty knock on your head — my security men needed to remove you from the hotel parking lot without attracting the attention of your assailants."

"What assailants?"

The man smiled, and the ghosts of laughter gained definition. "You don't think that hotel room exploded from spontaneous combustion, do you, Mr. Smith?"

"No offense, sir," Tom replied, "I *think* you've helped me and my family, and I appreciate that. But right now I'd just like someone to tell me what happened."

"None taken, son. I think introductions are in order, and then we'll get you up to speed. I'm Nicholas Walters. That imposing man at the door is Richard, head of my security detail. You and your family are guests in my home — and not by force, I would add. Your wife Amy has consented to your family's presence here."

Amy nodded.

"Where are we?" Tom asked.

"About five miles outside Charlottesville, which puts us about 65 miles west of the world's attention right now."

"OK. Why are we here?"

"Richard and I, along with the rest of the world, have followed your family's saga over the last day or so with great interest. We've also observed the parasites forming around you. It's been fascinating, really. Whatever happened in your church yesterday, it has attracted some of society's worst elements, like jackals to carrion: Carter Ray Jones, Chip Stone, assassins, our own esteemed governor, probably our equally esteemed president –"

"Assassins?" Tom interrupted.

"Yes. That's actually how you came to be in my care this evening."

Walters paused.

"I'm a pretty good judge of people, Mr. Smith," he continued. "It comes from a lifetime of dealings, in business, in family, in war and in peace. My judge of character is really my stock-in-trade. I decided early on that, whatever happened at St. Thomas's, it was not some underhanded trick by you or your family. You are the benefactors, or the victims, of something much bigger. It's my judgment that you're good people, caught in a confluence of four of our world's worst elements — politics, power, media and religion.

"During your well-intentioned — but perhaps ill-advised — appearance on GNBNC this afternoon, you let slip where your family was hiding, and I knew that you'd put your family in mortal danger."

Tom flushed. He'd nearly killed the two most important people in the world.

"Fortunately, several members of my security detail happened to be in Richmond," said Walters. "My men got to your family first, and here you are."

"I don't know how to repay you," said Tom, Amy nodding in agreement.

"No repayment necessary," said Walters with a smile. "I'm glad we could be of assistance. I'd recommend you remain here for the immediate future."

"You seem very familiar to me, Mr. Walters," Tom said.

"I should think so," laughed Walters. "You and your boy there knocked me right off the front page of the newspaper."

Tom still looked uncertain.

"I happen to be embroiled in some disputes with a number of parties — the Justice Department, Greenpeace, People for the Ethical Treatment of

Animals — hell, even my own family," Walters said. "I've been successful in business, and… It's a long story, but suffice to say: when you achieve a certain level of success, it brings new challenges."

Now Tom recognized Walters — the billionaire businessman under investigation by the government, and under attack from many others. But this man bore little resemblance to the despicable character in the news.

"Well, none of that is important right now," said Walters, waving his hand. "I'm sure you're exhausted. Why don't the three of you get comfortable? I've shown Amy another room for Billy, but I suspect you'll all want to stay together tonight. Whichever is your preference, of course.

"The phone is there on the nightstand," Walters said, motioning to the bedside. "It works just like a hotel. Pick it up and dial 11 to get the kitchen. Order whatever you like for dinner. You may want to flip on the TV. The news coverage has taken an interesting turn since this afternoon's incident.

"If you need me or my security men, just dial 0 and the operator will alert us." Walters turned, then stopped at the door.

"One more thing. I have a small chapel here on the grounds. You are free to use it. Just call the operator and she'll help you find it."

"I don't think I'll have any need for that," Amy blurted, then flushed at her own tone.

Walters raised his eyebrows, but smiled. "No? Well…, I begin every day there. Feel free to join me."

Amy, still blushing, clenched her jaw.

"Very well," said Walters, still smiling. "Get some rest. We'll talk more in the morning."

Walters and his security guard left. Tom glanced at their surroundings, realizing again how horribly awry his plan had gone.

"I'm sorry about all this."

"You did what you thought was right," said Amy. "You were trying to stop it, but there's no way."

"I guess someone thought they could stop it this afternoon," said Tom. "How did you get away?"

"We'd been watching you on GNBNC," replied Amy. "As soon as you mentioned the hotel, I knew we had to get out. I grabbed a few things and we left."

"We hid behind a truck in the parking lot, and a minute later this huge SUV comes zooming up. That was Mr. Walters's security men, but we didn't know it. They went into the office, then came out and went over to our room. They kicked in the door, and when they couldn't find us, they started looking around the parking lot.

"That's when our little talker here," and Amy motioned to Billy, "spoke up. He was so excited about the truck, and he yells 'big truck.' That's how they found us. They said 'we're here to protect you,' grabbed us and threw us into their SUV. They had guns out, so I just did what they said. They said they'd been sent by the man they worked for, but that's all. I was really scared, but there was nothing we could do. So we waited in their SUV for you to show up.

"Then two other guys drove into the parking lot next door, and one of them went over to the office. After he came back, they hid behind a dumpster, and we couldn't see them. Then you came skidding up in the van. One of our guys jumped out and ran after you, and that's when everything exploded. I thought you'd been killed until the security guy came around the back of the SUV, carrying you like you were dead. He said you'd be OK, and we took off. They brought us up here."

"Jesus, what an adventure," said Tom. "What do you think of Walters? Is he using us too?"

"Well, he didn't get where he is by missing opportunities to make money," Amy ventured. Tom nodded.

"But, on the other hand," Amy said, "he doesn't act like he wants anything. I don't know why, but I feel like I can trust him."

Tom nodded again. For him, the jury was still out on Walters. But the man *had* saved their lives. The good news was that his family was safe, for the moment, and Amy seemed to be coming out of the deep shock that had blanketed her since the incident. For the first time in a day and a half, things seemed to be looking up.

FORTY

"Chip, can you tell us more about what's going on there?"

"Yes, Preena. The entire hotel, or what's left of it, has been roped off by Virginia State Police as a crime scene, although no one's quite sure what actually happened here."

Using his well-developed peripheral vision, Stone checked his hair in the tiny monitor next to his cameraman's feet. Perfect.

"I've spoken with several witnesses who saw a bright flash of light, almost like a proverbial lightning bolt from the heavens, that hit a first floor room in the hotel," Stone continued, "immediately followed by a huge explosion that destroyed several rooms on the first and second levels of the hotel. The fire then spread to the rest of the structure."

"Was anyone hurt?" asked Preena breathlessly for the sixth time in the last two hours, knowing full well the answer.

"Police and fire personnel are searching the still-burning wreckage. As we get closer to sunset, the urgency is intensifying. So far, only three of registered guests are unaccounted for: a family matching the description of the Smiths."

"How ironic," commented Preena Squall meaningfully (and meaninglessly) back at the anchor desk.

"Yes, Preena, it certainly is," added Stone, not wanting to be left behind.

"Has there been any sign of Tom Smith in all this?"

"Yes, Preena. Witnesses describe seeing a man matching Smith's description speeding up to the hotel just before the explosion, and police found the family's van in the parking lot."

"Is Smith a person of interest?"

"My sources say they're not ruling anyone out," said Stone. "So, if the father is still alive, he's a suspect."

The Reverend Carter Ray Jones turned off his hotel suite television and slid two cubes of ice into a tumbler. He didn't want to wake his assistant, at least not quite yet, but he did want to do some thinking about the new shape of the situation.

The father might be alive or dead, but either way, it looked like the child was dead. *This completely changes the calculus*, Jones mused as he poured four fingers of scotch. The child was no longer a vehicle to carry Jones toward his goals.

What were his alternatives? The young preacher had turned out more idealistic than practical, so that option was dead too. Jones needed an ally with assets that Jones could capitalize on — such as perceived credibility or a platform — and whose agenda meshed with his. This person also needed to be practical enough to appreciate a solid business deal or naïve enough to take Jones at his word.

Jones stared at the dark TV screen and sipped his nightcap. His fallback alternative was clear.

With that settled, he put down his drink and refocused on his assistant.

FORTY-ONE

Chief of staff Scott Butler sat alone in the Governor's Office's communications staff room, on the third-floor in the southwest corner of the Capitol Building, flipping through cable news networks. The flickering picture reflected off the sunset framed in the office windows.

Since yesterday's incident at the church, the news had gone wall-to-wall on the story, but now the angle had shifted. For first 24 hours, the news (and the world) had debated whether the kid was a messenger from God, a pawn of the Devil, or an innocent victim of a calculating father. Now with the kid murdered, any gray area disappeared. The talking heads were picking one of the three options and sticking to it.

For some reason, the finality of the kid's fate seemed to demand finality of opinion, with little margin for maneuvering between the competing scenarios.

This would frustrate his boss, Butler knew. And when she was frustrated, her employees suffered, starting at the top.

To the rest of the world, the governor was sweetness and light, a perfect combination of good looks, grace under pressure and intelligence.

Her staff, however, had experienced a different side of Mary Rolfe.

There was the time that Republican majorities in House and Senate of the Virginia General Assembly passed an abortion clinic regulation bill so precise in its language that signing it would have pinned Rolfe to a very specific position on the issue. Rolfe hated to be nailed down on any issue, especially abortion. She vetoed the bill to maintain her options on the issue, costing her political capital with the conservative base.

Butler had been in the governor's office when she vetoed the bill. After doing the deed, Rolfe was so enraged she hurled a commemorative copper paperweight across her office with such force that it shattered a framed photo of her with President George W. Bush, plunged through the photo itself, and lodged in the wall.

Not satisfied, Rolfe stalked around her desk, grabbed a stuffed bobcat crouched on an end table (a gift from former governor and former senator George Allen, who cultivated an image as an avid outdoorsman), gripped the bobcat's head tightly and repeatedly smashed the bobcat's body against the corner of her desk. She grunted with every blow, like a noisy tennis pro. After five good swings, Butler heard the trophy cat's neck snap, and on the governor's next backswing the body spun crazily away, shattering dozens of crystal beads on a 135-year-old chandelier.

Red with rage and now holding only the bobcat's head, Rolfe launched the feline cranium at her third-floor office window. The skull ricocheted off the bullet-proof glass, whizzing by Butler's ear on its way to the other side of the office, where it rolled around on the floor in a rough oval.

Now, as Butler watched the maneuvering room disappear on the issue of the miracle kid, he felt a shudder of fear for the remaining occupants of the third floor of the Virginia Capitol Building, living or stuffed.

FORTY-TWO

Reverend Fogherty sat on the cold concrete steps outside the ministers' living area at the rear of St. Thomas's. His left hand cradled his chin, and his right held a damp handkerchief.

Reverend Waite pulled up to the residence in his aging Honda. He cut the engine and turned off the lights, and studied his superior on the stoop. Fogherty's head was in his hands, and his shoulders sagged from the weight of his grief.

He's a good man, Waite thought. He might be old-fashioned and slow to act, but his heart is true and his faith is pure. Now Waite worried about that faith. Fogherty seemed to think that if he'd just been a better preacher, God wouldn't have felt the need to teach a lesson in the middle of his homily. Somehow Fogherty had turned the miraculous event into a rebuke from the Lord. Now that the family had been killed, in the very hotel room they'd visited the night before, Fogherty's shame had ballooned into guilt and grief.

Waite got out of the car and walked to his friend and boss, placing a hand on his shoulder. Fogherty didn't move.

"This isn't something you did," Waite offered.

"Precisely," Fogherty replied, his voice catching. "It's something I didn't do. I didn't provide the spiritual environment that God wanted at St. Thomas's. I didn't provide the wisdom God felt our congregation needed. I didn't provide the counsel that would have eased Amy's pain. I didn't keep her and Billy from being killed. I didn't do anything. I failed."

"You didn't fail!" Waite implored. "You weren't the reason God chose our church. He blessed us!"

Fogherty looked skeptically at his lieutenant.

"I'm over that," Waite said, shaking his head. "I'm not looking at this as an opportunity to take St. Thomas's to the next level. I think God was saying maybe we're at just the right level. He wouldn't have chosen our church if He thought we were off-track. It's the world that's off-track. God was saying this is the place to get back on track."

Fogherty looked back at his feet. He wiped his eyes with the damp handkerchief.

For a long time, neither man spoke.

"I feel so badly for the family," Fogherty nearly whispered.

"Yeah," Waite murmured.

"Billy…" Fogherty choked out.

"Yeah," Waite said, fighting back tears himself. "Yeah…"

Now neither man *could* speak. Waite sat on the steps next to Fogherty. They sat a while in the cold, fading February light.

Over time, they noticed increased traffic on the road, and several cars entered the church parking lot.

"Strange…" Fogherty murmured.

Waite rose. When a minivan entered the lot, Waite headed up the sidewalk alongside the church.

"I'll see what's going on."

"I'll come with you."

As the ministers climbed the slight hill, more parked cars came into view.

Reaching the front of the church, they were surprised by a substantial crowd, perhaps 200 people. Many had settled in — there were lawn chairs, blankets, even a couple tents on the grass framed by the semi-circular driveway.

Since Sunday there'd been a lot of curious traffic — cars creeping around the curve of the driveway, stopping for a quick picture or to peek inside. And there'd been a lot of media. But this was new — a growing crowd digging in for a longer stay.

"Oh, good Lord!" Fogherty exclaimed, frustrated.

Several people cried out to them.

"Bless us! Bless us!"

The crowd surrounded the ministers. Many touched their clothing, several fell to their knees in prayer.

"Help me!"

"Bless me!"

"Heal me!"

As they shouted, the crowd pressed closer and more agitated.

"Help me!"

"Bless me, please!"

"What are you people…" Fogherty said, then stopped. The desperation in their voices shut down his righteous indignation mid-sentence.

He knew he was confused, was hurting, was searching for meaning. He felt as flawed and mortal as he ever had. But these people also were confused, hurting, searching. They'd come to him, to their church, for relief.

Compassion overwhelmed the grief.

"Come inside," he said. "Let's pray together."

He shepherded the crowd up the concrete stairs and into the church.

FORTY-THREE

"Mr. President," the NSA director called out as he entered the Oval Office.

"Jim!" the president answered, looking up from a political briefing book. An inveterate hard worker, he'd been at his desk for an hour, since 5:30 a.m. "What'cha know good?"

"Positive news, Mr. President. We've got a strong lead on Tom Smith's location."

The president motioned to a chair.

"NSA resources have determined that, not only did Smith survive yesterday's explosion, he's almost certainly being harbored in a private home near Charlottesville. Overnight we verified his exact location and put resources in the area."

"Harbored, eh?" the president said. "By whom?"

The NSA director smiled. Some days he loved his job.

He let the suspense build for a split second.

"Mr. Smith is being harbored in the home of Nicholas Walters."

The not-easily-surprised president was rendered speechless.

God I love this job! the NSA director thought again.

"No… SHIT!" the president finally shouted, breaking into laughter.

"Yessir."

"That… is… GREAT! That is *outstanding!*"

"Yes sir, it is."

The president spun his chair sideways and gazed out the window, contemplating the ramifications of this development.

"Does the FBI or CIA know this yet?" asked the president.

"No sir, not yet," the NSA director replied.

The president pondered.

"I guess we could arrest Smith *and* Walters," the president mused.

"Yes sir, that is *one* option."

The president nodded, acknowledging the alternative. "Or…"

"As your attorney general would remind you, Mr. Walters has weaseled his way out of our efforts to jail him on numerous counts," the NSA director said. "He remains a free man, flouting this administration's regulatory and criminal investigatory authority."

"Yeah," the president agreed. "And then there's…"

"Yes, the irresponsible, inflammatory allegations about you that he's made known to us."

"Yes," the president agreed. "There *are* those."

"If we successfully prosecuted and incarcerated Mr. Walters, he might make his allegations public, causing significant damage to your administration."

"And to the reelection campaign," the president added. "And even if we waited until after the election to put him away…"

The NSA director jumped into to prevent the president from having to verbalize the entire thought: "…Mr. Walters's irresponsible allegations could still damage your administration's second-term effectiveness, rendering you an immediate lame duck, and seriously damaging your legacy."

The president was no longer smiling. The NSA director waited.

"And then there's the kid's dad," the president said. "He's a dangerous guy to have out on the loose. I mean, it looks like he killed his family."

"Yes sir," the NSA director responded. The president pondered.

"I think I like the second option we discussed," the president said, which of course they had not actually discussed. "Can your boys take care of it quietly?"

"Yes sir, I think we can," the director said.

"OK," the president said. "Just the same, we need to line up the rest of the intel folks behind tracking down Smith by any means necessary. Can you do that?"

"Yes sir, at the 7 a.m. meeting," the NSA director said.

"OK, sounds like a plan," concluded the president.

FORTY-FOUR

"Although no bodies have been recovered yet, it is widely believed that the family perished in yesterday's explosion at the hotel," said the FBI director. "However, after comparing the time of the explosion with the time it would have taken Mr. Smith to get to the hotel from the television station, we think it is extremely unlikely that Mr. Smith reached the hotel before the explosion took place."

"So he's not dead," the president offered.

"We don't believe so, no."

"Have we confirmed it was the Venezuelans?" the president asked.

CIA jumped in. "Yes sir. FBI and NSA monitoring and NSA satellite intercepts all confirm that Venezuelan leadership ordered the hit."

"Good to see all y'all boys playin' nice," the president jabbed.

"What are the chances the rest of the family is alive?" the president asked the FBI director.

"Our best guess is 1 in 10 that they weren't in the room," the FBI director responded. "They might have faked their own deaths to engineer a disappearance and get out of the intense spotlight. However, Smith didn't make it there in time, even if that was their plan, and our monitoring suggests that the assassins are confident they succeeded."

"Do we know where the bad guys are?" the president asked.

"We believe they're still in the Richmond area, although it's possible they've slipped out. We are putting a wide dragnet into place."

The president glanced over at his National Security Agency director. Understanding passed between the men without a word, without the slightest movement.

"I don't believe that's a good use of our resources," the NSA director said.

"I'm sorry?" The flank attack caught the FBI director by surprise.

"What is your goal?" the NSA director asked.

"What is our *goal?*" the FBI man repeated. He looked at the president for support, but the chief executive's face was non-committal.

"Yes, your goal," continued the NSA director. "What is your goal? Say we catch these guys. What the hell are we gonna do with them?"

"We'll prosecute the shit out of them and use it as leverage against their crazy leader!" the FBI man could not believe he had to explain this to the NSA jerk.

"Who'd they kill?" the NSA man asked.

The FBI director looked at the president again, still waiting for the man to jump in and tell the NSA guy to get his head out of his ass. But the president didn't say anything. Didn't even move a muscle, as a matter of fact. The FBI man's political radar sprang to life. Something was up.

"They killed…" the FBI director began. "They killed… the family. The kid. The kid from St. Thomas's Church." *What the hell is going on here?*

"They killed the kid from the church? The child who healed his father's head with just a touch of his hand? The child who spoke as if he were an adult? The child that God chose as his messenger for a communication to the world? Is that what you want us to say: we allowed a tin-pot South American dictator to kill what may have been Second Coming of Christ?"

Oh, the FBI man thought. *Now I get it.*

Too late. The NSA director set the hook.

"Look," scrambled the FBI director.

"And what is the proper response from the most powerful nation in the history of the world to the assassination of what many believe was the Son of God? An extension of the trade embargo? Canceling an exhibition baseball game?"

The rest of the penguins unconsciously edged back in their seats, the president noticed, as the leopard seal ripped apart the first unfortunate bird in the water.

"I get your point," the FBI director stammered.

"*I don't think you do!*" the NSA director shot back. "The *only* response that the people of the United States will accept to a crime of this magnitude, a crime *literally of Biblical proportions*, would be a full-scale invasion of Venezuela and deposing their leadership! Are we all ready for that reality?"

The NSA director gazed around the room at the silent council, moving from face to face.

"While we're at it, how do you think an *honest-to-God martyr* will affect domestic politics, or for that matter, domestic terrorism?" he continued. "I'm no FBI man, but something tells me that brave new world would be a tad *unstable*. Do you *think*? Do you THINK??"

"Jim," the president said quietly. "Point taken."

The National Security Agency director nodded to his boss and leaned back in his seat.

The president allowed the gravity of the situation sink in.

"So," the president said in the direction of the FBI director, but really to the entire room. "What is the conclusion of the FBI regarding the apparent crime in Richmond?"

The FBI man balled his fists, then released them slowly, letting go of the truth.

"It appears that the family was killed yesterday...," he said, "by the father, Tom Smith. It also appears that Sunday's events were an elaborate hoax orchestrated by Mr. Smith. A manhunt is underway for Mr. Smith, who is considered armed and dangerous."

"Let's hope that, when he is captured, that he does not attempt to resist arrest," the NSA head added. "It would be tragic if he died before the world could determine exactly how he managed to stage this hoax."

"Yes," the FBI man concurred. "That would be unfortunate."

"Thank you all," the president said by way of adjournment. "If you'll forgive me, I have a meeting with my political team."

"Jim," the president added, standing and turning to his NSA director. "You keep me posted on the progress of our manhunt."

One last gratuitous slap at the FBI chief, whose agency, in theory, had jurisdiction over domestic crime investigations.

"Yes sir," the NSA director said, rising as the president left the table. "I sure will."

FORTY-FIVE

By 8:30 a.m. on Tuesday morning, Amy had been up an hour, showered, awakened her son and given him a bath, all to wash away the surprising amount of grime built up after just 36 hours on the lam.

Tom rolled over in the comfortable guest room bed to see Amy combing Billy's wet hair, both clean and decked out in what appeared to be new clothes.

"Y'all are up early," he said.

"I wanted to try to get a fresh start on what I hope will be a better day," said Amy, as she tried and failed to persuade Billy's cowlick to lay down and behave. "How do you like the clothes? Mr. Walters sent someone out last night to get them — a couple outfits for each of us."

"You seem pretty optimistic," Tom ventured, marveling at her newfound strength, despite what still seemed to be an impossibly difficult situation.

"I guess I am," she replied. "I don't know why, really. But I can't just take it any longer. Despite everyone who seems to be lined up to either use us or trash us, we still have each other, we have a safe place to stay for now, and Billy is OK. I can't say I think God is on our side, but at least He doesn't seem to be making things worse at the moment."

Tom took encouragement from Amy's point and energy. Maybe a hot shower is exactly what the doctor ordered, he thought, and dragged himself to his feet, heading for the bathroom.

"Mr. Walters left a note inviting us to breakfast when we feel like it. The note even has directions to his kitchen," Amy laughed. "In this house, you need either directions or GPS."

"I'll shower real quick and we can head down," replied Tom, scratching his stomach through his t-shirt.

"It's a date," Amy teased.

Geez, she is *in a good mood*, Tom thought as he walked to the shower. *Good.*

FORTY-SIX

Twenty-five minutes later the family was sitting around a beautiful walnut table in a large dining room on the southern side of the mansion. Billy played in Amy's lap while his parents eyed the room in amazement.

The sun was up over the mountains, and six sets of French doors flooded the room with light. Through the doors was a comfortable patio, and beyond that a picturesque valley covered in snow. Inside the dining room, bright walls softly reflected the morning light. Opposite the doors hung two paintings — collections of brush strokes that, taken as a whole, created lovely, colorful images of gardens. Simple, elegant crown molding accented the room.

A door opened, letting in the distant clatter of a working kitchen. Two women in neat uniforms carried in plates, silverware, cups and glasses. Smiling and efficient, the women set out places for the Smiths, plus one extra seat. The next visit brought large bowls and platters of food: scrambled eggs, bacon, sausage, croissants, biscuits, butter, jam, orange juice and coffee. As the women finished, Nicholas Walters entered the room through another door, wearing khakis, a button-down shirt and loafers.

Considering his age, Walters looked pretty fit, Tom thought.

"Thank you, Maria, Christina," said Walters.

Maria and Christina smiled and went back into the kitchen. Walters sat at the head of the table. "Eat, please," he encouraged.

Tom began putting a plate together for Billy.

"I hope you all slept well," he said, "and that you've found everything you need to be comfortable."

"We slept very well, thank you," said Tom.

"You have a beautiful home Mr. Walters," added Amy.

"Thank you," Walters replied. "I've been very happy with it."

"We really don't know how to thank you," Tom said. "The last couple of days have been very hard."

"I can only imagine. I would be happy to arrange for professional counseling if you feel you need it."

"That's very kind," said Amy. "But I think our first goal is to somehow straighten out this mess, and *then* maybe get counseling — as long as we can keep it together in the meantime."

"Yes, of course," said Walters.

"May I ask a question?" said Amy after a pause. "Why are you helping us?"

"First of all, please call me Nick," replied Walters. "As for why I would help you — I suppose the answer varies depending on how honest I am being with myself.

"I'd like to think that I would have helped you at any point in my life," he said. "You clearly are the victims here, minding your own business but pulled into the nasty worlds of national media, politics and corrupt televangelism.

"The situation reminds me of a sport popular in Afghanistan, called 'Buzkashi,'" Walters continued. "In this game, two teams of horsemen fight over the body of a beheaded, disemboweled goat, trying to drag the goat over their goal line to score, sort of like a gory polo match.

"As I see it," concluded Walters, "your family is the goat."

Tom and Amy blanched, but couldn't help agreeing.

"It would have been inhumane not to step in if I had the opportunity and the means," said Walters.

"But, if I were being honest with myself, which I try to be, I have ulterior motives," Walters added. "Many of the same institutions that are abusing you — the government and the media in particular — are using me and my companies as a piñata these days, and as the saying goes, 'the enemy of my enemy is my friend.' That, friends, is probably also a reason for my helping."

"But *we're* just innocent *victims*," Tom responded, and regretted it immediately, his reddening ears flagging his guilt.

"I see that my fans in the media have already reached you," smiled Walters. "Don't be embarrassed, Tom. I'm not surprised. Thoreau said that 'a mountain outline varies with every step, and it has an infinite number of profiles, though absolutely but one form.' The fact is that there are as many ways to view an issue as there are people looking at it — but the media can only present one or two of those perspectives, and that is not always the perspective that most accurately portrays the issue's true form. In other words, don't believe everything you see on TV. I am no more the man you've seen on the news than you are the father who is being branded a child abuser and murderer on the news-talk shows, even as we sit here this morning."

"I'm sorry," was all Tom could manage to say.

Walters released Tom with a kind expression. "Not to worry, son. I'm not overly sensitive."

"You mean it doesn't bother you when they say terrible things about you?" asked Amy.

"No," Walters said. "I long ago let go of the need for people to like me, and I don't care whether I get good publicity or not. Why should I? I am self-validating — I know if I've done good or not, and I decide whether I'm successful or not. Besides, God knows me and that's all that's going to matter in the end, isn't it?"

Maria slipped into the room, refilling coffee cups and glasses, and taking away empty dishes.

"Thank you, Maria," said Walters as the servant headed back for the kitchen.

"You are welcome, Mr. Walters," Maria answered with a strong accent.

"I've tried to get Maria and Christina to call me Nick, but they won't do it," Walters said after she left. "They are both from Mexico, both excellent employees, and both extremely conscientious — something I find increasingly lacking in American employees."

Walters gazed at Tom and Amy.

"Tell me, what do you do for a living?" Walters asked.

"I do CAD work in a machine shop in Richmond," Tom said. "CAD means--"

"Computer-automated drafting?" Walters cut in.

"Yeah," Tom said, impressed.

"Do you enjoy that work?" Walters continued.

"It's alright," Tom said. Amy made a face next to him.

"He's a computer whiz," Amy beamed. Tom looked down at his plate.

"Is that true, Tom?" Walters asked.

"Yes, he really is," Amy answered, clearly proud. Then an unreadable expression crossed her face.

"There seems to be more to this story," said Walters. Rather than pose the obvious question, Walters just stopped talking.

"Tom…," Amy began, not sure if she should go on. A glance from Tom released her to share.

"Tom went to Virginia Tech for computer science," Amy said. "But during his first year, his mother got sick, so he came back to be with her. At home he taught himself computer-automated drafting, and he was able to get a job at a machine shop."

"You must be very clever," Walters said to Tom.

"It's not that hard," Tom said, shrugging.

"It's *really* hard," Amy countered. Tom shrugged again.

"That's how we met, actually," Amy continued.

"At the machine shop?" asked Walters.

"No, his mom," said Amy. "I was an attendant at the assisted living facility where Tom's mother…" Amy looked at Tom, her eyes clouding.

"Tom used to work all day, until seven or eight o'clock," she continued. "Then he'd come sit with his mom, every night."

Walters glanced over at Tom. The young man was still looking at his plate.

"He was…," Amy started. "He was such a good son to his mother. He was so devoted. I couldn't help but fall in love with him."

Walters smiled.

"We were married four days before Tom's mother died," Amy said. "Right there in her room. It was beautiful. It really was."

"How wonderful," Walters said.

Tom looked at Walters — was this old stranger actually tearing up?

"We wanted to send Tom back to college right away, but we couldn't afford...," Amy paused again, embarrassed.

"We were out of money," Amy concluded after the pause. She looked over at Tom. "I'm sorry, Tom. I didn't mean..."

"It's all right," Tom whispered. Then turning to Walters, Tom added, "My mom's illness... it was hard. In a lot of ways."

"I understand," said Walters, letting Amy and Tom off the hook. "Do you still want to go back to school, Tom?"

"Yes," Tom replied. "And I will. As soon as we, you know... we're almost there."

The table talked turned to other topics. As breakfast progressed, Tom and Amy again complimented Walters's home.

"Thank you," Walters said, now looking a little embarrassed himself. "I've spent a good portion of my life making the money that allowed me to build this house. Until recently, I was CEO of a company that produced and marketed chemicals, oil and gas, and cattle."

Looking around at the expansive house, Walters's voice turned wistful. "It is a nice house... My money has brought me comfort, and the services of fine people like Richard, Christina and Maria, but it has not bought me happiness, in life or with my family.

"It's a cliché, but for a reason: If I could do it all over again, I would spend more time with my children, and less time working. I missed a lot of my sons' and daughter's lives. I was a very, very good businessman, but not such a good husband or father. By the time I realized my mistake, it was too late — I'd lost my family. I'm afraid they are not very fond of me now, and I can't say that I blame them."

"Where is your family?" Amy asked.

Walters opened his mouth to answer, but was interrupted by the beefy security man stepping into the dining room, stopping just inside the door.

"Mr. Walters," the large man called out. Walters walked over to him.

The two men spoke in low voices for a minute, punctuated occasionally by soft exclamations of surprise from Walters. Whatever the issue, it seemed serious.

Finally, Walters looked down in silence, then patted his security man's shoulder and said, "That sounds like the right plan. Let's get going."

Walters turned to Amy and Tom.

"Folks, I'm sorry to tell you this, but we need to leave this residence… immediately."

Tom half-stood at his seat, spurred to action by Walters's tone.

"Why?" Amy blurted.

Walters's pained expression conveyed the sincerity of his unhappiness.

"We've been alerted that some of the folks who were after you yesterday now know that you are here, at my home," Walters said.

"But how?" Amy asked.

"We're not sure, actually," Walters responded.

"Then how do you know?" Amy asked, frustrated, then started to apologize for the tone.

Walters extended a hand, as if to say *it's all right*.

"I know this is upsetting, but it's a bit complicated to explain right now," replied Walters, edging toward the family with a hand out, encouraging them toward the door. "And while I don't mean to be secretive, it really is critical that we leave *right now*. It is your choice, of course. But our information suggests this is, literally, a matter of life or death."

Amy looked over at Tom, who gritted his teeth and gave her a slight nod.

"OK," sighed Amy.

"Good," replied Walters, and before the older man had finished the word, his security guard was ushering the family back into the maze that was Nick Walters's home.

Snaking through hallways and down stairs, the group was joined by several other men — more security, judging by the guns.

Turning a final corner into a long hallway leading to an exit, Tom heard an odd noise — like a jet engine — growing louder.

FORTY-SEVEN

Tom's stomach hit the floor as the helicopter leapt straight into the air. Strapped into his seat, Tom watched, helpless, as Billy, secured next to Amy, burst into tears. Over the engine noise, Tom tried to sooth his son.

"It's alright! It's like a roller coaster! It's fun!"

Billy's pitch approached that of the rotors.

"Tom!" Amy shouted over the chaos. "Billy's never been *on* a roller coaster! He doesn't even know what that is!"

Tom reddened and glanced at Nick and Richard, seated facing them across the cabin. The security man stared out the window, face emotionless. Walters grimaced in regret.

"I'm sorry about this," Walters said. "It is necessary — I'll explain in a few minutes!"

Tom nodded. Not sure what to say, he peered out his own window, on the same side of the cabin as Richard's. The expansive mansion fell away quickly, floating on graceful swells of land covered in undisturbed snow. Immaculate. A paved road snaked from the house, through the trees and disappeared around a hill. Tom guessed it was Walters's driveway. On a second pad near where they'd taken off, another helicopter sat, rotors a blur. As Tom watched, the second copter rocked a little, then leapt up from the pad, pivoted from the house and accelerated in the opposite direction, hugging the rolling white landscape.

"Who's in the other helicopter?"

"The staff," Walters replied. "They're being taken to a separate safe location."

"A safe location?" Amy spoke up. "Your house wasn't safe?"

Walters paused, obviously hesitant to say something.

"Amy, Tom," he began, but was interrupted by the security guard.

"Mr. Walters! Come take a look, sir."

Richard wore a headset that left one ear uncovered. A microphone curled down along his cheek.

Walters unbuckled and crossed the wide cabin to Richard's window. Curious, Tom looked out his window.

There wasn't much to see. Tom could make out a dark SUV on the side of a road running along Walters's property fence.

"Is that who we think it is?" Walters asked.

"Yes sir, I believe so," Richard replied, then put a hand to his headset. "Johnson in the other copter reports another vehicle parked on the southern perimeter, along Route 671."

Another pause. "He says five armed individuals have breached the fence and are moving toward the house."

Tom looked again at the SUV below, smaller now. Despite the distance, Tom could see tiny dark figures against the snow, moving through the trees, inside the fence. A cold fear gripped his gut.

"Mr. Walters, what's going on?"

Walters moved back to his seat and buckled in before answering.

"Tom, Amy, it appears that your family has attracted the interest of some very powerful people. Based on information that we have, it may even be the federal government — or more likely, some element within the federal government — intent on getting in touch with you.

"I am not convinced," Walters added, "that they have your family's best interests at heart."

He let that comment sink in.

"I'll be happy to tell you what I know as soon as we get some quiet time," Walters said.

As if on cue, the helicopter jerked sideways, rolled nearly ninety degrees to the right, then pitched forward, diving toward the ground.

"Moommmyyyyy!" Billy cried again.

"*Are we crashing?!*" Amy yelled at Walters.

Before Walters could answer, Richard shouted, his bass voice vibrating in the cabin, "Stay calm, folks!"

Everyone on the helicopter, even Billy, stopped and looked at the security man. The helicopter's sickening drop continued.

"Our pilots are the best in the world!" Richard said. "We… will… not… crash!"

Then, turning to Walters, Richard said, "We've just received word that two military jets, probably F-18s, have scrambled from Langley."

Amy and Tom locked eyes, dumbfounded.

Like a Disney ride from Hell, the helicopter surprised the entire cabin with a sudden bottoming out of the drastic dive and a sharp roll left. Several Gs pressed the passengers deep into their seats.

As the copter's trajectory flattened, Richard spoke to Walters. "The warning got us out ahead of those armed teams, but now we have to evade the fighters. The captain is going to stay close to the ground to keep off their radar."

"How long until the jets get into the area?" Walters shouted as the helicopter swooped and swerved through a shallow valley in the rolling mountains.

"Five minutes, maybe less."

"How far to the safe house?" Walters asked.

"About two minutes," Richard responded. "We're far enough away now that the jets will miss as they head toward your house. We're below their radar, and there are no reports of AWACS getting into the air. The jets won't see us. We should be fine."

"We should be fine," Walters repeated, looking at the family. "We're going to be fine."

It sure doesn't feel like we're going to be fine, Tom thought, as a church steeple whizzed by the window.

"What's AWACS?" Tom asked, swaying as the helicopter juked and dodged.

Amy broke in.

"Airborne Warning and Control System — it's a radar station on a large plane that can pick up low-flying aircraft."

Walters and Richard were surprised, and impressed, into silence.

"With our aircraft so low to the ground and between these mountains," Amy continued, "the fighters won't be able to pick us up unless they get help from an AWACS."

"Amy paid her way through college in the Army," Tom bragged.

"Can they shoot us down?" Amy asked, not interested in kudos.

"No," Richard said, heavily wooded hills rushing past the window behind him.

"Since we're probably not on their radar, they can't use radar-guided missiles against us. We're too far away and too low for heat-seeking missiles, even if they knew where we were and our heading. If they got close enough to make visual contact, they could lock onto us with the heat-seeking missiles, or use their cannon within a mile or so. But since they can't see us—"

A violent turn of the aircraft interrupted his explanation.

Richard's eyes went distant and his hand rose to the headset.

"OK, try a few more," he said.

Immediately the copter rolled into a sharp, banking turn. Blue sky appeared through the windows on the high side and snow-covered ground spun past the low side. When the helicopter straightened out, Tom noticed they were much closer to the treetops.

The helicopter held this course for ten or fifteen seconds, then veered hard again, and straightened out.

Richard wore an intent expression. "Roger," he said. "Let me get back to you."

"We have a problem" Richard said to Walters. "This shouldn't be possible, but the jets are still tracking us, matching our course changes."

"How?" Tom asked.

"That is the critical question," Richard said. He looked hard at Tom. "Since Sunday, have any of you come into contact with other people — people you don't know?"

"A lunatic broke into our house," Tom said. "I fought him off while Amy and Billy got out — but he was actually crazy, I think."

"Other than that, we were in the hotel nearly the whole time," Amy responded, hanging onto her armrest through the wild gyrations.

"Except I went to the television studio," Tom said.

"Did you have any unusual interactions with anyone?" Richard asked.

"I've had nothing *but* unusual interactions!" Tom shot back, frustrated.

"I understand, sir," Richard replied calmly. "Did anyone touch you?"

Tom thought about his conversation with Governor Rolfe in the SUV, feeling a rush of shame. Then he remembered the parking lot takedown.

"The governor's security team threw me down in the parking lot. One of them kneed me in the back. Then they put me in handcuffs."

Tom realized Amy was staring at him.

"It's been a weird couple of days," was all he could think to say.

"Take off your shirt! Let me look at your back, and your wrists!" Richard ordered.

Tom unbuckled, yanked off his new shirt, stood and turned his back to Richard, spreading his legs for stability and grabbing any handhold that looked sturdy. A bruise in the center of Tom's back confirmed his account.

Richard leaned forward to examine Tom, froze for a second, and looked at Walters.

"The jets are closing, despite evasive maneuvers. He's gonna fly a straight line away from the jets to buy as much time as possible. He figures we have four or five minutes max until the fighters make visual contact, at which point they can use heat-seeking missiles."

Walters nodded, face drawn. Richard refocused on Tom's back, running his hands up and down like a blind man searching for Braille lettering.

"Your wrists," Richard commanded.

Tom spun around and sat, holding our both hands. Richard examined his forearms, turned the hands over, check the wrists, and shook his head.

"Any other unusual physical issues?" Richard asked. "Cuts, scratches, bruises, welts?"

Tom thought back to his shower this morning. Nothing jumped out at him. Except…

"I have a welt or something on the back of my leg," Tom said. "I think I pulled a muscle yesterday running to the car at the television station. Now it feels like a bump or something, in the same place."

"Drop your pants!" Richard ordered.

Tom glanced around the cabin, then yanked at his belt and pulled down his new khaki pants, revealing non-descript boxers.

Billy pointed and laughed, tears streaking his face.

Richard spoke up as Tom turned his back on the security man.

"Captain says the jets are two minutes from visual contact," he said. Then Richard leaned in toward Tom.

Almost immediately Richard circled a small lump on the back of Tom's thigh with his finger. "This the place?" he said.

"Yeah, I think so," Tom replied, looking back over his shoulder.

Richard examined the lump — a red welt with a dark spot in the center. "I think this is a tracking device," he said.

"In my leg?!" Tom shouted.

"Yes, I'm afraid so."

"What if they catch us?" Tom asked.

"They will shoot us down," Richard replied, his voice as calm as the situation was desperate.

Tom looked at Amy and Billy. He'd led the danger right to his family.

There was no question what to do next.

Tom lunged for the helicopter's sealed cabin door.

Richard was quick — far quicker than Tom's rusty high school wrestling reflexes. Before Tom could grab the door handle, Richard planted his shoulder into Tom's ribs. The two men crashed into the far wall as Amy screamed.

"Tom, what are you doing?!" she yelled.

Before Tom could answer, Richard was shouting.

"I can't let you do that, Mr. Smith!" he yelled, even as he scrambled to gain a pinning position on Tom.

Tom's eyes were wide and wild as he thrashed.

"Tom, stop!" screamed Amy. "Stop!"

"No, sir!" grunted Richard. "We're going to try something else! Stop fighting or you <u>WILL</u> get us killed!"

Tom stopped struggling, his face contorted in desperation.

"Done?" Richard asked, not yet relaxing a muscle. "I'm serious — you're gonna get us killed if you don't stop."

Tom nodded. "Yeah, OK," he grunted.

Richard relaxed his hold. "Roll over."

Tom obeyed, lying flat on his stomach, dressed only in boxers, breathing hard.

Richard got on one knee, grabbed Tom's shirt and threw it at Tom's head.

"Hold on to this," Richard said. Meanwhile he reached down to his ankle. In a flash, Richard was back leaning over Tom's leg, a short, gleaming knife in his hand.

"What are you *doing*?" Amy screamed.

"It's OK!" Walters shouted. "Richard has advanced medical training!"

Amy stared at Walters, disbelieving. "But what's he gonna do with a *knife?!*"

Richard ignored the conversation about him, pressing his left hand into the back of Tom's thigh, and leaned towards Tom's head. "Put that shirt in your mouth and bite down. This is gonna hurt like hell, but you gotta stay still."

"OK!" Tom shouted, then bit down on the shirt.

Amy clapped her hands over Billy's eyes, but kept hers glued to that knife.

Richard didn't hesitate, sinking his knife into her husband's leg. Tom went stiff, the shirt muffling his cry of pain.

Blood welled and spilled over the gash as Richard sliced a shallow circle around the welt with a twist of his wrist. Another flick and Richard pulled a small cone of flesh from Tom's leg. Tom grunted in pain through a clenched jaw.

"Gimme the shirt," Richard instructed. Tom released his hold on the fabric and Richard pulled the cloth onto the wound. "Press down hard."

Still kneeling, Richard held the hunk of flesh up to the light, inspecting it like a piece of fruit. Blood painting his fingers, Richard sliced into the pointed end, exposing a tiny, black embedded dot.

"Got it!" Richard yelled. "Excuse me."

"It looks like a licorice Tic Tac," Amy said, not loud enough to be heard, and not registering the comment's oddness given the circumstances.

Richard dashed to the bathroom in the rear of the cabin, turning sideways to squeeze through the door. The plastic seat on the john smacked open, and a jetting gurgle filled the space.

"I flushed the tracking device! Empty the latrine tank and take evasive action!" he shouted into his headset.

Richard popped back into the cabin and fell into a seat as the helicopter flipped 90 degrees in a maximum-speed turn to starboard.

Tom, on the floor in a fetal position, had no chance to grab a handhold. Turns out he didn't need one. The centrifugal force flattened him against the floor. Looking out the starboard windows (he had no choice — his head was pinned in place), Tom saw trees and the flash of a road. Tom could hear Amy soothing their screaming son.

Almost imperceptibly, the copter righted itself, then began a low, gentle zig-zagging course through a valley. Amy had unbuckled and was on her knees over Billy, whispering and stroking his hair. Billy, meanwhile, had a deathgrip on Amy's arm and was suspiciously eyeing the passengers (*including me,* Tom noticed), as if to say, "Which one of you idiots is putting us through this?"

Tom dragged himself with one arm to Billy's seat, rolled over and rested against the seat front, thighs pulled to his chest, shirt still soaking up blood under the bridge of his knees. Tom closed his eyes and used his free hand to alternately caress his son and wife.

After a minute of silence in the gently swaying aircraft, Tom looked at the security guard who'd just stabbed him.

"So…?"

"The captain reports that jettisoning the tracking device seems to have worked. We are headed 135 degrees off our prior course, but the fighters have not adjusted. They're still headed toward the area where we dumped the tracking device. We seem to have lost them."

Tom let his head drop back against Amy's leg. *Thank God*, he thought. "Thank God," he said.

FORTY-EIGHT

Reverend Fogherty had been energized by the previous night's impromptu service. He woke up a man restored, a bit disappointed that the cloudy day also looked to be a slow one, work-wise.

Eating breakfast across from his young assistant, Fogherty came up with an alternative plan.

"I think I'll call St. Michael's to see if they need any help this morning," he said.

Reverend Waite chewed his bran muffin. "Sounds good. I can hold down the fort."

Watching Fogherty cheerfully munch Cheerios, Waite asked, "What's got you so fired up this morning?"

"Well… I don't know, actually. I just feel ready to take on the world."

"These days I wouldn't be surprised to see 'take on the world' in our job description," Waite said.

"I'm ready," Fogherty said, getting up with a grin.

Waite watched Fogherty put his dish in the washer and stride to the phone. The old man was really charged up.

After a brief conversation, Fogherty headed for the door. "I'll be back in about two hours. Reverend Wilson has a confessional service this morning, and expects a large crowd."

Waite listened to Fogherty pad down the sidewalk to his Buick. The sharp click-click of Fogherty's purposeful gait sparked joy in Waite's heart, but he was honest enough to notice his own vague disappointment as well.

* * *

Two and a half hours later, Fogherty was still standing at the front of St. Michael's Church, meeting one-on-one with attendees. The service had been cathartic, as hundreds of congregants had listened to Reverend Wilson urge them to get right with God. Afterwards, the flock was invited to come forward in turn to unburden themselves of the weight of pain and regret for their mistakes. So many accepted the offer that both ministers had been kept busy for 90 minutes.

Yet Reverend Fogherty could see dozens of heads still in the pews, waiting their turn. Despite his new energy, he was in his 70s, and while the next worshiper slipped into the chair across from him, Fogherty bowed his head in a prayer for stamina.

"Hola pastor," a voice interrupted in a Latin American dialect of Spanish.

Fogherty slipped effortlessly into Spanish: "Cuál es medir en su corazón esta mañana, mi hijo?" *What is weighing on your heart this morning, my son?*

During his 50-year career, Fogherty made many mission trips to Latin America, and became fluent in Spanish. His skill helped nurture a strong Latino presence in the St. Thomas's community.

A pause in the conversation impelled Fogherty to look up at the man, and he was chilled by the man's eyes. "Hard" didn't quite capture the gaze. They seemed to pull in all the light in the room, reflecting nothing — no emotion, no pain, no joy — in return. An emotional abyss. Nonetheless, warmth and love for the man rose from Fogherty's heart and steadied his gaze.

"What can I help you with today, my son?" Fogherty murmured in Spanish.

"You cannot help me, and God cannot help me."

"Don't underestimate the power of God, and the power of good."

"Don't underestimate the power of evil, reverend," said the man.

Reverend Fogherty searched the man's face. Something led Fogherty to assume this man was a soldier, a veteran of some equatorial war between a dictatorial government and a dictatorial rebel force. Fogherty had seen and ministered to many poor soldiers over the years, particularly during the misnamed "Cold War" between the United States and the Soviet Union, when the killing and dying occurred on proxy battlefields in the Third World. Fogherty attempted to reach out to the cold soul from this world view.

"The sins of the past can be a heavy burden," Fogherty said.

"My sins are not committed in the past," the man said. "Nor do they burden me."

The implication was immediately apparent. Fogherty didn't know what to say. In all his years counseling the faithful, he'd never, to his knowledge, kneeled opposite a peace-time killer.

"God is ready to forgive any sin." The room grew warmer.

"Hah!" laughed the man, mocking Fogherty.

"As terrible as your sin might be, you must realize that we all are sinners, and equal sinners at that," said Fogherty, undeterred. "From the moment we enter this world, we are lost, and saved only by God's grace. You are not the only one."

The man gazed back at Fogherty without feeling. The reverend took that as permission to continue.

"We are dropped into this world like swimmers into the middle of the ocean. It does not matter how good a swimmer we are — how good a person we are — we will not be able to reach land without God's help. The best swimmer will still perish, along with the worst of us. You just can't be *that* good. God is your only hope. Only by acknowledging that can you really be saved."

"Then what is the point of trying to do the right thing?" the man asked, his tone implying he'd bested the preacher.

"Because it *is* the right thing," Fogherty answered. "It is impossible to acknowledge Him and still choose to choose sin. You *will* still sin. But you will do it out of weakness, not out of malicious intent. There is a difference to Him, if not to your victims.

"However, you still have an obligation to your victims," Fogherty added. "If nothing else, the police should know about the crime."

A grim smile. "The police know about the crime. The world knows about the crime."

And at that moment, Reverend Fogherty knew about the crime. His heart froze and his blood boiled.

"*You!*" Fogherty hissed.

"Yes," the man responded with an icy smile. "Yes. Me."

Fogherty's jaw clenched, and his muscles twitched with the impulse to grab the cold-blooded murderer.

"Buenas dias, reverend," the man said in English, then walked out of the church.

FORTY-NINE

Chip Fan @chipfan03 Feb 9
No doubt @Chipstone3 deserves a #Pulitser prize for his reporting on this sick hoax in virginia. Good looks and brians — spectaculer!

Chip Stone nodded in agreement with the Tweet on his phone screen. *I ought to forward this one to that meathead editor*, he thought. *Although I guess I'd need to correct the spelling error…*

Reading fan Tweets was one of Stone's guilty pleasures. After all, working in the newsroom was intense, with the pressure not to flub the copy, millions (even billions?) watching his every move, and constant attacks from political fanatics, conspiracy theorists and arm-chair critics.

It had been a difficult two days since the miracle-baby story broke — that is, since he'd broken the story — and Stone was exhausted. Sitting alone in his borrowed office at WSSS-TV, Stone figured he had earned some pampering.

ilovechip @missy4921 Feb 9
I'm w/ u! @Chipstone3 is a dreamsicle!

It's unanimous, Chip thought, nodding even more.

medialies @medialies Feb 9
what the hells a matter with you you idiots? @chipstone3 is as dumb as a bag of hammers! and its #pulitzer, not pulitser, you putts!

That was uncalled for! Stone sulked.

Chip Fan @chipfan03 Feb 9
Its speled "putz" not "putts"! And @ChipStone3 is the finest example of a television news reporter available in America today!

Way to go, chipfan!

medialies @medialies Feb 9
tell me something, chipgroupie, if @chipstone3 is so smart, how'd he miss the cut on the dad's head that healed in less than 20 seconds? http://bit.ly/1ljj3fE

Huh?

Stone stared at the screen for several minutes, trying to decode what medialies was saying. A cut on the father's head? Stone thought back to the last time he actually watched the video — it must have been... the day it happened, on Sunday.

He'd seen the video dozens of times since, but he hadn't really watched it. Stone had also watched footage of his own reporting during the crisis, which often included the video from the church, but he had fast-forwarded to get back to himself.

Stone grabbed a DVD off the stack on his desk and inserted it in his computer and hit play.

It was his field reporting from the night before, from the burned hotel. Stone fast-forwarded through his stand-up (which looked very good, given the circumstances — the flak jacket was a nice touch) until he reached the kid in the church.

OK, there's his dad. Alright, there is some sort of cut on his head, just like medialies said.

The kid is talking, the camera is zooming in... Jesus, the dad looked freaked! That *is* an ugly knot... Zooming in, zooming in... OK, most of the bump is out of the frame now...

Now the camera was in tight on the boy's face.

The kid was done, slumped over in the dad's arms. Then he wakes up and the church goes bananas. *What's this guy talking about?*

Stone looked back at the Twitter post, and noticed for the first time the link in the message. He clicked on it, and it went to a video of… *is that St. Tobias's Church? That's the kid, but from a weird angle. It definitely wasn't the news report footage. Someone must have shot this on their phone during the kid's rant.*

The view count on the video was over 40,000. Stone did a quick refresh, and the count jumped by 500 views. He refreshed it again, and it had already jumped another by 1,000 views. This video was going viral.

Stone clicked play, and watched the familiar event from an unfamiliar angle — and this time the dad's head was in the frame the entire time. *There's that ugly gash. The kid's talking… the dad looks… different? Wait… Wait! WAIT!*

"*Holy shit!!*" yelled Stone, as he realized what he was seeing — or more precisely, what he was *not* seeing — on the screen.

The ugly cut had healed in the time it took for the boy to say two sentences!

Stone lunged for the phone and dialed the Atlanta studios.

The veteran managing editor picked up the phone.

"Lou! This is Chip, in Richmond!"

"Yeah?" Lou had not gotten over Chip's nifty maneuver to get to Richmond.

"Lou, I got something that is really hot! Really really hot! I need to break in to the programming!"

"Really? OK, what is it?"

"The kid! His dad! His head!"

"Does this get better, Stone?"

"Listen, Lou! His head — the dad's head! It has a cut on it at the beginning of the video, and by the time the video is over, the cut's healed! Right there on camera!"

"Stone, the video is 33 seconds long! What the hell are you talking about?"

"It's on the Internet," Stone yelled. "Someone at the church took it. It's blowing up! I'm going to forward it to you!"

Stone fumbled with his phone, then hit send and waited.

"OK, I got it," said the managing editor. "Hang on."

Stone heard the managing editor breathing into the phone as he watched.

"OK, Stone, the video's running. What am I looking at?"

"Look at the dad's head. Do you see the cut on his head?"

"Yeah…"

"Watch it through the whole video!"

Another pause as the editor watched the drama unfold yet again. Stone could still hear the editor breathing into the phone as he watched. Then the breathing stopped.

"*Damn! DAMN!* We gotta get this on the air! Get down to the studio. How long 'til you can be ready?"

"120 seconds."

Stone heard the editor shouting at the control room staff, "We're cutting in for breaking news in two minutes folks!"

By the time the editor had said "breaking news," Stone was running flat out for the studio. In the hall behind him he heard GNBNC cameramen and the station's floor director scrambling up from their breakroom bagels and coffee as they got the word.

Stone burst through the studio doors like a missile from its silo and headed straight for the newly refurbished WSSS-TV news desk. As he reached the desk and the rest of the crew blasted in behind him, Stone heard his name called out.

"Chip! Chip! Could I have a quick word with you?"

It was Reverend Carter Ray Jones. Stone didn't know it, but Jones had come to put the move on Stone. The St. Thomas's story, while still hot, had turned to whether the father was a murderer instead of whether the kid was a messenger of God. Jones had struck out with the young minister, and there was no family now to piggyback on, so Jones figured he could work the morphing story from his home studios at the Jones International Ministry and Christ Almighty Family Theme Park in Nashville. He was flying out later this morning.

All around, crew members grabbed headsets and powered up cameras and set lights. Stone's perfect internal clock registered 20 seconds to air time, even before the voice in earpiece confirmed it.

"Chip! It's Reverend Jones… I wanted to have a word with you before…"

"Hey, Rev, love to baby, but I'm going on the air in 16 seconds!"

"I can wait until commercial break to –"

"There ain't gonna be another commercial for two hours!"

"What's going on?" Jones asked, finally grasping the organized chaos all around him.

"Wait and watch, Rev! You'll know soon enough, along with the rest of the world!"

FIFTY

For the second day in a row, Governor Rolfe found herself gazing into the black hole of a robotic camera lens in the tiny remote broadcast booth, trying to look comfortable while precariously perched on a stool. When her interviewer on the other end of their electronic connection finished her question, Rolfe smiled, and spoke.

"I am *so* glad you raised that issue," said Rolfe, carefully avoiding the reporter's name.

In truth, Rolfe couldn't remember the reporter's name. One of the cardinal rules of media interviews is to repeat the reporter's name as often as possible. But Rolfe had found it impossible to remember the names of all the blow-dried, fat-lipped, beauty queen "anchorwomen" she'd talked to during the past 36 hours. It was remarkable how many were pulling down paychecks from major network news operations.

Where do they find all these News Barbies? Rolfe wondered with part of her brain, even as she formulated the answer using another part of her brain.

Much of Rolfe's irritation with the gorgeous anchorwomen grew out of the frustration that, usually, these newswomen were more or less immune to one of Rolfe's key weapons: her looks.

As she rose in Virginia politics, Rolfe had been a big hit on the campaign trail, especially with men. But like JFK, Rolfe's formidability extended well beyond her looks, and she used every weapon in her arsenal, as appropriate.

But her beauty, even her sexiness, had a dual value for her.

The flash of a thigh or extended, deep eye contact reduced most men to malleable mush, and the technique, if employed with discretion, was useful. But a subtle yet visible sexiness also worked to counterbalance one of her main vulnerabilities as a political candidate: the combination of her gender, advancing age, single marital status and lack of children.

The whole marital thing had been a problem from the start. As Rolfe's star had risen, so too had the inevitable lesbian rumors that swirl around single female politicians. To counter these rumors, the statuesque Rolfe had allowed herself to be seen on the arm of various high-profile men, like Dwayne "The Rock" Johnson and Robert Downey, Jr. This wasn't difficult to arrange, thanks to her beauty and bright future. And that bright future got a little brighter every time she was escorted to the Altria Theatre in Richmond — called The Mosque back in a less politically correct age — by a world-famous celebrity.

No one thought Rolfe could be dating The Rock and still be a lesbian. The fact that Rolfe secretly preferred the gardener and or the groundskeeper as lovers only proved to herself that she was keeping her private vow not to sleep her way to the top.

But these domestic partners were hardly acceptable marriage candidates in her view, and the no-husband, no-family issue still loomed. In the Virginia gubernatorial race, however, her high-profile dating life was enough to reassure nervous conservative voters.

Now, just as she was hitting the national stage, one of her most reliable assets had been devalued by these News Barbies in two ways: her beauty didn't soften the tack of a hard questioner; and, she couldn't capitalize on the contrast between her and her inquisitioner. Next to these women, Rolfe appeared merely attractive, rather than stunning.

"There's no doubt that, no matter what we find in our investigation of the explosion, we need to talk to the father," Rolfe said. As she spoke, she massaged a yellow, foam-rubber toy telephone book in her hands, which she'd received at a recent speaking engagement at a marketing awards dinner.

Rolfe stress was spiking with each passing day of the crisis, as she lost her wiggle room around whether Tom Smith (and possibly his family, if they were still alive) were being truthful or were committing fraud on an anxious world. Now the ends of her fingers were whitening as she kneaded the rubber phone book.

"Look, I saw the video of the child speaking, just like you did. I can't explain what happened any more than the hundreds of experts that have pored over the video. But there is one person who can explain a lot more than we can — that is Tom Smith."

As she spoke, Rolfe clamped down even harder on the little rubber phone book. Both hands were straining as the governor pulled and squeezed and yanked and scrunched the toy. Her face was calm, but her guts were boiling at being so close to a committed position, and the pressure cooker inside her was venting through her hands into the promotional souvenir.

"One would think," continued Rolfe, "that Mr. Smith would be cooperating with state and local authorities to help determine, and frankly, to explain, what happened to his family. I am beginning to have grave concerns about Mr. Smith and his role in all this, given his reticence."

The yellow pages bauble was now stretched to twice its width as the governor fought to stop short of calling Mr. Smith a suspect in the family's fate. For all she knew, he was dead with his family, or maybe the whole family had somehow escaped and were about to come out of hiding. If she committed to an opinion on Smith, then her future maneuverability would be dramatically reduced. She didn't want to be caught questioning the father's motives if he turned up alive and unassailable.

Problem was, the rest of the world had already crossed that line. The polls showed that even those who had believed in the kid were coming around to the conclusion that Tom Smith had some underhanded role in the death of his family.

With the parade marching toward a speedy conviction of Smith for *some* sort of criminal activity, Rolfe was in danger of falling behind the public she supposedly was leading.

Though most in the news media would not or could not admit it, they also hated to be left behind the public opinion parade. Now public opinion was turning against Tom Smith, and the media was rushing to stay ahead of that wave of opinion.

All that was to say that Rolfe should have expected the anchorwoman to try to pin her down on the issue of Tom Smith.

"Governor," the Barbie intoned, "Many experts…"

Experts? the governor wondered mockingly *Experts on the families of children used as a mouthpiece for God?? There* is *such a thing?*

"…are voicing serious concern about Tom Smith, saying it seems likely he played a role in the death of his family. Children's rights groups are calling for his immediate arrest. Your own attorney general in Virginia stated this morning that he will — quote, 'hunt down Mr. Smith and bring him to the righteous seat of judgment in the Commonwealth of Virginia.'"

The governor's face betrayed no emotion, despite the attorney general's statement being news to her. But her shoulders jerked as she ripped the little yellow phone book into two ragged foam rubber pieces. *That stupid, Bible-thumping, holier-than-thou scrawny sorry-ass excuse for a team player*, the governor raged within herself. *I'm gonna stick my foot so far up his ass that he's gonna be picking toenails out of his nose.*

News Barbie continued.

"Sources tell GNBNC that the president may form a special FBI investigation team to look into Mr. Smith's role in the explosion. Polls show most Americans believe Mr. Smith had a hand in the family's death."

Rolfe had an urge to stuff one half of the foam rubber yellow pages in her mouth, chew it up and spit it at the camera. She tapped the heels of her red pumps to distract from the compulsion, repeating "there's no place like home" three times in her head. Nearly every stakeholder was forming a posse to find the father, and she was still back at the crime scene, appearing to make excuses for the man. And this, after Smith had insulted her on worldwide TV yesterday.

"And finally," said the animated children's toy on the other side of the split screen, springing the carefully laid trap, "your own party's presumptive presidential nominee, Mike Montegrande, is rumored to be preparing call for the immediate detention and interrogation of Mr. Smith."

As best as Rolfe could tell, she now was the only person left on the planet who hadn't tried and convicted Smith of murder. Not only was she out of maneuvering room, she was in danger of appearing to join forces with Mr. Smith if she didn't condemn the guy right here and now. A bolt of frustration shot through Rolfe's brain, and she bit down so hard on her tongue that a rush of warm blood flooded the back of her throat. Swallowing, she gave in.

"Well, I should tell you that my staff is, as we speak, readying a statement I've prepared about this situation," Rolfe lied. Her press secretary, Stonewall Jackson, stuck his head through a seam low in the red velvet curtains, eyes wide in disbelief — understandable given this was the first he'd heard about any such statement.

Rolfe saw Jackson's shiny moonface emerge from the seam like a big, oily, knuckleheaded baby. With a flick of her wrist, betraying no motion to the camera, Rolfe backhanded Jackson sharply on the forehead, her way of saying, "Start writing the damn statement, you idiot!"

Jackson understood — it was not the first time the governor had struck him. Yanking himself back out of the booth, Jackson grabbed his laptop and began typing everything the governor said.

"Yes, uh," Rolfe stumbled, nearly uttering the name "Barbie," then recovering. "You and this network," Rolfe could not quite recall which network she was on at the moment, "are getting the scoop."

I don't make these kinds of mistakes, she thought.

Taking a breath, Rolfe regrouped, and prepared to simultaneously create and announce her new position. What the hell, the rest of the parade was already a mile down the road toward the lethal injection chamber — she needed to be bold.

"As of this morning, the commandant of the Virginia State Police has placed Mr. Smith on our Ten Most Wanted List in the Commonwealth of Virginia," Rolfe announced in a firm voice.

The Virginia State Police commandant, watching the interview in his office, started in his chair at the news of what he apparently had been doing this morning.

"Mr. Smith is now at the top of that notorious list," Rolfe continued, emboldened. "Anyone who knows me knows children are my highest priority, When I think about little Billy Smith and the way he and his mother died, I am just heartsick. Mr. Smith is a wanted man in Virginia, so much so that we're offering a $25,000 reward for information leading to his arrest."

News Barbie allowed the slightest smile. *Gotcha!* "To restate your point, governor… [pause] GNBNC News has learned that the state of Virginia is offering a $25,000 reward for information leading to the arrest of Tom Smith, father of Billy Smith, the boy involved in the still unexplained incident at St. Thomas's Church outside of Richmond on Sunday. Mr. Smith, who Virginia has placed at the top of its Most Wanted List, is being sought for questioning related to the explosion yesterday at a Richmond hotel that apparently took the lives of Billy Smith and his mother, Amy Smith. GNBNC News will bring you more information as it becomes available."

Rolfe knew that the anchor was no longer addressing her, but instead was speaking to the broadcast's audience. Rolfe waited, steaming, while the News Barbie finished her lines, paused, and then answered in a confident voice, "That's correct."

"We are going to go to commercial break, and when we come back, more from Governor Mary Rolfe of Virginia," said Barbie, finishing out the segment.

"And we're out, back in two minutes," Rolfe heard the director say over the ear piece. Then, "OK, folks, let's cue up the news bulletin lead-in."

"Thanks for the exclusive, governor," News Barbie said with satisfaction.

"Certainly," Rolfe responded, shooting death wishes over their communications link.

Rolfe listened as the News Barbie's words, beginning with "GNBNC News has learned…", were mated with a pre-recorded news bulletin intro in a bass male voice:

"We interrupt this broadcast to bring you a GNBNC News Bulletin…"

Within three minutes, the News Barbie's recap of Rolfe's announcement, paired with the news bulletin lead-in, would play on all of the television and radio networks in the GNBNC media empire: BNC, the company's entertainment network; GNBNC2, the company's financial news network; *Radio*GNBNC, the company's national radio network; and, GNBNCNews.com, the company's news web site.

Just then, Big Head stuck his giant orb back through the seam.

"Phone — it's Montegrande," Jackson said in a whisper.

Rolfe grabbed the phone.

"Mike!" Rolfe purred into the mouthpiece.

"Hello, Mary," Montegrande replied, just as smoothly. "You're doin' great! Took real guts to get out in front on this issue like that. I like that in a leader."

"Thank you, Mike," Rolfe replied, grimacing to herself at the memory of the News Barbie stampeding her toward the Ten Most Wanted list announcement.

"You heard the bubblehead repeat our leak that we're holding a news conference later today," Montegrande continued. "We'll come down very close to your position."

"I'm glad to hear that," Rolfe offered.

"Too bad you and your boys didn't get Smith at the town hall," Montegrande added in an unexpected jab.

That would have been difficult, since he hadn't actually committed murder yet, you asshole, Rolfe thought, angry about the unfair shot. Montegrande was probably testing her ability to suffer unearned blame and humiliation, a prerequisite for the second-highest office in the land.

"Yes, too bad," Rolfe allowed, willing to acquiesce, but not to wallow in the humiliation.

"Well, hindsight and all that," Montegrande offered generously.

"Yes," Rolfe replied, wringing one of the mangled halves of the toy telephone book again.

Rolfe was still nervous. Once Montegrande had taken his position, the limb she was on would morph into the trunk of the truth tree, and she'd be safe. But for the moment, she was exposed, risking her entire, carefully planned career on Montegrande joining her in the near future. This was not something Rolfe risked lightly, but she was confident the risk was acceptable.

So she was unprepared for what happened next.

"We interrupt this broadcast to bring you a GNBNC News Bulletin…" a deep voice interrupted the conversation, both on the ear piece and on the television in Montegrande's office.

"That should be the report of the reward for Smith's head," Rolfe assured

Montegrande.

"We now go to Chip Stone in Richmond…"

That's odd, Rolfe thought. *Why would Stone deliver this bulletin, when News Barbie just recorded it?*

Within 60 seconds, Rolfe's credibility, reputation and chances at winning the vice-president spot on the GOP ticket would disappear, as if they'd never existed. Once she saw it coming, it was too late.

FIFTY-ONE

"Good morning," intoned Stone in his best bass news bulletin voice. "GNBNC News has uncovered a major new fact in the case of Billy Smith."

The Reverend Carter Ray Jones stood confused behind camera number one.

And in a small, curtain-walled television booth, just steps away from Chip Stone at his temporary anchor's desk, sat Governor Mary Rolfe of Virginia, a now ill-fated former up-and-comer in the Republican Party. Alone in the booth, Rolfe sat bound and tied by audio wire and her own words as surely as the peril-plagued Pauline, listening, through a tiny speaker in one ear and a cell phone held to the other, to the sound of a train coming around the bend and barreling down upon her career. Except she didn't realize what was happening.

"As reported here earlier," Stone continued, "The Smith child and Amy Smith, the child's mother, appear to have been killed yesterday in an explosion at a hotel. Tom Smith, the family's father, has not been seen since just prior to the explosion. Virginia Governor Mary Rolfe announced just moments ago on GNBNC that Mr. Smith has been placed on the state's most wanted list."

There it is, though Rolfe. *Although he really didn't punch it like it merited a news bulletin…*

"He doesn't seem too excited about the most wanted list," noted Montegrande through the phone. Through her other ear, Rolfe heard Stone continue.

"But in a development that *precedes* yesterday's tragic events, GNBNC News has uncovered new information regarding the original incident at St. Thomas's on Sunday."

There was dead silence on the cell phone. A cold lump began congealing in Rolfe's stomach.

"We are going to show you a *new* video of that same occurrence that we have just obtained from a source [Stone figured the Internet was a source, so he was technically telling the truth], and I want you to watch the part of the screen highlighted by the light circle, just above Mr. Smith's right eye."

Rolfe had to imagine what Stone was describing. In her mind, Rolfe saw the jerk's face and forehead — nothing remarkable there.

"What th' hell?" Montegrande muttered over the phone. *Uh oh*, Rolfe thought.

"Note there is a sizeable wound on Mr. Smith's head as this video sequence begins," Stone narrated. "Now keep your eyes on that wound."

In the silence of the next few seconds, Rolfe labored to remember Smith's forehead. She would have noticed a "sizeable wound" on his head. All she remembered was a very average looking face. No head wound.

"What're we lookin' at here?" Montegrande said, obviously to someone in the room with him.

Almost at the same time, Stone's voice came back on the air. "In the original report, the camera shot was tight on the child — that is news jargon for close. Let's freeze it here — but as you can see in this new video, the father's head is still visible. And if you are very perceptive, you've noticed a slight change in the wound."

Silence.

"Hhm," Montegrande sounded intrigued.

"Now, as the video continues running, and the boy continues speaking," said Stone with a "wait-til-you-see-this" tone, "*watch that head wound…*"

Silence.

Silence.

Silence.

"*HOLY SHIT! HOLY SHIT! HOLY SHIT HOLY SHIT!!*"

The phone vibrated with Montegrande's tinny voice.

Montegrande wasn't alone. All around Rolfe's curtain-walled dungeon, unseen people gasped, shouted and cursed. Rolfe was cut off, with no way to know what was going on. The dark camera lens across the booth gave no hints.

Over the din, Rolfe heard Stone's voice explaining the action on the screen.

"You can see that the wound that was on Mr. Smith's head has actually *disappeared*. In the space of only 20 seconds, as Billy Smith appears to act as a messenger of God, the significant gash on Billy's father's head *completely heals*."

More shouts and swoons in the studio added drama to the moment. But Rolfe didn't need special audio effects to understand the importance of the last minute of her life.

She had *just* finished calling Mr. Smith the scum of the earth, a manipulating father and probably a murderer, and declared her police force was hunting him down like the jackal he was. Meanwhile, Montegrande hadn't gone public with his condemnation of Smith yet — and he sure as hell wouldn't now. How on earth could Montegrande consider adding her to the presidential ticket after this?

Montegrande! On the phone!

There was chaos leaking through the phone from wherever Montegrande was.

"*Mike!*"

"*Mike!!*"

"Get Wilson and Calaman in here!" Rolfe heard Montegrande shout to someone on his side of the line. "Somebody pull up that video on a laptop pronto!"

"*MIKE!!*"

Montegrande's voice was suddenly louder.

"Governor," he said, addressing Rolfe. "Governor…"

"Mike, listen," Rolfe pleaded. "It could be a trick. Some kind of magic trick…"

"No…"

"Mike, *please*, listen," Rolfe was unaware of the desperate tone in her own voice. "Mike, this guy's bad news. He killed his family!"

Nothing.

"Mike…"

"Sorry governor," Montegrande sounded distracted. "I've got to go…"

"*Mike!*"

The phone went dead, as dead as her career now appeared to be.

FIFTY-TWO

In the living room of a small safe house in rural Virginia, Amy stared at Tom's head, mouth agape. Slowly, haltingly, like a cat sneaking up on a sleeping Doberman, Amy reached out to touch her husband's smooth, unblemished forehead.

While watching the video, Tom himself had, without thinking, touched his forehead. His fingertips rested on smooth skin while the video showed him with the ugly wound. Tom felt confusion when the bloody image on the screen conflicted with the reports from his fingertips.

Then, as the video continued, the gash and the blood disappeared, and Tom floated into a stunned, waking unconsciousness.

Stone prattled away on the screen, but Amy and Tom, and Walters in the doorway behind them, were not listening.

"Tom…" Amy whispered, eyes brimming.

Tom kept staring at the screen, a finger brushing across his forehead.

"Tom…" Amy repeated.

Tom didn't move.

Amy glanced around the room and locked eyes with Walters.

"Mr. Walters," she said. "*This* house doesn't have a chapel, does it?"

"Uh, no," Walters replied. "But I think we can make do…"

FIFTY-THREE

Stonewall Jackson yanked open one of the seams in the curtain.

"Governor, we gotta get out of here!"

Rolfe sat, shocked and motionless.

"*Governor!*"

"GNBNC News is pulling together experts in medicine, video tampering and illusions, cosmetic alteration and faith healing," Stone announced in the nearby studio. "We'll have this panel assembled within 15 minutes, and at that time we will bring you a special GNBNC report. Until then, we return you to your regular broadcast."

"Governor, let's go before they cut back to you!" Moonface stage-whispered. Rolfe didn't acknowledge. She stared at something in the distance, bewildered.

"*Governor!*" Jackson hissed, tugging on the hem of her skirt.

From within her trance, Rolfe backhanded Jackson again, hard, across the bridge of his nose. Jackson yanked back his hand and dabbed at his nose. Bright red blood dripped down his finger as he pulled it away. Rolfe's ring had laid open a healthy gash.

"*Screw* this!" Jackson barked.

Jackson pulled his head out of the booth. The curtain wall closed behind him like the Red Sea as he stalked away, to freedom.

"Governor?"

Rolfe was still lost in thought.

Her career was over. In the minutes prior to the bulletin, she'd tied herself, with knot after knot after knot, to the theory that Tom Smith was a fake and a murderer, and now there appeared to be a significant chance that *something* supernatural had happened last Sunday in that damned church.

"Governor? Governor, we're back on the air. Can you hear me?"

It was News Barbie. But Rolfe didn't register. Her path to the White House was dissolving before her…

…unless… *somehow*, Smith could be proven to have killed his family.

Rolfe's mind wandered to a passage from Sun Tzu's *The Art of War*, one of the books that, along with Machiavelli's *The Prince* and Chris Matthews' *Hardball*, formed her combined Bible of politics.

Sun Tzu wrote, "When an army burns its boats and smashes its cooking pots, it is at bay and will fight to the death."

Her boat was burning. She was committed. Either Smith would be convicted of murder, or Rolfe's career would end. She was on death ground.

"Governor, we're back on the air. Can you hear me?" News Barbie paused. "We seem to be experiencing technical difficulties…"

"No, no, I can hear you now," Rolfe broke in.

"Governor, it seems that the world has been turned on its head yet again, this time by the remarkable discovery on the second St. Thomas's video," said News Barbie. "Minutes ago you said that Tom Smith is on Virginia's Most Wanted List. Do you still believe that Mr. Smith belongs in custody, if he is still alive?"

Minutes ago you were pushing me to have him shot on sight, Rolfe nearly said out loud.

Instead, Rolfe responded with conviction: "I am convinced now, more than ever, that not only is Mr. Smith responsible for a massive deception played on the entire world, but that he murdered his own family and remains a dangerous threat to other Americans."

"But, governor, how can you still feel this way after seeing what the world just saw on that video?" the reporter asked.

Well, since I didn't get to see the video…, Rolfe inner voice fumed.

"To the contrary, what the world just saw was further evidence that Tom Smith played a key and highly suspicious role in this entire affair!" Rolfe snapped back. "The waters are muddier, not clearer, than they were prior to your news bulletin."

"But..."

"'But' nothing!" Rolfe kept rolling. "I am specifically instructing my Virginia State Police commandant, through this broadcast right now, to double the manpower on this case. I *will* bring Tom Smith to justice!"

FIFTY-FOUR

The Reverend Carter Ray Jones could not believe what he'd just seen.

Jones had built his career on "faith healing": raising paralyzed men and women to their feet, curing cancer-stricken youngsters, restoring sight to the blind, hearing to the deaf, and relieving the dumb of their money. All walked away from his stage healthy. Of course, they'd all come *onto* his stage equally healthy.

No, despite this long career of "faith healing," Jones had never seen such a healing actually occur.

Now he not only had witnessed a healing by God — *can you believe that?* — but he was close enough to the principals to smell the potential profits.

The *world* had just seen this occur! Billions of those people had access to significant money reserves — savings accounts, checking accounts, retirement accounts, CDs and cash management accounts. Jones had come to the studio today simply to strengthen his ties with Chip Stone, his only point of leverage in this opportunity. Now he knew that he needed to tie himself *inextricably* to Stone, because Stone was his access point to the global congregation. Just beyond his reach, Jones could see a payday that would dwarf his career earnings!

"OK folks," echoed a voice from unseen speakers. "We're out for ten minutes while Atlanta pulls the panel together."

Stone pulled off his microphone and ear piece. "I'm going to the can," he announced to Atlanta and the Richmond crew as he trotted from his desk.

Jones fell in behind him.

"Chip…"

"Not now, preacher," Stone replied over his shoulder. "The Story of the Millenniums just got even better and I've got to piss."

"Chip, I've got a proposition…"

Jones paused, looking around to make sure no one overheard. He followed Stone into the men's room, then resumed.

"I've got a proposition I think you'll be interested in," Jones continued.

Stone had already assumed the position and was standing with his hands on his hips. "Preacher…" Stone began, but stopped when he saw Jones on his hands and knees.

"What the hell are you doing?"

"Checking the stalls," Jones replied, as if it were obvious.

The compulsively neat anchorman was horrified that the preacher was touching the bathroom floor with his bare hands.

Jones didn't notice. He stood up and wedged a foot against the base of the door, then gave Stone a look.

"I could make you a millionaire by Friday," Jones said.

The tinkling sound emanating from the urinal stopped. Stone eyed Jones, then nodded that Jones should continue. The tinkling resumed.

"I proposed a synergistic merger of your reach and credibility and my fundraising power."

Jones didn't bother with the "reaching the spiritually needy" bullshit. That baloney wouldn't push Stone's buttons.

"In a nutshell: you make sure I'm on every panel for the next three days, and give me a chance to get my 1-800 number out when I can. I won't overdo it, so you won't get in trouble. In return, I give you…"

Jones paused. Despite the massive potential, he loathed giving away profits. But there was no other way.

"…I give you 25% of every dollar I raise."

"Keep dreaming preacher," Stone snapped.

"35%."

"Listen, you bloodsucking fake," Stone said. "I'm a nationally —

internationally — known television journalist! What makes you think I'd sell that kind of credibility to some BS artist like you for 35%?"

"45."

"50," Stone replied, finishing up his business.

"Done," Jones jumped.

Jones reached out his right hand, and Stone instinctively grabbed it to shake on the deal. Jones felt a warm wetness in Stone's handshake.

At the same time, Stone realized he was shaking a hand that seconds ago touched the nasty bathroom floor.

Small price they each reasoned. The deal was done.

FIFTY-FIVE

"Then the man left," Reverend Fogherty said, recapping the St. Michael's encounter for Reverend Waite. They sat in the living room of their shared quarters behind St. Thomas's Church. The TV had been off all day — continuous reports of the explosion were too painful.

"You think he killed Amy and Billy?" Waite asked.

"I suspected it," replied Fogherty. "Then, when I asked, he all but confessed."

"Do we go to the police?" Waite wondered.

"But what about the confidentiality of our worshipers?"

"This man is a murderer!" Waite exclaimed.

"I understand. But how will we build a bond of trust between ourselves and our flock, or between them and God, if every illegal confession is brought to the police?" Fogherty countered, his forehead worrying into creases and folds. "The sanctuary provided by a church must remain that — a sanctuary."

"But our duty *cannot* be to protect and shield someone who has taken a life — taken *two* lives, maybe *three!*"

"Our duty is to God, and to His principles," said Fogherty. "'Vengeance is mine,' sayeth the Lord. Not 'vengeance is yours until I get my shot.'"

"That's cra—…"

Waite nearly bit through his tongue stopping the sentiment from escaping.

"Reverend Fogherty, God *will* deal with him, as only He can, when this man goes on to judgment," Waite managed to say. "But in the meantime, man has the rule of law, which even the Bible says we should follow, even if we don't like it."

"I'm sorry, son," Fogherty replied. "I don't see flexibility on this."

Waite fumed. Sometimes there was no talking to the old man.

FIFTY-SIX

The red-faced president was spitting-mad.

"GNBNC figured out the dad's head healed up during the kid's speech!"

"Yes sir," replied his NSA director.

"*They're running that damn video every two minutes!*"

"Yes sir."

"And *the family is still alive and out there somewhere!*"

"Yes sir."

"Do you mind telling me how in the HELL you and your boys missed the family?"

"We're not quite sure, sir," the intelligence chief stammered. "They got away in a helicopter."

"SO… I… GATHER!" the president thundered across his desk. The NSA boss shrank into his chair.

"Let me be more specific," the president continued. "I actually have *several* questions. One: how did they know we were coming? Two: how did they have enough time to warm up a chopper and get away? Three: why didn't you have air cover as part of this operation?"

"Well, we did scramble jets—" the NSA boss cut in, regretting it immediately and bracing himself.

"I KNOW," the president roared, "So does the Joint Chiefs, and they'd like to know WHY. I think we bought you fellas several dozen drones and helicopters in the last appropriations bill. Next time, I'd recommend you use one of those instead of alerting everybody and their sister at the Pentagon."

The two men sat for a moment. The president's rage began to ebb. No longer shouting, he ticked off the remaining questions. "We also need to know how they got away from our jets, and where the hell they went."

The president covered his face, leaned back in his chair and breathed deeply.

"All right. Listen, our top priority is finding the family and Walters. The longer they're out there, the more problems they gonna cause, especially now.

"You know," the president added, "I think I know someone else who might be able to help us find them."

FIFTY-SEVEN

Tom reached for the ham with his fork. Outside, through the safe house's dining room window, the gray light of the day was in full retreat. Inside, Tom continued his explanation between bites.

"… so I bent over to grab Billy's shoe, and that's when he kicked open the van door, right into my forehead. I don't remember anything else until I came to on the driveway, with Amy standing over me. I probably should have gone to the hospital, but Amy wanted to get to church on time because it was Reverend Fogherty's fiftieth anniversary as a preacher. Besides, my head hurt, but I didn't really feel like I'd done serious damage, like a concussion or anything. I was surprised when I saw the size of the bump."

"You wanted to get to church on time, did you, Amy?" Walters smiled over at the young woman.

"Yeah, I guess I did…" Amy replied.

"You don't strike me as the spiritual type, if you don't mind me saying so," said Walters.

"No, you're right," Amy conceded, then continued. "This whole thing with Billy… and then all the weirdoes around our house and the jerks in the media and the people saying that Billy should be…"

She paused.

"Well, you know what I mean," Amy continued. "And then there's the creepy preacher guy from television, and *then* someone tries to kill us yesterday… it just doesn't seem like God is really looking out for us in all this."

"That's certainly understandable," Walters replied. "You and your family have been through a lot."

Silence.

"Tom, you don't seem to be having the same reaction," said Walters.

Tom and Amy smiled at each other.

"No — it's kind of strange, actually," replied Tom. "Amy was the one high on religion, and I was skeptical. My dad died when I was a kid, and since then, I haven't had much faith in God."

Walters nodded.

"As I got older, and especially after Billy came along, I realized that I was getting close to my dad's age when he died, and I've been having a hard time putting that out of my mind," Tom continued.

"An early mid-life crisis," Walters said.

"Yeah, it was, I guess. These past few years, I've had trouble sleeping, worrying about dying, about losing Amy and Billy, about not existing…"

The fear had returned to Tom's voice and his face. He hand moved back and forth along his pants leg, where his leg wound's dressing formed a slight bump. He stopped and looked at his fingers.

"I was so paranoid about dying or getting sick that I didn't want to touch elevator buttons or anything else that someone else touched before me." Tom was smiling again.

"I ended up getting this callous on my knuckle, because I'm afraid to touch anything with my fingertip," Tom said.

"That's interesting, because you haven't struck me as someone obsessed with dying," Walters said, then added with a smile, "You didn't seem afraid to die when you tried to jump out of the helicopter."

"No, no, you're right," Tom replied. "It's weird, but since the whole thing with Billy in the church, I've felt more at peace about all these things that worry me. And I've gotten a little closer to being on speaking terms with God, I guess."

"So Amy," Walters said. "You've lost faith, and Tom, you're experiencing a growth in your faith."

The couple smiled at each other again.

"I guess we're not much of a match," Amy said.

"To the contrary. In my experience, the healthiest couples are rarely in stride with each other — spiritually *or* emotionally. Usually, the best you can hope for is that one is strong when the other is weak, and vice versa. I'd say you're perfectly matched."

"Well, even if *both* of us had been strong, we would have been in trouble if you hadn't come to our rescue," replied Amy. "And we're grateful for your help and Richard's help and your helicopter pilots… although I'm still confused about how you knew we needed to leave your home, and how you knew so much about the fighters chasing us."

Walters did not answer. Amy searched his face.

"Well, it's complicated," Walters said. "I am a member of an organization…"

Another pause.

"Why don't I start from the beginning?" he resumed. "Years ago, during the Cold War, a small number of successful businessmen began realizing, independent of each other, that when totalitarian governments dominate the world, the available markets are reduced and freely operating economic systems are undermined. This, of course, runs counter to the interests of business, and to basic morality for that matter.

"As often happens, these like-minded men began to find each other, and a consensus started to jell around the issue," Walters said. "Still, these businessmen didn't do much about it.

"Then came 9/11, which was horrible, of course. And it was understandable that the governments of the West would increase security measures to prevent any future attacks. But then the U.S. took it too far, ramping up surveillance of all citizens, and particularly those who might disagree with whichever president was in office at the time. That kind of centralized power became very concerning, and spurred these businessmen and a handful of businesswomen into action.

"A loose organization of business people was formed. Our goal is to monitor the geopolitical landscape, and in particular the governments. The key to our success is our information-collection capabilities. In order to match the immense intelligence services of the world's largest governments, this organization has built a very capable security cooperative, where we share information from around the world. We don't try to influence political events — that is up to the people in a given country, of course.

"It kind of sounds like you control governments, like those Star Chamber conspiracies," Amy said. "I'm not sure I like the idea of business in control of governments."

"Nor would I," Walters responded. "In fact, in very rare instances, we do act in a concerted way to influence world events, but only to prevent genocide if we can."

"But our ability to do so is limited. We could never control a government, and within our organization, there is no desire to. We recognize that democracy is, generally, a business-friendly form of government that can spur opportunities that we might not have anticipated. So we simply monitor all governments, particularly dictatorships, and otherwise leave the democracies alone. The main purpose is information gathering."

"Do you try to help a particular candidate during elections?" Amy persisted. "I don't want business to have an ability to steer our elections. I mean, these corporations… Some of these people are just evil. Look at all the scandals with bookkeeping and all that."

"Well, as for steering elections: no, we do not," Walters replied. "We have intentionally kept the movement non-political, because it needed to be a check against politics and demagoguery. It also needed to be non-religious, since the group could foresee themselves having to act to prevent religion-driven genocide one day.

"As for your point about the moral character of corporate leaders, I'm afraid I have to agree — many companies leaders have lost their sense of right and wrong. But, by and large, the leaders of corporations are just people who worked in companies and did well, moved up. They are in powerful positions, but most still are regular people nonetheless. I believe most of the business leaders involved in this organization do have a moral sense of right and wrong — myself included, I should hope.

"All this brings me to the answer to your question of how we knew about the armed men and the military aircraft," said Walters. "We have sources in most of the armed services and security departments of the world's governments.

"That's how we knew that team was coming to my home, probably to kill all of us," concluded Walters. "That's how we knew the F-18s had been scrambled. That is how Richard was able to figure out so quickly that you might have a tracking device on you, Tom. And that is how we came to be in this safe house — it's a shared organizational asset, sort of a 'timeshare-of-trouble.'"

"Are all the world's businesspeople in this thing?" Tom asked.

"No, very few, actually," Walters said. "One must be invited. It is a lifetime subscription, and once you have made the decision to join, your security people become tied in to the information flow, even if they are not quite aware of where it all comes from.

"Speaking of decisions, I think the two of you now face a decision," Walters said.

Amy looked up, pulling her hands through her hair. "I can't decide whether it's good or bad that the world thinks we're dead."

"Well, right now, it does no harm that everyone assumes that you were killed," said Walters. "But the intelligence agencies know Tom is alive and probably assume you and Billy are alive. I wouldn't be surprised if our distinguished president were behind this afternoon's assault.

"It's simple, really," Walters added, seeing the couple's startled expressions. "The last thing a corrupt, philandering, immoral president needs is a nationwide religious revival. He's afraid this incident will spark that revival, and he needs to stop it before it happens. That means getting rid of your family.

"…and me too, now that he knows I'm helping you," Walters added, smiling.

"Geez, Nick!" Tom said. "How are we going to survive if the president wants us dead?"

"Well, so far so good," said Walters. "Besides, I have a trick or two up my sleeve when it comes to this president. If you think he's slimy now, you should have seen him back when he thought no one was watching him. But I was watching him."

Tom and Amy mulled this new information.

"However, the president doesn't yet realize the position he is in," Walters stated. "So the government will keep looking for you. But even if they weren't, hiding in safe houses is no way to live life, or bring up your son."

Tom agreed. "Sooner or later we have to go back out and try to get the situation back to normal... or closer to normal, anyway."

"Yes, but with every passing day, the craziness goes up a notch," said Walters. "Until your miracle healing there on the video, the whole world thought you were a murderer, Tom. Now I'm sure they don't know what to think about you, but most still seem to believe that Amy and Billy are dead. It's hard to keep up."

"Maybe all this will die down on its own?" Amy ventured.

Walters knew he had to speak the hard truth to these kids.

"It's not going to just die down, I'm afraid," he said. "Look at who you've got after you. Rolfe has staked her political career on bringing Tom in as a murderer. Anything less ends her White House aspirations.

"Chip Stone and GNBNC have built their entire schedule on this story," said Walters with a rare scowl. "As long as this story is alive, their ratings are through the roof, and their ad revenues are not far behind. This could be a billion-dollar story for them — the last thing they're going to do is let it die down.

"And then there's the good Reverend Jones. I think it's clear what he wants out of this story, and the longer it goes on, the more money he will collect. I don't think this story goes away on its own any time soon."

The Smiths sank into their chairs.

"But..."

Walters's tone pulled their eyes up from the floor.

"We may be able to settle it down some — maybe enough for you to have a real life — by showing the world and these dimwits that you are a normal family."

"How?" Tom asked.

Walters explained his plan.

It sounded risky to Tom. But what was the alternative? He thought about his son. How could his life ever be normal if they didn't try? Tom grimaced. If he'd handled the whole thing differently, somehow, Billy wouldn't be in this jam.

Walters read Tom's mind and leaned forward, eyes sympathetic.

"Son, you can't blame yourself," Walters said in a soft voice. "You're a good dad, dealing with a tough situation, and you're doing a good job. Keep your chin up."

Tom was surprised how comforting Walters's confidence was. He lingered in the comments, soaking up the support, as the theme song to *SpongeBob Squarepants* floated in from the other room.

Are ya' ready kids?

Aye-aye, captain!

I can't heeeaaaar you!

AYE-AYE, CAPTAIN!

It was time to regain control of their lives, to take action. Tom cracked a grin and locked eyes with Amy.

"Let's do this," Amy said.

Tom nodded, and the decision was made.

"SpongeBob Squarepants!" sang the TV one room over. *"SpongeBob Squarepants! SpongeBob… Squarepaaaaaaants!"*

FIFTY-EIGHT

Beaufort, North Carolina sits at the elbow of America's East Coast, where the north-to-south shoreline veers east-to-west, running even with the 35th-parallel before sliding southwestward once again toward Wilmington.

Two miles due south of Beaufort, across the marshy Rachel Carson Reserve and the Back Sound and through a narrow channel separating the southern-most slivers of the Outer Banks island chain, are the open seas of the North Atlantic, and a straight blue-water shot to the Bahamas and the Caribbean.

Jutting out into the Atlantic, Beaufort early on earned favored-port status among traders, shippers and buccaneers seeking shelter after a long sail from the Caribbean or Africa. Some sailed directly into port, their vessels heavy with rum, spices, molasses, coffee or human cargo. Some slipped in with discretion, carrying the spoils of piracy.

In modern times, Beaufort has capitalized nicely on its history and sleepy-eyed beauty, and tourism has replaced trade and piracy as the settlement's chief industry.

Still, the call of the North Atlantic and the warm southern waters echo in the wind — the same wind that filled Blackbeard's sails 300 years ago. A young sailor in North America seeking passage to the West Indies could do worse than walk the docks of Beaufort. Often, sailboats headed for the islands touch here, their final stop before setting out across the broad swath of sea that washes up along both the concave coastline of the Mid-Atlantic states and

Jimmy Buffett's former haunts.

On this Tuesday night, though, the wind carried more than a siren's song from the Caribbean. The jet stream that, for much of the winter, had been slicing almost laterally west to east across the entire continental United States, took a turn for the confusing, confounding the models by swerving southward as it passed over Kansas, following the Mississippi all the way to the warm Gulf of Mexico. There the jet stream wheeled around, executing a neat U-turn and barreled northeastward between the beaches of the East Coast and the Atlantic Gulf Stream. Dragged northward along with the jet stream was warm, moist air that had been loitering over Florida and the Gulf.

The shift was so unexpected that the imminent warm air and rainfall didn't make the marine forecasts that night along the North Carolina coast.

An old sailor, working around the deck of his 51-foot Little Harbor sailboat nestled in a Beaufort slip, may have been the first to witness the wind shift just before midnight, blowing his vessel's flag toward the mainland, and feel the soft, warm rain begin.

Over the next few hours, night owls in North Carolina, Virginia and southern Maryland saw the same changes as the jet stream whipped north to Washington, D.C., and then east across Delaware and out over the Atlantic.

Nearly simultaneously, residents of the upper Midwest and Ohio Valley were suffering the sting of a grim cold front scattering sub-zero temps from Chicago to Pittsburgh to Charleston, West Virginia.

In the Weather Channel headquarters, a gaggle of meteorologists gaped, amazed, at a large, digital wall map of the nation.

After a few minutes watching the new weather patterns develop, the senior meteorologist spoke for the group.

"Holy shit, I've never seen anything like that."

The group nodded. The veteran continued.

"I guess the pot stays. Everyone ante up another five bucks for tomorrow's pool."

Mumbled agreements and jangling pocket change signaled consensus as the weather wizards stuffed cash into a fish bowl by the main forecasting computer.

"I thought for sure I'd win today," one said.

"Yeah, me too," said his colleague. "I haven't been that surprised since the housing bubble popped in 2008!"

The two men shook their heads in resignation.

"Well, who could have predicted *that*?" said the other in sympathy.

FIFTY-NINE

Chip Stone reclined on his makeshift office couch at WSSS-TV. The door was closed.

He needed rest after nearly 18 straight hours of broadcasting since the father's head wound-healing story broke on Tuesday afternoon. Television critics had dubbed Stone "the Ironman of St. Tobias," which served as both a tribute to Stone's stamina and a dig at GNBNC for getting the church name wrong for the first 24 hours of the story. Stone considered the moniker, net-net, as a compliment.

Garbed in a white hotel robe, slippers, a cucumber slice on each eye and a towel on his head, Stone breathed slowly, so the lime-green mud mask could perform its magic on his tired, aging, expanding pores.

Drifting through light REM slumber, Stone sensed unsatisfying warmth in his nostrils, as if someone were exhaling inches from his face.

Groggy, Stone pulled off the cucumbers and strained to focus…

"Eeeeeeeeeiiiiiiiiiiikkkkkkkkkkkkkkkkkkkk!!!!!!!!!!!!!!!!!!!!" Stone shrieked once his brain recognized what his eyes were reporting.

The huge man leaning over the couch jumped at the gunk-covered person's scream.

"Sorry to disturb you," the man apologized. "Can you help me?"

Wide-eyed, Stone scrunched and cowered into the far corner of the couch.

"I'm looking for Chip Stone," the man said. Stone didn't really hear — he was too busy noticing the man's massive forearms, as big as his editor's. Stone shivered involuntarily.

"Chip Stone," the man repeated. "I'm looking for Chip Stone. This is his dressing room, isn't it?"

In a flash, Stone realized the man hadn't recognized him! Stone took this as another compliment, this time to his formidable undercover skills.

Stone fancied himself a master of disguise, and had assumed many personas through his career. He donned a white suit and fedora when posing as a rich horse-owner, trying to crack the underground gambling industry around the Kentucky Derby. He had sported the costume of the famous, fan-favorite mascot-for-hire, the "Cheering Emu," when reporting on the sexcapades between pro football players and cheerleaders. Stone shivered at the memory of the unpleasant turn that investigation had taken when, still in costume, he'd somehow wound up in a smelly training room with three drunk defensive linemen, a coked up female body builder and five bottles of Dom Perignon.

The painful memory bounced Stone out of his reminiscence. The newsman, safe under his veil of anonymity, decided to play along to learn what the man was looking for.

"Aye don' ayam deese Cheep Stoyan," Stone replied, affecting / inventing an accent. The master of disguise realized his accent was an awkward mix of Scottish and Mexican, with former-Eastern Block leaking in at the tail end. Oh, well, too late now.

"Watt are yew licking at for heem?" Stone continued, improvising.

"Pardon?" asked the big man.

"Deese Stuune," said Stone. "Watt need heem for yew?"

The intruder worked nearly ten seconds, trying to decipher the mud-person's words.

"OH!" the big man said in sudden realization. "I have a delivery for him."

"Watt deese ayam?" Stone asked.

The intruder's lips moved slightly as he repeated the phrase "watt deese ayam," sifting for the hidden meaning. Stumped.

Stone grew impatient.

"*Watt arra deese yew need?*" Stone barked.

The man registered nothing. Out of desperation, the man explained his mission.

"I have a video for Mr. Stone. It's from the family of the boy at the church — the Smith family."

"*OY!*" Stone yelped. "Aya knewa Meester Stoyan! Aya heeyem to geeve!"

"You-ah heeyem to geeve?" the man repeated.

"Jes!"

"Jes?"

"*Jes!*"

"Are you sure?" the intruder asked. "Do you work with him?"

"Jes, ayam wurk heeme too weeith!" Stone answered, then grabbed one of his cards off the vanity and gave it to the man.

"Well," hesitated the large man. "OK. Please make sure he gets it."

"Seer, werra arra deese fameely?"

"I can't say."

"Oy, OK," said Stone.

The man handed a thumb drive to Stone, then moved toward the door.

The big man turned, just before exiting the room. "Thank you very much for your help, ma'am."

SIXTY

"We do not know exactly what happened on Sunday," said Tom, Amy at his side, nodding. "We are as mystified as the rest of the world."

Billy sat on Tom's lap, gleefully ripping apart a newspaper page his father had just displayed to the video audience as proof of the date: Wednesday, February 10. Shreds fluttered to the ground.

"But we do know this," Tom continued. "Our son, Billy, is a good boy. He's not the devil, or God, or possessed or anything else. He's just a normal little boy who deserves a normal life. Our greatest fear is that he, and we, will never have that. We didn't ask for this. If anyone can find good in what happened Sunday, and can improve their life or the lives of others… well, that's great. But our lives have been destroyed. We've been chased from our home, nearly murdered, and portrayed as criminals, con men, child abusers and worse. But we're not any of those things. We're just a normal family, trying to make a life for ourselves.

"Please, please, please leave us alone. Leave our son alone. We can't tell you the meaning behind what happened Sunday — that's up to each person to decide in their heart. All we can tell you is that we don't need to be a part of that process. Please respect our wishes, and stop the craziness that's gone on since Sunday. Please."

SIXTY-ONE

Scott Butler flinched as the mirror shattered just over his left shoulder, the target of a gubernatorial projectile. He envied his departed friend, Stonewall Jackson, who had quit yesterday as press secretary and gubernatorial piñata. A shriek shook Butler from his emotional crouch just in time to spot a glass statuette rocketing his direction.

Butler dove off the couch, and the statuette exploded against the wall, where his head had just been.

"Governor…"

"SHUT UP YOU MORON!"

"Governor!"

"*SHUT UP SHUT UP SHUT UP WHAT DO I HAVE TO DO TO GET YOU TO SHUT THE HELL UP?!*"

Rolfe strode toward Butler, heels clicking with each syllable. Butler scrambled backward and rolled over a table. Rolfe tried to step onto the table but her tight, thigh-length skirt thwarted the move.

"Governor, you couldn't have known!"

"I *know* that *I* couldn't have known, you *idiot*!" Rolfe snapped, stalking Butler like a tiger. "That's *your* job!"

"How was I supposed to know they were still alive?" Butler whined, circling to keep furniture between him and Virginia's top government official. "They just made the video this morning, for God's sake!"

"EXCUSES EXCUSES!"

Beyond Rolfe's beet-red face, Butler saw Chip Stone's perfectly calm, smooth features as he discussed the video released by the family this morning, showing all three of them alive and well in an undisclosed location.

Not only was the family still alive, their coziness strongly suggested that mother and son were not running for their lives from a homicidal father.

Butler and the governor had been in the executive office on the third floor of the Virginia Capitol planning the day's media strategy when Chip Stone had cut into programming — again — to bring the world this latest development in the "story of the millenniums," as Stone called it from time to time.

The minute it became clear the family was still alive, Governor Mary Rolfe had gone Mt. St. Helens. Smith's soliloquy was drowned out by a curse-laden diatribe, punctuated by breaking glass and heavy objects thumping against walls, the floor, even the ceiling.

Butler knew the news report was important, but he had to prioritize his own safety, so he ignored the television while dodging Rolfe's deadly missiles.

"*I... told... the... world... that... I... thought... Smith... was... a... murderer!*" Rolfe struck her desk with an honorary billy club she'd received in the Dominican Republic during a "business development trip." On her last swing, a large chunk of dark cherry wood splintered off the desk corner and bounced to Butler's feet. In a flash he'd tossed it to the far side of the room, to deny the enraged governor a potentially lethal weapon.

"How could you let this happen?!"

"Governor, you got boxed in, then the video came out — there was no way we could have seen this coming," Butler said.

Rolfe glared at Butler, shoulders heaving and hair matted.

"OK, then, genius, what do we do now?"

"I don't see what we *can* do, except to stay with our strategy of demonizing the dad," Butler said. "We can't walk it back now — besides, who's to say that the dad didn't orchestrate this whole thing? Even the fire at the hotel?"

Rolfe tapped the end of the billy club in the palm of her hand, considering Butler's point. The dad is abusive, using the family for his own purposes. The family, scared out of their minds but still feeling loyalties to the father, falls victim to Stockholm Syndrome, in which hostages empathize with and experience true affection for their kidnappers.

Rolfe's spreading smile emboldened Butler.

"Governor, our White House strategy is still intact," he said.

The reminder of her wrecked ambitions re-enraged Rolfe.

"Listen you nit-wit! Don't tell me about strategy! You're the reason we're *in* this mess! Don't you *forget it!*"

As the governor punched out the last two words, she flung the billy club at Butler, scoring a perfect strike on both of his shins. Butler collapsed to his knees, whimpering. Fortunately for Butler's scant remaining dignity, the intercom buzzed, drowning out his pitiful whine.

"Governor, the President of the United States is on the line for you," reported the governor's executive assistant.

Even through the pain, Butler was astonished when Rolfe shot him an incongruent look of pleasure, as if sharing a special moment with a trusted confidant, rather than being interrupted while abusing an underpaid office punching bag.

"*Wow!*" the governor mouthed to Butler with a big smile as she picked up the phone.

"Mr. President, how are you?"

The president might be the leader of the opposing party, but right now friends trumped party distinctions.

"Hello Governor Rolfe. How are you? Surviving the chaos?"

"Of course, sir — I thrive on it," Rolfe replied. "To what do I owe the pleasure?"

"Before I begin, is this a secure line?"

"Of course, Mr. President," Rolfe said. Rolfe had, during the first week of her term, installed a secure phone line the FBI would have had trouble cracking (in fact, the NSA *did* have trouble, but they eventually succeeded).

"Governor, I've watched your positioning on this church issue, and I think you've done an admirable job under difficult circumstances."

"Thank you, sir."

"But it looks like the faith healing development and now this morning's video have put you in a box," he continued.

Rolfe paused. "Yes sir," she was forced to admit.

"Seems to me, any opportunity you had at being Montegrande's running mate has gone down the crapper. And with Virginia's one-term limit on governors, this was probably your best opportunity to become vice president. No Virginia members of Congress appear ready to step down either, so unless you win the governor's race after sitting out a term, I'd say your one shot at the brass ring may be slipping away right now."

Rolfe did not need the president's assistance to understand the desperation of her current situation.

"That seems to be how the math is working out, yes sir," Rolfe conceded. Then she went on the offensive.

"However, all due respect, sir, I doubt you're happy with the way things are working out, either."

This one is sharp, and ballsy, the president thought.

"Oh?"

"Yes sir," Rolfe continued. "Again, all due respect, but the last thing a president constantly under attack on moral grounds needs is a wave of national religious revival."

"I admire your candor," the president said evenly.

"Thank you, sir. Not to put too fine a point on it, Mr. President, but the most advantageous outcome for you would be for Tom Smith to be found clearly responsible for perpetrating a hoax at the church, and then of kidnapping and even killing his family."

Silence. Just as Rolfe thought that she might have overplayed her hand, the president spoke up.

"Well, governor," the president said. "You and I are both known as ferocious defenders of the defenseless, especially children."

"Yes sir."

"And I believe, as I'm sure you do, that if Mr. Smith did in fact perpetrate a hoax at the church, and if he is holding his family against their will, and if he does end up murdering his wife and son, then he should be brought to justice swiftly," the president said.

"No question."

"In fact, law enforcement should consider Mr. Smith armed and very dangerous, and should use all means necessary to protect the public from him," the president said.

"Absolutely."

"Can I count on you and Virginia's law enforcement agencies to pursue Mr. Smith as aggressively as possible?"

"Definitely."

"And will you be out in front on this issue, ensuring the public understands how dangerous Mr. Smith is?" the president asked.

"Yes sir, I will be."

"Good," the president said.

"May I ask you a question, sir?" Rolfe said. "How are you feeling about your chances for re-election?"

"Good, thanks!" the president said. "Better, in fact."

"Good for you," Rolfe said. "Do you expect a lot of turn-over in your administration as you begin your second term?"

"Oh, you know," the president toyed a bit. "There's usually *someone* ready to go over the private sector and collect their reward for years of public service."

"Yes sir," Rolfe said. Her proposal was on the table. So she stayed quiet and waited for the president to either accept or decline. Finally, the answer came.

"You know, governor," the president drawled slightly. "Come November, I may very well need to get back in contact with you. It is difficult sometimes to find qualified candidates for these cabinet and ambassador positions. I may need to see if you can offer any suggestions come then."

"Mr. President, you know where you can find me," Rolfe said, closing the deal. "And I will be more than happy to help out the leader of my country — in *any* way I can."

Rolfe tossed in the suggestive touch, knowing the president had a weakness for attractive — and unattractive — women. Anything to help the cause.

"Of course," the president answered. "If things work out right, you will definitely hear from me."

SIXTY-TWO

Wednesday afternoon turned out to be one of those semi-rare Virginia winter days when a southerly breeze carried balmy tropical air that smelled like a Florida afternoon. Sitting on the south-facing patio of the safe house, Walters, Tom and Amy soaked in the unseasonably warm weather.

The plan was in motion. Early this morning the family recorded the brief video, which Richard delivered to WSSS. Sure enough, minutes later GNBNC broadcast the clip around the world. Step one accomplished: the world no longer thought the family was dead, and no longer thought Tom was a murderer.

Now, in the early afternoon, the fugitives sat, warmed by the weak winter sun and the southerly zephyrs. Tom couldn't stay still — every five minutes he stood and stalked around the patio and into the small clearing of grass separating the safe house from a dense stand of trees. Amy leaned back in her Adirondack chair, eyes closed, breathing easily.

"Before we head out on the next stage of our plan, I need to complete a task," Walters said, relaxing in the chair next to Amy's. "I think we'll be ready to go around 5 o'clock."

Amy cracked her eyelids against the sunlight and turned toward Walters.

"Mr. Walters…" Amy began, then caught a playfully sharp look from the old man.

"Nick, I mean," she said with a shy smile. "Why don't you give a lot of money to a charity or some good cause, so everyone would know you're not the jerk that the news makes you out to be?"

"How do you know I don't already?"

"Well, I've never heard anything about it on television or in the newspaper," Amy said.

"So it must never have happened, eh?" Walters countered, smiling.

"Well…"

"Real altruism is anonymous," said Walters. "*Real* altruism isn't about getting good press. I have to laugh at people like Jack Munroe over at GNBNC, donating all that money to Greenpeace and then issuing a press release and going on a media tour. He thinks it buys him respect, and I suppose it does, on the superficial, bullshit cocktail circuit he rides. But it's not any kind of respect I'd want, and it says a lot about why he's giving away the money."

Amy pondered Walters's point, still unconvinced.

"Sweetie, when you started taking church more seriously, were you doing it to get me to respect you?" Tom asked, standing on the edge of the grass.

A pained "Hah!" was all Amy could manage to say.

"I deserve that," Tom allowed.

"When I started getting serious about God, you turned off!" Amy finally said, irritation lacing her words.

"Well, then, why didn't you stop going to church?" Tom asked.

"Because I wasn't doing it for *you*, *or* to make you *like* me," Amy snapped, the anger still fresh. "I was doing it for *me*."

"Exactly," Tom said.

"And I admire that, for what it's worth," he added.

Amy looked at Tom, then at Walters. She'd just figured out something important about all three people on the patio.

"OK, Nick," Amy said, still squinting. "What about you? You're the only person I know with a chapel in his house. You *must* be religious."

"Well, yes and no," said Walters. "I find myself in line with thinkers like Emerson, who said that God is within us and part of us. God is what animates us. 'Man is a stream whose source is unseen' is something Emerson wrote once. He also said, 'Our soul descends into us from we know not where.' I like that."

"So you don't like religion?" Tom asked.

"Well, no, that's not necessarily true either," Walters responded. "I sure as hell don't like the kind of religion that that con man Carter Ray Jones is selling. Money is his god, and he takes advantage of the spiritually needy to get it. What I *do* like is what organized religion can do by virtue of its organization. St. Thomas's is probably a good example. Do you have a program to feed the poor?"

"Yes," Amy answered. "We collect food for the homeless and feed them every week. We also collect clothes, toys and that kind of stuff. We adopt families during the holidays to make sure the children get something. I think we do a lot."

"Precisely," said Walters. "I hear people like Robert Redford say that he's a spiritual person, but that he doesn't like 'organized religion.' I think I know what he's saying, but I also think he's missing the point. He may be thinking of Jones's brand of organized religion, or of the hierarchical games that you see sometimes in religions. But from where I sit, spirituality without religion can easily become just a higher state of self-absorption. To be complete, spirituality has to manifest itself in action — the kind of action that organized religion is very good at carrying out. The power of numbers is what gives organized religion the ability to positively affect the world. One doesn't have to be part of an organized religion to do good, of course. But churches like yours are responsible for a tremendous amount of good at the grass-roots level.

"Sometimes I watch the television service for a church in downtown Richmond," Walters continued. "They have a preacher, Flemming or Flamming or something, who really moves the congregation, and they do good things all over the place."

Amy glanced at Tom, and was startled to see how engrossed he was in Walters's comments.

"These churches — they make a difference in people's lives," concluded Walters. "That's what separates good organized religion from charlatans like Carter Ray Jones and his so-called ministry."

SIXTY-THREE

Reverend Carter Ray Jones sat cool under the hot lights of the WSSS-TV set, positioned across a corner of a triangular desk from the equally cool Chip Stone. A network make-up artist brushed some late lunch crumbs off Jones's ample tummy terrace. After the staffer walked away, Stone leaned toward the reverend, put his hand over the lavaliere mic pinned to his jacket, and motioned Jones to do the same. Jones did so obediently.

"OK, preacher," Stone said, with no hint of reverence, "you've got to pour it on for this to work."

"Yes, yes, I know," Jones said. "Don't worry, news boy, I'll hook this fish."

Stone nodded, then grimaced as Jones's phrase reminded him of his news editor back in Atlanta.

You didn't catch this fish — it jumped into your friggin' boat! the cranky old newsman had said.

We'll see who the fisherman is and who is a reporter, Stone thought.

A woman's voice interrupted Stone's reflection.

"Gentlemen, I hope you have room at the table for a woman," said Governor Mary Rolfe, cross-stepping seductively onto the set.

Neither Stone nor Jones was able to conceal his admiration for the governor's form as she slid slowly into a chair facing the third side of the triangular table.

"Whatsamatter, boys? Y'never seen a lady guv'ner before?" Rolfe purred quietly in a pitch-perfect Mae West, busting the red-faced representatives of God and the Fourth Estate. Rolfe took the opportunity to knock the men off balance because, since she wasn't mic'd yet, the other microphones wouldn't pick up her low-volume remark — they'd be set at low levels to avoid feedback.

The make-up artists rushed onto the set to powder down the sudden moisture on both men's faces.

Rolfe regarded her counterparts with triumphant satisfaction. Then she put them on their heels again.

"Don't you two look like peas in the same pod! What little plan have you co-conspirators cooked up?"

Both men were speechless — a simultaneous event of astronomically low probability.

"Let me guess," Rolfe continued, speaking low, still un-mic'd. "Chipster, you are getting tired of being spoon-fed the story of your lifetime — you'd like to get in the driver's seat and steer this puppy for a while, right? Maybe get a crack at this family, live and in person, instead of by video?

"And you, preacher," Rolfe said, turning toward the rotund reverend. "Right now this family's about as useful as bourbon in a barrel — no good to you unless you can get at it, right?"

Jones and Stone exchanged sideways glances.

Jones realized the governor had guessed right — the two men were in cahoots — but had missed in her guess at how.

Employing considerable restraint, both men managed to keep their mouths shut. Rolfe mistook the stony silence for a *nolo contendre*.

"Well, gents, what we have here is a confluence of interests," Rolfe delivered. "I'll help you get a shot at the family, but I want in on the broadcast when it happens. It needs to be a live panel, not a prepackaged story" — shooting an accusatory glance at Stone — "maybe just the three of us, daddy-dearest and the kid. How's that sound?"

Reverend Carter Ray Jones's mind was spinning and checking options like a safe-cracker. The governor's audacious approach was impressive. But with her shot in the dark, she'd claimed the least profitable stake in the alliance — participation in any future interview of the kid and his family. The plan Stone and he had sealed with a damp handshake wasn't about journalism or access. It was about bank, lots of it, and the governor didn't have a clue. Nonetheless, she could cause trouble if she went public with allegations that the two men were in league. And on the upside, if she could somehow deliver the family, that would create a second tsunami of tithing. Jones decided to bring her on board.

Stone's mind was also working overtime. *She is so* hot! *I wonder what she's trying to do here?*

"Uh, sure, governor," Jones said. "You're in."

Stone's expression went from barely disguised lust to barely disguised confusion. Jones patted the air gently with a bejeweled hand.

"It's alright," he mouthed. Stone nodded without understanding.

"Wonderful!" Rolfe beamed as the sound technician leaned in front of her to attach a lavaliere mic to her blouse. "I can't wait!"

SIXTY-FOUR

"Welcome to a special three-o'clock edition of *News Talk Today Now* on GNBNC," crooned the abnormally tan (for February) Chip Stone. "*Wazzzzupppp!*"

Eyes rolled throughout Atlanta's News Vortex.

"Today's top news, just as it was yesterday and the two days prior, is the miracle child of Richmond, Virginia. Truly, this is a story that has riveted a nation, riveted a world, as day after day we find out more and more about the child and the event that occurred Sunday in that small church."

Stone ended the scripted run-on sentence wondering if he shouldn't toss in some ad-libbing, just to give the broadcast the kind of spontaneity that kept viewers tuning back in. What the hell…

"It has been a long time," Stone freelanced, "since we've seen a story of this magnitude, a story that has grabbed the attention of a nation so thoroughly. For me, I think back to the blockbuster story of autumn three years ago — *Pachyderm in Peril* — wherein a newborn elephant from the Richard Richardson and Son Traveling Circus fell into a sinkhole in Santa Cruz, California. For eight tense days and nights, a nation watched as workers and volunteers labored desperately to reach the big baby and to extract her from her loamy predicament. Thanks to GNBNC's 24-hour coverage, America watched a parade of Boy Scouts, Girl Scouts and animal rights organizations march by the sinkhole dropping in peanuts to nourish the trapped behemoth. Through the

GNBNC coverage, a nation witnessed bittersweet moments as activists advocating world peace, workers' rights, women's rights, men's rights, children's rights, spirits' rights, circus trainers' rights and a car full of clowns took turns singing anti-war songs, workers' party songs, show tunes, college football fight songs, Helen Reddy songs, nursery rhymes…"

Rolfe stared at Stone, wondering not only where he was going but where the hell he was right now. She glanced over at Reverend Jones in time to catch him pulling a fat pinky finger from his ear and inspecting it for wax.

"… then of course came that horrifying moment when the clowns were assaulted by anti-circus activists…" Stone continued, now lost within in his own wandering story.

Rolfe kicked off a shoe, and without a move above the waist, drove her stockinged foot deep into Stone's crotch, and not in a nice way. Stone suppressed a yelp, but stopped talking, mid-thought on the subsequent movement to ban gun ownership for circus clowns.

After a two-second pause, Stone looked over at his guests.

"With us today…"

SIXTY-FIVE

"This guy Stone is an odd bird," Nick Walters offered to Tom and Amy, who were sitting across from him on a comfortable couch.

They were watching *News Talk Today Now* on the safe house's large-, but not huge-, screen television.

"That's an understatement," Tom answered. "When the wind blows, his ears whistle." On-screen, Stone introduced his two guests.

"Now *she's* dangerous," Tom added as the camera focused on the governor.

Tom had only briefly covered off with Amy on his encounter with Rolfe in the SUV outside the WSSS-TV studios, and he'd not delved into the details of Rolfe's green eyes, her fragrant perfume, and the way her voice slides into a low, husky purr when she whispers.

Tom shook his head to free himself from the memory. He marveled at the enormous potency of a direct advance from a woman like Rolfe — strong enough to spin his compass needle, even momentarily, from the true north of his family and of Amy.

A verbal altercation on the television achieved for Tom what shaking his head could not — a change of subject.

"All I'm saying is that we don't know for sure that the video of the Smith family is genuine," Rolfe was arguing.

"Governor, what about the newspaper they hold up in the video?" countered Stone. "How could that be faked?"

"I don't know how, but it can be," Rolfe argued. "Digital video technology can achieve amazing results.

"The only solid evidence we have right now is a questionable event at St. Thomas's last Sunday, a destroyed hotel room, a missing family and a suspicious-acting father," Rolfe continued. "That is plenty enough for me to ask the Virginia State Police to track down Mr. Smith and bring him in for questioning."

"So Mr. Smith is a suspect in some crime?" Stone asked.

"I think the term-of-art these days is 'person of interest,'" Rolfe replied dryly. "But I've made it clear what *my* interest is in bringing him in. In fact, I've asked my State Police commandant to offer a $100,000 reward for information leading to the arrest of Mr. Smith."

At State Police Headquarters in Southside Richmond, a weary commandant sighed and buzzed his administrative assistant.

"Susie, get me Tips and Rewards again, please."

The governor kept rolling. "I will not rest until this man is brought to justice, and this family, this child — if he is still alive — is placed in the protective custody of the Commonwealth of Virginia."

Amy's stomach dropped. "She's talking about taking Billy!"

"We're not going to let that happen," Tom reassured her, not so sure himself.

"With all due respect, governor, I have not come to the same conclusion," Reverend Jones weighed in, filling the screen. "In fact, I've spent a lot of time in prayer this week, a lot of time with the Lord, and God has chosen to speak to me, directly, on this matter."

Rolfe and Stone showed only poker faces to this seemingly momentous disclosure.

"It's true," Jones insisted over silent skepticism. "God Himself has informed me that this family is special in His eyes, and that I am to serve as their shepherd, to bring them safely through this valley of darkness.

"Now, I willingly accept this solemn responsibility," Jones said, gazing into the camera. "But even though my spirit is willing, my resources are limited. So I ask that anyone who trusts in the Lord and His judgment in this case help me

229

raise the financing I need to successfully shepherd the blessed family through this crisis. Our brand new toll-free number is 1-999-GO SAVE 'M — that's 1-999-467-2836. We will need a great deal of additional resources for this effort, because it may take months, maybe even years, to guide the Smiths through the many perils they face in this world of heathens and non-believers."

"I can't believe this jerk is using our situation to raise more money for his outfit!" Amy exclaimed.

"That's the only reason he's here," Tom said.

"He sure doesn't give a damn about you three," Walters added. "He's in it for the money."

"I know," Amy stammered. "But I just can't believe he'd be that bald-faced!"

"He's a piece of work, all right," murmured Walters, with the distracted look of someone figuring out a math problem in his head. He blinked, then turned to Tom and Amy.

"You know, I've met Jones before," he said. "In first class, one time, on a flight from L.A. to Dulles. He was in the next seat, spiking his orange juice with vodka from one of those little airplane bottles.

"He looks over at me and sizes me up — suit, tie, briefcase, first class — and must've figured we were birds of a financial and philosophical feather. When the flight attendant, a man, came by to freshen Jones's juice, Jones gave me this little sideways look, sort of mocking the guy."

Walters's expression soured.

"Then, when the flight attendant left, Jones starts whispering jokes about the guy's sexual orientation. How the hell would Jones know what this guy's sexual orientation was? All the guy had done was pour orange juice. And what business was it of his? It pissed me off."

The preacher, unaware of the lancing he'd just endured somewhere in the undulating hills of Virginia, continued his pitch.

"My operators are standing by, ready to take the tithes and offerings of the people of this nation and of the world, to assist me in guiding this poor family through this terrible crisis."

"Shouldn't the reporter be stopping him from doing that?" Tom asked no one in particular.

"Yes, he should," Walters replied. "But Stone's just sitting there. Something's not quite right about this."

The group watched in silence for a moment.

"And speaking of not quite right," said Walters, "it just came to me: 1-999-GO SAVE 'M also spells 1-999-I M SATEN — Satan with an 'e-n,' though."

"Idiot can't even spell!" Tom laughed.

Amy snorted. "I'm surprised it's not 1-666-BEELZEBUB!"

Tom just shook his head as the three returned their attention to the television. Chip Stone began to speak.

"Well, here we have represented Truth, in Reverend Jones's claim that this is a Chosen Family for which he is responsible. We have Justice, in Governor Rolfe's quest for an alleged murderer. All we are missing is The American Way, and I will assume that mantle for myself and my colleagues in the Fourth Estate.

"*Our* mission is to find out what's really going on, and satisfy the public's right to know every single detail about this family. 'The Public Right to Know': it's in the Declaration of Independence, and it is our 'religion,' if you will."

Walters laughed sharply. Stone continued.

"I pledge to you, viewers at home, that I will not stop pursuing this story and this family until I have brought them on the air, into the courtroom of public opinion and gotten the answers the American people and the world deserve."

Walters glanced at the young couple. *There's no way these two understand what they're up against. And that's probably just as well.*

SIXTY-SIX

Reverend Waite pushed his body hard through the light, warm afternoon rain, willing it up the hill along Woodman Road. When he reached the halfway point on the hill he would be able to see the steeple of St. Thomas's, signaling the last mile of his five-mile run. The slap of his running shoes on the black pavement kept rhythm with the sound of his breathing.

Normally this steady percussion-and-woodwind orchestra transported the reverend into a sort of meditative trance, allowing his stress to flow from his body. Often he reached the end of his run feeling like he'd hardly run at all. Time passed quickly on those days, like the hours during deep slumber.

Today the cacophony in Waite's head clashed with the music of his legs and lungs, contributing to the chaos in his heart. For most of his relatively short career, Waite had labored at Reverend Fogherty's side, patiently biding his time and learning what he could about pastorship, while still aching for the chance to take the reins of St. Thomas's and bring her into the modern world. He wasn't unhappy, but neither was he fulfilled. His was a pastor's heart.

Despite these longings, the arrangement had been acceptable because he knew Fogherty would not likely remain in the pulpit for much longer. Fogherty, with 50 years in ministering, had grown weary, and ready for the next stage in his mortal life.

Until recently.

The hill steepened, and Waite pushed harder against gravity and fatigue.

After last Sunday, Reverend Fogherty initially had suffered a crisis of confidence. He'd taken God's actions as a personal rebuke. Ol' Fogey's heart took another hit when it appeared Billy and Amy had been murdered. However, as the week progressed, Fogherty found inspiration in his ministry to the many who were touched, frightened or simply confused by Sunday's occurrence. Then came this morning's video showing Tom, Amy and Billy alive and well, leaving Reverend Fogherty as ebullient as a new seminary graduate.

Of course, Waite's own initial interpretation had been equally incorrect, and malevolent to boot. Waite grimaced at the memory. His first conclusion had been that the event was an opportunity to raise the profile of St. Thomas's, to increase the weekly tithings, to upgrade the facilities, even to put St. Thomas's on local (or, he'd dared to dream, national) television. Unsaid but understood was that Waite would lead this progress (to his own greater glory, he realized later).

Fortunately, he'd encountered that slime bag Carter Ray Jones in the make-up room of WSSS-TV. Jones embodied the logical extreme of all of Waite's secret desires — most notably, the desire for money and self-glory.

The run-in left Waite disgusted with himself, and prompted a 180-degree turn in his perspective. Waite now felt his understanding of the event was properly aligned with God's will, and that revelation brought him peace. The family's video appearance added joy to that peace.

However, as healthy as his transformation had been, it had been even more revitalizing for Reverend Fogherty.

A pick-up truck piloted by a good ol' boy yapping on a cell phone rounded the curve at the top of the hill and barreled toward Waite, right tires hanging over the pavement edge. Waite stepped into the ditch. The truck roared over the asphalt where Waite had just been jogging. The driver never even noticed Waite.

Waite began running again, and so did his mind.

St. Thomas's spiritual rebirth was finally happening — except Waite wasn't leading it. Fogherty was. And Waite was honest enough with himself to admit to conflict in his heart.

Hadn't he paid his dues? Hadn't he put in his time? Hadn't he worked and waited for the chance to lead St. Thomas's to its potential? Why would God now ask him to postpone his dreams while Reverend Fogherty enjoyed a resurrection in his career and his will to lead? What sort of cruel succession management game was God playing with Waite's career? With his life?

The very top of St. Thomas's steeple rose over the road ahead like the sun. Waite knew from hundreds of laps around this suburban track that even though he could see the tip of the church from here, he needed to continue pushing up the hill and down the other side for some time before reaching his objective.

Waite increased his cadence, knowing his body would respond. He always felt strongest nearing the top of a hill.

Waite recalled a seminary instructor's words: God always answers your prayers, but not always by giving you what you ask for. He has His own plan, and it may or may not correspond with yours.

Waite initially rejected this. What of free will? If God is steering our lives, what's the point of choice? What's the point of trying to live righteously?

Eventually, Waite came up with a competing theory: we're like children driving the old-style motorized cars at an amusement park, the kind that follow a raised metal guide bar that runs along the center of the concrete course. We can steer a little left and right, but the metal bar determines our ultimate path.

One would think the relatively small degree of freedom allowed the child drivers would frustrate them. But quickly the children learn and accept the reality of the predetermined path, and they take up the challenge of steering the car smoothly along that path, without banging too many times into the metal guide. There's even some comfort for the child, knowing that, no matter how poorly he steered, he'd eventually reach his destination — a long as he kept his foot on the gas and did not stop dead on the course.

Who knows? In the next world, we might graduate to cars without tracks, or even stock car racing... But in the meantime, our job was to do the best we could with the life that God gave us.

Waite crested the peak, and surveyed the shallow slope curving toward St. Thomas's driveway, which cut left and up the hill where the church was perched.

He knew St. Thomas's was his destination, but Waite struggled to accept that the path might not be straight, and might yet curve away before ultimately looping around to the pulpit in the small sanctuary.

The best he could do, he concluded reluctantly, was keep his foot on the gas, and try to steer along the road as best he could. Yes, it was frustrating. But the certainty in his heart of what lay at the end of this road offered comfort.

SIXTY-SEVEN

"Dig in guys!" Walters said. "I know it's an early dinner, but we've still got a lot to do today."

The family pounced on the food, and in the silence of four mouths chewing, a light, steady rain pattered on the windows. The day had clouded quickly, then opened up.

After a few minutes, Tom spoke. "I have to admit, I never thought I'd be eating dinner with a billionaire."

Walters smiled with him. "Heck, stranger things have happened to you *this week!*" he said.

"Still…"

"That sounds like the old question: If you could have a meal with anyone, living or dead, who would it be?" Amy asked both men.

"Chip Stone, Mary Rolfe and Carter Ray Jones," Tom laughed. "And I want to cook it, too."

"How about you, Nick?" Amy asked.

"I used to think it would be Jesus," Walters said. "Then it dawned on me that saying 'Jesus' reflected some doubt in my own faith. If all the religious stuff is true, won't I get a chance to talk to Him in Heaven?"

Walters looked at Amy. "Would *you* would pick Jesus?"

Many emotions flickered across Amy's face and through her heart.

"Do you doubt your faith, Amy?"

Amy returned Walters's gaze.

"I am learning to have faith in my faith," she said. "I think I'm getting stronger."

Walters smiled. "I'm glad."

"But you didn't answer my question," Amy countered.

"Nor have you," Walters parried.

"You first."

Walters had one arm of his glasses in his mouth, like a pipe, while he considered. "It's a tough choice. I think I would have liked to have Tom Wolfe over for dinner — the man was a genius.

"But I wouldn't want just him and me talking to each other. That'd be like playing catch with Joe Montana — if you really want to witness the brilliance of Joe Montana passing the football, you have to have a Jerry Rice there to catch it. If Montana were throwing passes to me, he'd have to underhand it. What good is that?

"Same with Wolfe," Walters continued. "He'd have to lob ideas to me that were easy enough for even me to catch, just to keep the conversation going. I'd need someone else there sharp enough to play catch with Wolfe across the table — Mark Twain, Herman Wouk, Florence King, Oliver Wendell Holmes — someone like that. I'd just watch the fireworks."

The gray-haired man looked into the distance, lost in the imaginary conversation he could witness. Breaking away from the scene, he looked at Amy. "Your turn."

"Mine would be Tom's mom and dad," Amy said. "Just so I can tell them what a wonderful son they have, and how grateful I am for him."

Tom was gazing at Amy, his face a mixture of grief and gratitude. Amy placed her hand on Tom's.

Richard's soft footsteps approaching in the hall brought Amy and Tom back to the table.

"Mr. Walters," said Richard, leaning in. "Michael Perry is here."

"Thank you, Richard," Walters said, getting up. "You kids keep eating. I have some business to attend to. I anticipate we'll depart by 5 p.m. or so."

After Walters left the room, Amy caught Tom's eye.

"He's a kind man."

"Yeah."

"I think these past couple of days have been exactly what we needed," she continued. "Nick's been a lifesaver."

Tom nodded.

"I *do* think I'm stronger," said Amy. "I *do* think that my faith is stronger now, after a couple of days away from all the craziness — a couple of days in the safety Nick has given us."

Tom couldn't really put words around how strongly he agreed with Amy, but he felt it.

The young parents spent the next several minutes in silence, watching their son gobbling the late-afternoon meal.

"Maybe we're near the end," Tom said.

"I hope so."

SIXTY-EIGHT

Just before 5:00 p.m., Nick's visitor left in a sparkling Jaguar, wipers sweeping away the warm, light rain.

Walters entered the TV room. Billy rolled around on the rug, giggling and spitting, and Tom and Amy sat curled on the couch watching the Weather Channel — anything but the news.

The weatherman… that is, the meteorologist… was dumbfounded at the climatic conditions over the eastern part of the country.

"We have a fairly strong cold front pushing down toward the mid-Atlantic from the Ohio Valley," the coifed climatologist said. "At the same time, a column of warm air is marching up the Eastern Seaboard, due to a dramatic, and unexpected, turn in the jet stream. That means warmer, wetter conditions for all of you along the Atlantic — so for all you folks in Charleston, South Carolina, if you're thinking of heading out this evening to perhaps look at the beautiful harbor, you better bring a raincoat… and all of you out by the aquarium, overlooking the harbor, you can be comfortable there, sitting on those cement steps between the building and the water, watching those big ships coming in and out of port, especially those big freighters riding low with their cargo…"

"Why do they have to try to convince us that they're really local weathermen?" Amy mused. "Everyone knows they're in Atlanta."

"And all of you in Fredericksburg, Virginia," the meteorologist continued.

"That's right — over by Mary Washington College, there in downtown Fredericksburg… you'll be seeing the warming trend continue into the evening, with light rain likely… so if you're driving down Route 17, by the river, you might want to use your wipers… particularly as you go by the park… with the swings… and the… uh… sliding board… you know what I'm talking about… there might still be some kids out there, playing in the rain… like that blonde haired one… the little boy… keep an eye out…"

"Well, gang, we're all set," Walters announced with a clap. "Who wants to go for a ride?"

"Are we sure this is the only way?" Amy asked.

"Nothing is ever for sure, sweetie," Tom replied. "I just know we can't stay hidden forever, and this looks like our only chance to break out of this story and get our lives back.

Amy looked back to Walters.

"I can't guarantee anything, of course," Walters answered. "But I agree with Tom. I can't see this ending without you taking this step."

Amy looked at her precious Billy. This was no life for him. How long could they lean on Nick Walters anyway? He'd been kind just to shelter them for the past three days. It was time to take definitive action. Amy stood.

"Well, if this is it, then let's do it!" she said.

"OK then!" Walters joined in.

The family filed out the front door and into a large SUV waiting in the circular drive.

SIXTY-NINE

It certainly had been an exciting week for young GNBNC associate director Lewis Plinkdunk!

First, on Sunday morning, he was put in charge of his first broadcast — and the *ALL & Then Some!* show, no less!

Sure, it was a years-old encore broadcast, but it came off without a hitch! And despite that last-minute emergency with the lights going off! *Thank God he was cool under pressure*, Plinkdunk thought, *or the Global World News Leader might have had a minute or longer of dead air* — the broadcast equivalent of a naval officer running his ship ashore.

Not good for one's career, to say the least.

But he'd kept his composure, and somehow — Plinkdunk could not quite remember how, in all the excitement — the show ran despite the blackout. Magnificent!

Then, later that day, this whole God-speaking-through-the-kid story hit the fan, and things hadn't been normal since!

Now it was late Wednesday afternoon, and the crew for *ALL & Then Some!* was preparing for the evening's broadcast. The subject, of course, would be the so-called Miracle of St. Thomas's, and tonight Alexander Langston LaMourgan's guest would be Michael Moore, film maker and general gadfly.

In the control room, the regular director was barking commands, lining up camera angles, loading graphics into computers, and generally running a tight ship.

I must watch and learn, Plinkdunk thought.

"Ex*cuse* me, but can you not sit on my work station?" a video technician snapped.

"Huh?"

"Get your ass off my work station!"

"Right! Yes!! Of course!!" Plinkdunk yelped, jumping off the desk like a cat off a hot stove.

On the wall next to the door, a sleek black telephone rang.

"Get that, will you?" the director said to Plinkdunk.

After two more rings, the director turned to her associate, who was gazing at the brightly lit set of *ALL & Then Some!*.

"Will you GET THE PHONE, *PLEASE!*"

"Huh? Oh! Yes! Yes!! Of course!!"

Before picking up the handset, the associate director paused to silently rehearse his greeting.

ALL & Then Some! — go!

ALL & Then Some! — GO!

ALL & Then Some! — YO!

The phone rang again.

"*Get the damn phone!*"

"Right!" said Plinkdunk, picking up the handset. "Alice Langin Lanny Some and Then! — *GAW!!*"

A moment of silence as the caller recovered from the salutation and the crew in the booth, to a person, brought their hands to their foreheads.

"Yeah, uh, who's this?" said a voice on the line.

The associate director switched to his basso voice: "This is Lewis Plinkdunk, associate director on the Hall — I mean, the *ALL & Then Some!* Show."

"You're with the Alexander Langston LaMourgan show?"

"Yes sir, I am."

"Is Alexander Langston LaMourgan there?"

"Mr. LaMourgan is preparing for this evening's show with Michael Moore.

Now, ex*cuse* me, but who is calling please?"

"Uh, yeah. This is Tom Smith."

"And your reason for calling?"

"Uh, I'm Tom Smith. I'm the father of the little boy from St. Thomas's this week — the little boy on the news."

Lewis Plinkdunk was halfway into his "talk to the hand" bit before he heard the caller's words.

"Well, I am *sorry*, mister, ahem, *Smith*! Mr. LaMourgan is not avail--… Wait, you *did* say… did you say you are the *father* of …"

"Yes sir, Mr. Plinkdunk. We… I mean, I was thinking that we might want to come on Mr. LaMourgan's show tonight. That is, if Mr. LaMourgan was interested."

"We?"

"Uh, yes. We. Me and my family."

"And Carter?"

"Billy? Yes. Is that OK?"

Lewis Plinkdunk automatically turned to seek out the director's permission, so as to cover his ass before landing the Interview of the Century. Then his common sense took over. Well, almost took over.

"Yes! Yes! Yes! Of course! We'll see you then!"

Then Lewis Plinkdunk, associate director of *ALL & Then Some!*, hung up on the Interview of the Century, without so much as a "can I give you directions?"

In the SUV, Tom Smith pulled the phone from his ear and looked at it.

"He hung up on me."

Four mouths hung open. Then one drooled.

In the *ALL & Then Some!* control booth, the director asked, without really caring, who was on the phone.

Plinkdunk was not quite sure how to answer.

"Hey! Plinkdink! Who was on the horn?"

"Aaaah…"

The director straightened up from a monitor and looked at her assistant.

"Yeah?"

"Aaah… No one… really… not… really… not anyone, really."

"Ohhh kaaayyy…," the director said.

The phone rang again and Plinkdunk nearly ripped it from the wall answering it.

"HELLO!" Plinkdunk yelled.

"Mr. Plinkdunk?"

"YES, yes, yes, yes!"

"Is there any more information you need or we need?"

"Of course, yes, yes. We got cut off. I apologize."

Minutes later, the Smith family had instructions and Lewis Plinkdunk was on his way to a completely undeserved promotion.

SEVENTY

"They've got *who?*" Chip Stone asked his editor over the phone from his dressing room at WSSS-TV.

"The kid, the dad, the whole freaking family!" said the news vet, rubbing it in that Stone wasn't getting this interview. Instead, Alexander Langston LaMourgan, a.k.a., "The Automaton of Nighttime News" (per the *Washington Post*'s Tom Shales), had somehow, again, landed the hottest interview in town.

"But this is *my story!*"

"Well, take a picture, 'cause your story is rolling by and headed up I-95 for *ALL & Then Some!*"

"This is *bullshit!*" Stone screamed before slamming the phone down, smashing his fingers.

"Damn, damn, damn, damn, damn!!!!" he screeched.

The plan had backfired! He had to tell Jones!

When Jones picked up the phone, Stone could have sworn he heard an odd, mechanical noise in the background.

"Jones! The Smith family — they're going on *ALL & Then Some!* tonight!"

After a muffled "*Get that off me!*" the preacher spoke.

"Are you shittin' me?"

"Yes! I mean, no! They're on the way to D.C. to do the show tonight."

"Oh for chrissakes! You said that *we'd* get this interview!"

"I thought we *would!* I thought that the way we were baiting them, the dad would want to answer us for sure!"

"Well, you blew that one, sport," Jones replied. "Now what?"

"Well, we're not going to get in on this sitting in Richmond," Stone said. "Let's get up to D.C. — maybe there's something we can do."

"What about Rolfe?"

"*Screw* Rolfe!" Stone spit back. "She can land her own damn interview!"

"Whatever, son. I can be at the studio in 20 minutes."

Jones paused, then spoke.

"Well, sport, we better get going. They're already running commercials that the family's gonna be on the show."

Stone could hear the GNBNC "Miracle at St. Thomas'" theme song in the background.

"I'll be out front!" Stone said. "See you in twenty minutes!"

SEVENTY-ONE

Lewis Plinkdunk chewed his fingernails in a plush armchair outside *the* Alexander Langston LaMourgan's dressing room. Across the room, his producer was talking on the phone. Plinkdunk could hear half the conversation as the producer tried to tell Michael Moore that he'd been bumped.

"Mr. Moore. Mr...--. Mr. Moo--... M--."

The producer stopped and listened.

"Yes, Mr. Moore. Yes, I do. I realize that. Yes sir — right into the lobby. Yes sir. The CEO of GM, right there. I know. Really gave him what-for. Yes sir, an Oscar. No, I know the American people hang on your every--. Yes sir. But here's the thing sir... Yes sir. Yes. Of course. No, I do—I do not think you're... Mr. Moore, that's just negative talk from trolls. Yes sir. I know, yes. Uncorruptable. Yes sir, definitely sour grapes. I know. Pardon me? No sir. I mean, yes, of course, God will probably draw a bigger audience than you. Is that what you meant? It wasn't? Still, you have to admit, this is a big story."

Again the producer stood, gritting her teeth, looking at the ceiling. She caught Plinkdunk's eye and made a "shoot myself" motion. Plinkdunk's heart leapt, gratified to have been invited to share in the producer's misery. He smiled broadly, as if he'd had the same problems with Michael Moore, then shook his head in empathy. When he stopped shaking his head and refocused, he realized the producer was no longer looking at him.

"Yes sir. I have no idea, sir. I'm sure you would win. Yes sir. But Jesus Christ probably would make a pretty good movie, don't you-- Yes sir. Righteous. Yes sir."

Another pause.

"I have no idea. Really, I don't. I wouldn't want to guess — I don't even know what a high IQ would... No really. Really. *Please, no...*"

Deep sigh.

"OK. Um, 110. No, really. R--... OK, uh... 115? Right. Of course. Of course. OK, what?"

Pause.

"Well! That... that sure is... uh... 141... oh, yes, and a half! I mean... I wouldn't have guessed... is that high? It is? OH, really? Wow. Yes sir. Absolutely sir."

The door of Alexander Langston LaMourgan's dressing room opened, and a thin, efficient looking young man stepped half-way out. He looked at Plinkdunk, furrowed his brow, and then saw the producer.

"*He's ready for you!*"

"*OK,*" the producer signaled, and began trying to wrap up the call.

"Sir, I have to... Yes sir. No, I think we'll need to reschedule you, as I said before. I'm not sure when. Yes. No. I'll call you. No, really. OK. You can call us when you're ready. No sir, it's really just because the family has not been interviewed yet, and... Yes. Yes. A scoop. Yes sir. No, you're a scoop too. You're just a scoop of a different flavor. Right? Ha ha! Yes sir. OK sir. Thank you. Thank you. Yes. OK then. OK. Thanks. Bye bye. Yes sir. Culture-shifter, yes sir. OK. Good-bye then. Yes. Good-bye. Yes sir. Bye. Bye then. Bye. OK. Bye."

SEVENTY-TWO

The preacher picked up the phone on the first ring.

"Reverend Fogherty?"

"Yes."

"This is Eleanor Sweetwater."

Mrs. Sweetwater was an active, gray-haired 73-year-old wisp of a woman who'd been in the pews for Fogherty's first sermon 50 years ago.

"Oh, yes, hello Eleanor. I haven't seen you since — well, since everything went crazy last Sunday. How are you?"

"Oh, I'm *fine*, Reverend. Except for the fact that my daughter-in-law left me for dead when that demon-child began shooting lightning through the church."

Fogherty sighed. Since Sunday, he'd been getting one of three different types of calls from members of his flock. The first were from those who'd decided to find a spiritual meaning within Sunday's event. These were deep and rewarding conversations. Fogherty had no doubt that God was using the little boy's outburst to strengthen many people's faith.

The second was from congregation members searching for what to think. Often they called just to talk, to vent fears or hopes. These conversations also were rewarding. Few things energized a preacher more than meeting a mind open to the possibility of God.

Then there were the third type of phone calls. These callers challenged Fogherty's patience. They invariably theorized Sunday's event was the work of the Devil, or the Communists, or the CIA, or Glenn Beck, or any number of religious denominations.

They also often remembered the event far differently than Fogherty, and differently than it appeared on the now-famous news report. Often they reported pyrotechnics, levitation, speaking in tongues, death and dismemberment, and treachery by fellow worshipers.

Eleanor Sweetwater clearly fell into the third group.

"Wasn't your son there, too?" Fogherty asked.

"Yes, yes," snapped Mrs. Sweetwater. "But the first thing my boy heard was that woman telling him to get out and take her coat with him! She didn't give a fig about me! She was worried about that damn coat."

Fogherty had noticed increased profanity among these callers, even the elderly, and without regard to the fact that they were talking to a man of the cloth.

"I'm not sure I remember lightning, Eleanor," Fogherty offered as an anchor to reality. Mrs. Sweetwater had no interest in such limitations.

"Oh, I'm sure you don't, Reverend. After all, you had been blinded by the first thunderbolt from that little bastard's hands! You were laid out on the altar, shaking and trembling."

Fogherty gave up.

"What can I do for you tonight, Eleanor?"

"I just thought you'd like to know that the devil-child and his family will be on Alexander Langston LaMourgan at nine."

"Really!?" Fogherty exclaimed.

"Yes! They're showing commercials every five minutes," said Mrs. Sweetwater. "You'd think it was the Second Coming of Jesus H. Christ himself!"

"Well, thank you for the heads up, Eleanor," said Fogherty, suddenly nervous.

"You're certainly welcome, reverend," replied Mrs. Sweetwater. "Oh, and Reverend Fogherty?"

"Yes?"

"You take care of those testicles, now — I heard they took a real beating from the lightning bolts."

"Yes. Ah, well, thank you Eleanor. Have a nice evening."

Fogherty hung up. He turned on the television, and sure enough, GNBNC was running promos for the interview at every commercial break.

"TONIGHT, on *ALL & Then Some!*," a bass voice rumbled over the "Miracle at St. Thomas's theme music, "Alexander Langston LaMourgan talks live to the Smith family, and to Billy Smith, in his Washington, D.C. studios! Don't miss this Interview of the Epoch!"

Flipping channels, Fogherty saw GNBNC's parent company was running promos on every other network in its empire, from BNC to GNBNCSports to the CritterWorld Network.

Reverend Waite entered the room, having just finished the evening service. Fogherty filled him in.

"That's in an hour and a half. We should watch it," said Waite.

"The whole world is going to be watching," Fogherty said. "After all these commercials, there isn't a person on the planet who doesn't know."

"Oh, God!" Waite exclaimed.

"What?"

"The guy you talked to, the guy who tried to kill them! He'll know!"

"Oh, sweet Lord!" Fogherty shouted. "We have to warn them! Quick, call the network."

After three busy signals and three "all circuits are busy" recordings, Waite tried the Washington, D.C. police. Again, all circuits were busy.

"We've got to reach them!" Fogherty said. "Come on!"

The old man actually ran from the room and out into the warm winter evening, jumping into his 1994 Chevrolet Corsica.

Waite slid into the passenger seat as Fogherty turned over the engine, and they turned left out of the parking lot onto Woodman Road and headed north to I-295, which would take them to I-95 North to Washington.

"I just pray we're not too late," shouted Fogherty over the four-cylinder's knocking and rattling.

SEVENTY-THREE

"I think we're all set," Tom said as the SUV trekked up Route 29 through the rolling hills of Virginia horse country, toward Washington.

"Good," said Walters. "I think this is really the only way, son."

"I'll bet Chip Stone is mad!" said Amy. "We really pulled a fast one on him."

"Yes," said Walters. "You can tell by the way he talks, Stone thinks he owns your story *and* you."

The group rode in silence.

"You know," Tom said. "I heard a professor on one of the morning talk shows saying that faith is a superstition, like a lucky rabbit's foot. He was saying that there is no proof of God, and that until he sees it, he's going to keep believing that spiritual people are idiots."

Walters smiled.

"You know, when Napoleon's courtesans argued there was no God, Napoleon would point to the stars and say, 'Then what of all this in the sky?' He said that if someone could explain where all that came from, he might agree there is no God. Until then, the stars were the proof."

Walters shook his head.

"It's as if some people don't want to admit that their magnificent intellects are a credit to anyone but themselves, so they say they aren't spiritual," Walters laughed. "*Everyone* is spiritual. Denying that is like denying that you have blood in your veins — it may make you feel more in control, and you may even believe it, but that doesn't change the reality."

Walters looked out at the gentle swells of green pastures and farms, shaking his head and still amused. Amy watched Billy spitting on his fingers.

"I think you were about to tell us about your family, Nick, back at your house," Amy invited. "Where are your children?"

Walters paused. *I've never seen a sadder smile*, Tom thought.

"One of my sons lives in Richmond, not too far from where you live," answered Walters finally. "He is a successful businessman, but he has learned from my mistakes and, from a distance, he appears to be a good father as well. My other son is a very accomplished writer, out in San Luis Obispo, California. My daughter is in Northern Virginia, and works in Washington as an advocate and lawyer for the homeless. None of them want much to do with me, or with my money, for that matter. They've turned out well — people of character and principle. I suppose their mother gets the credit for that, although I provided a fairly compelling example of what *not* to become. In a perverse way, I suppose, I helped them become the good people that they are, but I would have preferred to do it differently."

Amy and Tom were engrossed.

"When the kids were young, and my career had not yet really taken off," Walters continued. "I remember playing with them on the floor, reading to them, lying in bed next to them when they were sick."

The old man paused while strong emotions played across his face.

"I remember the joy, the infinite, absolute, unending joy, of hugging each of my children, of smelling their hair, of holding them close, of feeling their heart beating inside them and knowing it was a gift from my wife, from God…

"I'm not really sure when that ended," Walters continued, pausing now and then. "I just remember getting some promotions, some raises, more responsibility. I remember feeling this perverse pride walking out of the office to see my car, parked closest to the building because I'd come in so early, and still the last in the parking lot because I was leaving so late.

"Somewhere along the way, I lost my perspective," he said. "I lost my family. I lost my children. I lost that joy that came from just being with them…"

"Where is your wife?" Amy pressed gently.

"Northern Virginia, near my daughter," Walters responded. "She is happily remarried now, to a good man who has made their marriage his top priority. We still talk from time to time, and I think she understands that I'm not the same man who ignored our marriage and neglected our family. It's obviously too late for us, but I am glad she's found happiness."

"Can't she convince your children you have changed?" Amy asked.

"I don't know that they'll ever forgive me," Walters said, sadness creeping deeper into his voice. "They were 15, 13 and 11 when our marriage ended, and the man they spent most of their childhood getting to know was not a very good man. Two years after the marriage broke up, I began to understand, to grow — I don't know why, but I am glad I did — and I began to see how I'd misspent my life. But by then it was too late to change my children's perception. So for the last 15 years, I've tried to improve myself as a person, to be more like the person that God probably hoped I would be, to give to good causes and make my money more of a blessing to others than it had been to me. But I've also had to come to terms with the fact that, barring some unexpected revelation on their part, my children will never really like me, never really love me, and never really consider me much of a father."

Walters eyes reflected the gray, overcast sky.

"I have my doubts whether I'll get into Heaven," Walters said. "But if I do, I hope it is a place where we relive the most precious times in our lives, where that wonderful moment of snuggling with your child or hugging your mother or kissing your wife… that moment expands infinitely, in all directions, and lasts forever. That would be heaven."

Amy smiled, then reached over and put her hand on his.

"Thank you, Nick. For the shelter, and the food, and the protection. Thank you."

Nicholas Walters actually looked embarrassed. "It has been my pleasure, really. You're good people, with a good son, and you don't deserve to be sacrificed in the name of these false prophets. I just hope I can keep providing the help you need."

"Oh, you've done so much," Tom said. "Thank you."

"Actually, that reminds me," Walters replied. "I still have one more thing to do before we get to the studio."

Walters pulled out his cell phone and punched in a number. Then he put it on speaker and a ringing filled the SUV.

"This is the White House," said a pleasant female voice. "May I help you?"

"Good evening. This is Nicholas Walters calling for the president."

"Hold please."

Walters glanced over at his charges. Tom and Amy were sitting dumbstruck. Walters laughed. "You have no idea how nice it is to be around people who still can be surprised!"

"Yeah?" a grumpy, familiar voice echoed through the speakerphone.

"Mr. President. Good evening, sir. I trust you are feeling well tonight?"

In the Oval Office, the president glanced over at his NSA head listening in on a separate, muted line.

"I don't think you give a rat's ass how I'm feeling tonight," the president answered.

"Very true," chuckled Walters. "I *don't* care how you're feeling. But I do care to know that you are *thinking* this evening.

"Sorry we couldn't give a warm welcome to your men yesterday at my home," Walters continued. "Can I assume they left everything as clean as they found it?"

"Cut the shit, Walters."

"As you probably know by now," Walters said, showing no concern at the president's hostility. "The Smith family has been in my care for the past few days."

"As *you* probably know, the whole bunch of you are wanted by the FBI," the president countered.

"Perhaps, but I think the folks at the FBI don't realize yet how valuable we really are to them," Walters replied.

"What the hell are you talking about?"

"Knowledge is power, Mr. President. And right now, we are in a very powerful position."

Across the Oval Office, the president noticed his NSA boss wore grim expression. What was this?

"Stop talking like a fortune cookie and get to your point!" the president barked.

"I am in possession of some important information about you, Mr. President," Walters said. "And if you want this information to stay out of the public domain, you need to leave the Smith family alone."

"Oh, really?" the president mocked. "And what information do you have that the Republicans haven't already accused me of? If you hadn't noticed, the American public couldn't give two shits about the moral character of their president."

"Sad, but true," Walters observed. "But I think the public attitude would change if they saw rock-solid proof that their president had been compromised by avowed enemies of our nation."

"And that's happened, has it?" the president baited. Still, the Leader of the Free World couldn't help riffling back through the mental file of his indiscretions to see if there were any that might qualify as compromising the nation's security. He couldn't think of any.

"My information is about your involvement with a young woman," said Walters.

"Are you kidding me?" the president broke in, laughing. "That's the best you've got?"

"The young woman is a Saudi," continued Walters. The laughing stopped.

"You spent time with her during your trip last summer to the Middle East," continued Walters over the now quiet connection.

The president snuck a glance at his NSA director who, to the president's keen eye, was feigning surprise.

"Again, that's all you got?" the president spat.

"What you don't know, and what even your intelligence people don't know, is that this young lady...," Walters paused for effect..., "is the sister of the current security chief for al-Qaida."

The president felt a spear of panic plunge through his gut. The intelligence man also appeared shocked by that last detail.

"You're bluffing," the president croaked. "That's bullshit."

"I am not bluffing, and this most certainly is true," Walters said, "...as your intelligence people will confirm within the hour.

"Now, before you get any crazy ideas," Walters continued, "I have taken care to plant this information — with ample proof of its veracity — in numerous places, with numerous people. None of these people, by the way, are close associates or relatives of mine, so it won't do you any good to start knocking off everyone I know.

"These folks do not know what the information is, specifically," said Walters. "My arrangement with each is that if the Smith family is *ever* harmed in circumstances that are even the *slightest* bit suspicious, then these people should immediately release the information to the media.

"This condition is effective immediately," added Walters. "Meaning that if the Smith family is harmed even tonight, as we travel to the GNBNC studios, the plan kicks in.

"I'd add that, not only does this mean that *our* government better not harm the Smiths," Walters said. "It means that *no one* — no other government, no criminals, no terrorist group, *no one* — had better harm the Smiths — or this information will be released. Remember, the circumstances need only be suspicious for my plan to commence."

Silence.

"Nothing to say, Mr. President?" needled Walters.

The president managed to speak. "Are you telling me that I am supposed to keep the Smiths safe from the entire world? I'm supposed to use United States security assets to protect these people?"

"Very good, sir — that is *exactly* what I am telling you," Walters said. "Oh, and this commitment does not end with the conclusion of your administration. The release of this information, even after you are out of office, would be a setback for our nation. However, since I don't expect such high-minded motives to move you, I would also point out that the release of this information, even after your term is over, would forever stain your legacy."

"So I have to make sure the Smiths are safe from *anyone* for the rest of their lives," the president concluded.

"That is correct," said Walters.

The line was quiet for quite some time. Walters's calm expression belied the tension of the moment. But, in the tradition of great salesmen, Walters remained wordless, waiting for the fellow on the other side of the desk to break.

"You're a rotten little piece of crap, you know that, Walters?" the president exploded.

Walters waited a couple beats, so it was clear he wasn't responding to the president's remark.

"Mr. President, I want you to know that I am not proposing a deal," said Walters. "And I wouldn't trust you to hold up your end of a deal anyway. This is purely and simply a statement of fact. If the Smiths are harmed, you will be brought down. End of story.

"Good day, Mr. President."

Walters hung up, and the inside of the SUV was silent again.

Walters smiled in satisfaction. The Smiths said nothing. Tom's mouth opened and closed once or twice, as if trying to speak, but he couldn't find words. Amy blinked several times.

"He doesn't seem very nice," Amy said.

"No," Walters smiled. "He is not very nice."

"But we're safe now?" Amy said. "Could that be true?"

"That's right," Walters soothed. "He can't hurt you or Billy or Tom, and no one else is allowed to hurt you either."

"No one," Amy continued. "Not the freaks in our front yard, or on TV, no one."

Walters smiled. "That's right. You're safe."

Tom finally managed to find his voice. "Thank you," he said. "Thank you."

"Well, I still have a few more ideas of how I can help you all," Walters smiled. "I certainly hope I can."

SEVENTY-FOUR

"Listen, Walters, let's talk about this," the president said, a new tone in his voice.

"*Walters?*"

"He's hung up, sir," the NSA head said.

The president slammed down the phone, cracking the handset lengthwise.

"*DAMMit!*"

His disposition did not improve when saw the NSA director's disapproving, even angry, face.

"What the hell are you looking at?" the president snapped.

"An idiot."

"Watch your damn mouth!"

"How about you watch your damn *behavior*?!" the NSA director volleyed. "For chrissakes, you and your horny-college-kid antics have tied our hands!"

"How is this *my* fault?!" the president stood up, firing his chair into the bureau behind him.

"How… how is this *your fault??* Are you *kidding* me?"

"You or one of the damn penguins should have warned me about that girl!"

"We *did*, you moron! We told you, 'Don't sleep with women who aren't your *wife!*'"

"Oh, great!" the president threw up his hands. "What's your next pearl? 'Be careful, there are terrorists in the world?' Could you be any less specific?!"

"I don't think we could have been any *more* specific!" the intel man said, spinning away from his boss. He took five steps across the presidential seal emblazoned on the carpet. Halfway across the room, he paused, raised closed eyes to the ceiling, and took several deep breaths.

"Alright," he said, turning around. "Let's think about this…"

President and head spy stood quietly. The chief executive shook his head several times, dismissing faulty schemes that would fail to get him out of the jam.

At last the NSA director broke the silence: "We're stuck."

"Yeah," the president mumbled.

"I'm going to alter my instructions to our men in the field," the intelligence man said.

The president nodded. "And coordinate with the penguins."

The NSA director stared at the president before speaking again.

"Good *day*, Mr. President," he said, disappointed and sarcastic and angry all at once.

The president didn't bother to watch him leave.

SEVENTY-FIVE

"I am looking forward to interacting with this child."

The producer's briefing concluded, Alexander Langston LaMourgan leaned forward in his chair, bent at the waist, back perfectly straight, head tilted 30 degrees off vertical as he gazed, unblinking, at the producer. It occurred to the associate director that LaMourgan resembled the RCA dog looking into the phonograph trumpet — if the dog had been a member of the Royal Family.

Despite LaMourgan's odd posture, Plinkdunk was still awestruck and shaking with nervousness.

"Have you interacted to any degree with this family?" he asked the producer.

"No."

Has he blinked yet? Plinkdunk wondered.

The head swiveled in Plinkdunk's direction, while maintaining a slight upward tilt. Plinkdunk found himself looking up Alexander Langston LaMourgan's nostrils.

"And you, Associate Director Plinkdunk?" LaMourgan asked in perfectly clipped words. "Have you interacted to a significant degree with the child or his mother and / or father?"

"Uh," Plinkdunk stammered, unnerved. "Well, uh, not really… uh, your honor."

The producer shot Plinkdunk an angry look, which Plinkdunk missed entirely in his near-hypnotic state.

The head swiveled back toward the producer with a questioning look.

"He's new," the producer said.

"I see…" LaMourgan said. Then he swiveled back in Plinkdunk's direction. "Associate Director Plinkdunk, would you please assemble some background material and questions which I may utilize in my conversation with the child's family?"

"Huh?"

"Yes!" the producer jumped in. "He can do that."

"I will be grateful," said LaMourgan. "Yes. Grateful."

SEVENTY-SIX

By the time the preachers reached Doswell, Virginia, darkness had fallen. The warm rain continued, apparently unaware that it was February.

The bright red lights atop the one-third-scale Eiffel Tower at Kings Dominion slid past the streaked passenger-side window of the Chevy Corsica.

Reverend Waite missed the tower sighting; he was too consumed with worry as tractor trailers and passenger vehicles roared by them on both sides. Rooster tails of water coated the car windows with every passing vehicle. The speedometer confirmed what was obvious through the windshield: Reverend Fogherty was absolutely the only driver on I-95 obeying the 70 miles per hour speed limit.

With the exception of a few NASCAR race tracks sprinkled through the southland, I-95 was by far the most terrifying high-speed stretch of pavement on the East Coast. And, of the many hundreds of white-knuckle miles of I-95 between Miami and Maine, the 100-mile stretch between Richmond and Washington, D.C. was among the worst. Convoys of big rigs barreled up the road in the center and right lanes, tailgating slowpokes and blowing past state troopers who never seemed inclined to do anything about them. Packs of SUVs, pick-up trucks, sports cars and sedans swerved and cut through traffic at 85+ mph. Even the slowest cars on the all-too-narrow ribbon of concrete and asphalt usually traveled at least 75.

Then there was Fogherty. For most of his life, the main north-south highway had not been Interstate Highway 95 but, instead, rural Route 1, a stop-and-go, slow-mo tour of small towns and farmland, where the average speed limit was 40 miles per hour and, thanks to tractors and other farm equipment, the average speed was 30 miles per hour.

In the 1960s, former President Dwight D. Eisenhower's dream of a national highway system brought about the construction of Interstate 95, the kind of road that beckoned to the bank heist get-away driver in all Americans. Fogherty had never been comfortable driving on 95, and his discomfort was not eased when the speed limit was raised from 55 mph to 65 mph, and then 70 mph in some places.

Add to that Fogherty's belief that speed limits are indeed speed *limits*, and you wound up with a driver who functioned as a rolling traffic barrier wherever he went.

Waite long ago came to terms with his older colleague's penchant for obeying the speed limit, but never would the young preacher have guessed how orthodox the Fogherty's belief was.

"Should we go a little faster?" Waite asked.

Fogherty looked with surprise down as the speedometer, then exhaled in relief when he saw he wasn't wasting one mile per hour of the speed limit.

"No, we *can't* go faster," Fogherty assured Waite. "I'm already going 70."

"But, maybe this once, you should break the speed limit," pleaded Waite. "The family's probably already in Washington, and who knows if the assassins are there too. We don't have a minute to lose."

"I agree," answered Fogherty. "But what good will we be to the Smiths if we get pulled over and spend 30 minutes getting a speeding ticket? Or, worse, get in an accident?"

Fogherty's last few words were drowned out by a double-length tractor trailer howling by the right side of the car, and a monster truck roaring by on the left.

A conscientious rear-view-mirror minder, Fogherty glanced up to see a pair of bright headlights approaching quickly from behind. He squinted in irritation and flipped the mirror to the "night" setting to dim the glare.

"This freaking moron has no idea he's blocking traffic," said a reverend to his fellow passenger.

"So go around the idiot," Stone responded to Jones.

"I'd like to, except there's cars passing him on both sides. I can't get out of this lane."

"There's a break coming up on the right side," Stone said, peering into the rear view mirror.

"OK. Hang on."

The big minister floored his big car and made a sweeping, sloppy, swerving cut over to the right lane.

"*Jesus Christ*, reverend! Where the hell did you learn to drive?"

Jones glared at Stone in indignation.

"Oh, sorry, reverend. No offense."

"No offense *my ass*!" Jones shot back. "I'm a goddamned *good* driver!"

The boat-like sedan pulled along the right side of the dinghy–like compact car. The two men inside the small car were oblivious to the speeding sedan.

Jones lowered his window.

"*GET IN THE RIGHT LANE YOU DUMBASS!*" he bellowed as they went by.

"You should consider anger management," Stone said.

"*You* should consider …"

Jones bit his tongue. He still needed this blow-dried airhead.

"So what's our plan, Mr. Cronkite?"

Stone accepted the comment as a compliment without a second thought.

"I have an idea how to get LaMourgan off the show," Stone replied. "Then I'll be in the perfect position to take over the interview. You'll be a panel member…"

"And you're gonna let me talk up my toll-free number and web site, right?" Jones asked.

"Right," Stone said. "And you're gonna give me 50% of the take, right?"

"Yes, yes, of course. A deal's a deal."

The traffic on the three-lane race track thickened as the two made their way into greater Washington, D.C. Jones was driving like Denny Hamlin, drafting trucks, cutting through openings not six inches longer than his car, and using every bit of his lane and some of the shoulder to boot.

Focused on closing the distance to the GNBNC studios, Jones was even less cognizant than usual of his blind spot. So he was surprised when a white van honked in protest as he swerved to pass a tractor trailer that was doing only 85 mph.

"Holy shit, where'd that joker come from?" Jones muttered as he cut back in behind the truck.

The white van accelerated by, blowing right through 90 miles per hour.

"Shithead doesn't even realize he's blocking traffic," the van driver said in angry Spanish. "You oughta shoot his ass."

The man in the passenger seat just grunted under his cowboy hat.

Yeah, right, he thought, half asleep despite the jerky driving style of his partner. *The person who's gonna get shot tonight isn't in that car.* The drowsy man's hand slid to the pistol in his shoulder holster.

With the driver focused on the traffic and the passenger focused on the insides of his eyelids, neither noticed the running lights on the helicopter above as it overtook the van, headed north.

"The flight to Washington should take no more than 20 minutes," shouted the governor's assistant deputy press secretary — correction: the governor's newly promoted *press secretary*.

"Wow!" shouted Rolfe to the eager young man. "Have you made this trip before?"

"No!" gushed the press secretary.

"Well *I* have, about 50 times," snapped Rolfe. "So cut the tour guide shit and just be sure that I don't forget my coat or pocketbook, OK?"

Ten thousand feet above the helicopter and one hundred miles to the northwest, the leading edge of a mass of warm air rushing up the East Coast made first contact with the cold front that marched southeastward across the United States. The cold front's frigid air forced the warm air steeply upward. In the darkness, it was difficult to see the cumulus and cumulonimbus clouds forming.

The governor's helicopter pilot didn't need to see the clouds, however, to understand the brewing danger they posed. An air traffic controller out of

Reagan National Airport, just south of D.C., advised the pilot of the growing chance of thunderstorms.

"It's a good thing we left when we did," the pilot said to his co-pilot. "Another hour and we'd be in the middle of some nasty shit."

SEVENTY-SEVEN

Walters's SUV pulled into an alley behind a huge, white stone building and crept down the narrow passageway.

In the darkness, a garbage truck at the far end of the alley hefted and emptied huge dumpsters into itself, smashing them against its metal shell and then back to the concrete.

About 300 feet into the alley, the SUV pulled to a stop in front of a gray door with a small, faded metal plaque embossed with "GNBNC." A well-groomed young woman and two beefy, blazer-clad guards stood next to the entrance.

Amid the din of the garbage truck's appointed rounds, the SUV emptied into the dark alley: Richard and two other security men, Amy, Walters, and Tom, holding Billy and still limping from the impromptu surgery in the helicopter.

"Hi, Mr. and Mrs. Smith," the smiling young woman shouted over the echoing trash truck. "I'm Stacy, an assistant producer on *ALL & Then Some!*. I'll take you and your family upstairs to our green room and get you settled in!"

A GNBNC guard opened the door. One of Walters's security detail led the way, with Amy, the GNBNC producer and a network guard moving through the door behind him. As Walters's second security guard went in the door, a movement ten yards down the alley caught Tom's eye. A homeless man had risen from a pile of debris and was swerving out of the rainy darkness toward the group.

Richard read Tom's face and followed his gaze, spotting the homeless man, who had closed to 20 feet, both hands in the pockets of his bulky green Army coat. The second GNBNC guard also saw him, and moved toward the interloper. Richard slid around and in front of Tom, Billy and Walters.

The network guard raised his hands, as if to push the man away.

"Can I help you, sir?" the guard shouted with a hint of bluff in his voice.

The man stopped about 15 feet away. He mumbled, incomprehensible against the noise. His hands remained in his pockets.

The network guard turned to motion the rest of the group into the building. In that split-second, the tattered street person rushed forward, running a circular path toward Tom, Billy and Walters, and pulling his hands from his pockets. Tom thought he saw a flash of metal.

Richard pushed Tom and Billy toward the open door, then grabbed Walters's arm and yanked him in the same direction.

A sharp crack split the chaos, and everyone but Richard ducked. A gray object leapt from the homeless man's hand and slapped against the wall, then ricocheted down the alley, rattling with a hollow sound along the cement. It was a small metal cup, with two perfectly round holes cut cleanly through each side. The homeless man cried out as the cup was ripped from his grip and he collapsed to the ground, shaking his hand in pain, shock and fear.

"Get down! Get down!" Richard yelled from a crouch, a pistol in hand.

Everyone in the alley obeyed Richard's command (actually, they already were ducking down), including the GNBNC security guard and the homeless man, who rolled onto his side, knees pulled up to his chest and arms over his head.

"Get inside!" Richard shouted, pistol high and back against the stone wall next to the door. Tom and Billy, Walters and the security guard rushed into the network's building and Richard followed them in, leaving the vagabond trembling on the concrete.

With the door shut behind them, the frightened group came to a noisy stop in the hall. Around a corner, Amy's voice drifted back, "Tom, are you coming?"

Tom couldn't answer. His breath betrayed him, his thigh throbbed and his knees threatened to give out. He wasn't alone — the network security guard hyperventilated as he forced out words.

"Someone... shot... at us!" he said, eyes wide. "We're lucky they hit that bum instead!"

"They weren't shooting at us," Richard replied coolly. "And they didn't hit the homeless guy."

"What the hell're you talking about?!" the GNBNC guard countered. "Didn't you see--"

"If they'd been shooting at you, you'd be dead," Richard interrupted. Turning to Walters, Richard continued.

"Whoever it was shot that cup clean out of the guy's hand as he was running," he said. "They weren't trying to kill us. I'm guessing they thought the homeless guy was a threat. Their goal was to stop him."

Walters pondered the theory for a second.

"Why would there be a sniper here to begin with?" he mused.

"Based on the armed force that attacked the house, and the fighter intercept of the helicopter, I would guess that the sniper was on a similar assignment," Richard said.

"But he didn't kill us..." Tom jumped in.

Walters cocked his head, a glint in his eye. "No, he didn't, did he? Instead, he stopped what appeared to be a threat to your safety."

Richard nodded, and Walters allowed Tom to catch up. Tom's eyes widened.

"He was protecting us!" Tom said.

Richard nodded.

Walters laughed and slapped Richard on the back as he turned to catch up with the others down the hall.

"Who says politicians don't listen to their constituents!?"

SEVENTY-EIGHT

Alexander Langston LaMourgan looked up from his leafy salad and sprouts at the sound of the knock on the door.

"Enter!"

As the door opened, LaMourgan dabbed the corners of his mouth with a linen napkin. A somewhat familiar face leaned in.

"Mr. LaMourgan?"

"I am. And you are?"

Chip Stone, GNBNC anchor, was genuinely hurt, then insulted, that Alexander Langston LaMourgan, from his own network, didn't recognize him. He chafed at having to introduce himself.

"It's me…"

LaMourgan gazed at Stone for a moment, then tilted his head 30 degrees to one side, and looked at him some more.

"Chip?" Chip offered, hoping LaMourgan would finish for him.

Alexander Langston LaMourgan merely looked at Stone, not a muscle moving. *Is this guy alive?* Stone wondered. LaMourgan reminded him of a cross between C3PO and Prince Charles.

LaMourgan's head rotated 60 degrees in the opposite direction, reversing the tilt.

This conversational genius, known around the world for his interviews, was not even going to ask Chip for his last name.

"Chip," Stone stated.

Nothing.

"Chip Stone," he finally conceded, sure LaMourgan would recognize him now.

LaMourgan retracted his head over his shoulders, pivoting into a vertical position in the chair.

"Chip Stone. I am a GNBNC anchor. In Atlanta. I'm here covering the Miracle of St. Tob-- of St. Thomas's. The miracle kid."

"Yes, of course," LaMourgan finally said. "The child who will be my guest on the program this evening."

"Yes," said Stone. "I've come up to brief you on the story, so you can hit the ground running in the interview."

"Excellent," LaMourgan said. "Please, recline anywhere."

He sat down across from this broadcasting legend as LaMourgan's head followed Stone's movement.

After a long moment, LaMourgan asked, "Am I to understand you are in possession of information regarding the child and his family?"

"Yes," Stone said. But he was in possession of more than just information. In his jacket pocket, Stone carried a tube of liquid so vile that the tiniest dose would cause an adult to vomit within seconds. Stone figured a teaspoon of the stuff would leave a victim retching for hours.

Stone had acquired the potion in the Middle East during an assignment several years ago. He *had* planned to use the liquid on the next member of Congress he interviewed, figuring that, if President George H. W. Bush throwing up Japan's prime minister could make news for weeks, then a congressman yacking straight into the camera would be good for at least a night of top-of-the-broadcast coverage.

But Stone had been unjustly discredited before he could use the trick. Tonight, though, the drug would finally be deployed. Stone just needed to distract LaMourgan from his meal.

LaMourgan lurched forward. "Please," he said. "Prior to your initiating this briefing, I must visit the facilities."

"Sure," Stone said. "I'll be here when you get back."

SEVENTY-NINE

The green room wasn't green. That was Tom's first thought when the family was escorted into the room by the nervous little man from the Alexander Langston LaMourgan show. The green room was blue — a kind of powder blue, like the joke tuxedo.

"It's not green," Tom said to no one in particular.

"No, that's a common myth among people who don't work in the television business," said the skinny kid — Kerplunk? Even though Tom had spoken to the man on the phone and then met him again minutes ago, he was having a hard time retaining his name. Kerplunk's voice was oddly low, like it hurt his throat to talk.

"Where did the green room get its name, then, if it's not green?" Amy asked.

There was a uncomfortable pause as everyone looked to the associate director for an answer. Kerplunk stared at the ceiling, Adam's apple bobbing. Finally he looked down.

"Uh…"

Nick Walters jumped in, out of sympathy. "Where are the facilities?"

"You will find restrooms down at the end of the hallway," Kerplunk said, relieved.

"I'm going to go check on Mr. ---… on Alexander Langston, now," Kerplunk continued. "We'll be back to take you into make-up in about 30 minutes. The show begins in an hour. Just try to relax in the meantime."

"Thank you," said Amy.

After the door closed, the family exchanged smiles.

"Not exactly what I expected so far," Amy ventured.

"No," said Tom.

"I think that's a good question to ask yourselves before this goes much further," Walters said. "What do you expect tonight?"

"I expect LaMourgan to be skeptical," said Tom. "I expect a lot of angry viewer phone calls. I expect to spend an hour talking about what a great, normal kid Billy is, and how the world needs to understand that what happened on Sunday was not something that we arranged or faked — or wanted, for that matter."

"Do you expect the world will believe you?" Walters asked.

"I don't know," said Tom. "But I do know that this is our best chance to show them Billy is a normal kid, we are normal, and all we want is a normal life."

"What if it doesn't work?" Walters asked.

"Then we did the best we could," Tom answered.

"And that's all we can do," said Amy.

Walters leaned back in his chair and smiled, looking like a professor whose students have just achieved a hard-earned Eureka moment.

"Exactly."

EIGHTY

What a week! What a week! What a week! What a week!

Lewis Plinkdunk was beside himself with excitement!

And now the most unbelievable thing yet: when Plinkdunk checked on Alexander Langston LaMourgan, the show host was in the bathroom, violently ill, with just minutes before the big, live broadcast!

Thank God that Chip Stone, who apparently also is an anchor as GNBNC, happened to be in the studio — actually, in Alexander Langston's dressing room — at the time! Without missing a beat, Stone offered to fill in for the fallen LaMourgan, and the show *will* go on!

"I... I'm going to put this lavaliere mic on your tie, Mr. Stone," stammered Plinkdunk, leaning over the desk on the talk show's set.

"Yeah, sure, fine kid," Stone replied, not looking up from his notes.

"Mr. Stone?"

"Yeah?"

"Um, what... um, there's a spot on your shirt here, near the middle?"

The fastidious Chip Stone looked down at this shirt.

That's odd. I'm sure I would have seen that when I was putting the shirt on...

"I don't know..." Stone said. Gingerly, he touched the spot... it was moist. Without thinking, Stone raised his finger toward his nose — but the digit was still six inches away when Stone's head whipped back at the unmistakable odor.

That could only mean... that the spot was...

"Oh… my… God!" Stone shrieked.

Plinkdunk, stunned by the pitch and volume of Stone's outburst, cried out and fell sideways away from the anchorman, rolling across the desk top and off the far side.

Up in the control booth, the audio technician preparing to set Stone's mic level tore off his headphones in pain, eardrums all but shattered by Stone's screech.

Standing up, facing the world map on the back wall of the set, Stone tried to regain his composure and put out of his mind what he'd figured out was on his shirt: Alexander Langston LaMourgan's vomit.

I need a new shirt. I need a new shirt!

"I NEED A NEW SHIRT!"

"Mr. Stone! Are you OK?" Plinkdunk shouted from the floor.

"I need a new shirt!"

"Yes sir, Mr. Stone! *I'll* get one for you, Mr. Stone!"

With that, Lewis Plinkdunk leapt to his feet and ran as hard as his skinny legs could carry him, wing-tipped shoes slapping the tile floor, out of the studio and down the hall. Headed for wardrobe, he took a short-cut through a back hallway. As he accelerated through a corner, his wing-tips' poor traction betrayed him.

Plinkdunk's feet slid out, and he was horizontal to the ground, falling and flailing like a shot duck.

His round, thin shoulders struck first, but his head soon followed. The last sound Plinkdunk heard before blacking out was the hollow thud of his skull striking the floor.

Associate director Lewis Plinkdunk lay there, unconscious in a back hallway, for the rest of the evening, missing the biggest show of his life.

EIGHTY-ONE

At 7:45 p.m., a well-groomed intern appeared at the green room door to escort the group to the *ALL & Then Some!* studio.

The family was greeted in the studio by the producer, who brought them to the famous *ALL & Then Some!* Set, explaining the chain of events that led to Alexander Langston LaMourgan ceding his seat for the evening to a replacement.

"It was horrible," she said. "I don't think I've ever seen someone get so violently sick so suddenly. It must have been something he ate."

The producer shook her head to rid her mind of the disgusting smorgasbord of food that LaMourgan had told paramedics he had eaten that day.

"Anyway, Mr. LaMourgan is on his way to the hospital now, and they think he's going to be OK," the producer continued. "But they need to keep him under observation until tomorrow. For some reason, we heard that news from a detective."

"Who is hosting the show?" Walters asked.

"I am," announced a voice from the wings.

Chip Stone emerged from the shadows. There was a large wet spot on the front of his shirt, and Stone meticulously swabbed his hands with a wet wipe.

Tom and Amy glared at the contemptible news man. Well, they were going to tell their story, regardless who the host was.

"Thank God Chip just happened to be up here from Richmond," the producer was saying.

A few steps behind Stone came the famous, rotund figure of Reverend Carter Ray Jones, rings sparkling and white suit reflecting the studio lights. The producer looked surprised.

"May I speak with you privately?" Stone asked the producer.

Stone and the producer retired to a quiet corner of the studio, where they engaged in quiet but animated conversation. Jones turned to the family with a broad smile.

"And how are you folks this evenin'?" he drawled.

Tom was dizzy with rage. He felt an overpowering urge to punch Jones but, before he could, Amy spoke up.

"We are fine, no thanks to you," Amy said, jaw muscles flexing with every syllable. "You here for another free meal at the kill, you vulture?"

"Now, just hold on a minute…" began Jones.

"Stuff it, jerk!" Amy snapped. "You're lucky I believe you're going to Hell, you son-of-a-bitch. If I thought for a moment you weren't, I'd kill you right here."

Amy didn't as much speak as snarl. Clint Eastwood couldn't have delivered a more chilling line.

"Mr. Jones, I don't think further conversation is a good idea," Walters interjected firmly, impressed with Amy's steel.

Jones was stunned by the very real threat.

The producer and Stone returned, interrupting the exchange. The producer looked miserable.

"Reverend Jones will be joining us on the panel," Stone announced, to the producer's clear disgust.

"Wonderful," Jones smiled.

Amy lunged at Jones. "You fat motherf--"

Tom caught her by the waist.

"Come on, honey," he said, steering her away. "It's all right. We can deal with him."

Amy stalked away, eyes locked on Jones with lethal intensity. The family fell behind her like cubs behind the lioness.

Then the producer strode off set. Stone gave Jones a shrug.

"You can't please everybody."

"Amen brother," Jones replied, and the two men stepped toward the desk to get mic'd up.

EIGHTY-TWO

The producer burst through the control room door. The technicians spun toward her in surprise. On the wall, the phone rang.

"That fat-ass preacher is on the show! Stone says he'll walk off if we don't put Jones on!"

The phone continued ringing. Meanwhile, the technicians, not Fourth Estate purists, shrugged at the news.

"And if the preacher throws in his toll-free number, you gotta let it go," the producer continued over the din of the phone, disgusted with herself for acquiescing.

The electronic trill of the phone sounded again.

"Will you get the damn phone, Dinkdung?!" the producer shouted out to her absent assistant. "*Where the HELL is that twerp*?!"

On the floor of a nearby deserted hallway, Plinkdunk lay oblivious, unconscious but otherwise OK, dreaming of accepting his second Emmy.

Exasperated, the producer picked up the phone.

"*What?!*"

"Ah…"

"*WHAT?!*"

"Um, this is the press secretary for Virginia Governor Mary Rolfe…"

"*Oh for chrissakes…*"

"Pardon?"

"What?! What do you want?!"

"Governor Rolfe is en route to your studios. We are 10 minutes away. She would like to participate in tonight's *ALL & Then Some!* broadcast."

The producer looked at the ceiling in frustration. *That's it,* she said to herself. *I'm drawing the line.*

"NO!"

"She says no," the youngster said to his boss, who was sitting in the front seat of the cab directing the driver.

"*Gimme the phone!*"

The press secretary nearly threw the phone at her.

"Listen, sweetie," Rolfe began. "I'm going to play a hunch. Is Chip Stone involved in tonight's broadcast?"

The producer was surprised. There had been no public announcement about Alexander Langston LaMourgan's illness.

"I can't discuss that," the producer said, not used to being the one hiding behind "no comment."

"Yes, I'm sure you can't, honey," Rolfe said. "Do me a favor. Tell Stone I want to be on the show. Tell him that if I'm not on *this* show, I will be going on *another* network's talk news show tonight to discuss the relationship between Stone and Reverend Carter Ray Jones."

The producer paused. She hated giving in to the politician, but the mention of a relationship between Jones and Stone was enticing. Stone had been a pain in the ass from the word go. The producer loved the idea of Stone getting another humiliation added to his distinguished list, and she certainly didn't want to let another network get the scoop.

"I don't have to ask Stone," the producer said. "You're on."

"Beautiful."

"There are protesters out front," the producer continued. "Come in through a door on the west side of the building. I'll have security meet you there."

Ten minutes later, Governor Mary Rolfe was striding through the back hallways of GNBNC, headed for the ultimate do-or-die moment of her notable career.

Unseen in the shadows outside the building, two men managed to catch the door before it closed behind the governor and her aide, and slipped into the building, ski masks in their pockets and a long traveling case in one man's hand.

EIGHTY-THREE

"What on earth is with your shirt, Stone?" Jones asked.

Chip Stone shivered at the reminder, then pulled his suit jacket around to cover the drying spot. "I... someone... spilled something on it. I don't want to talk about it."

Jones shrugged. "Whatever."

Across the triangular desk sat the Smith family: Tom, Amy, and Billy on Amy's lap. Amy and Tom wore mics, and a large set microphone hovered just a foot-and-a-half above Billy's bobbing, drooling head. All three were squinting under the bright set lights. Nick Walters crouched with his head between Tom's and Amy's, dispensing some last minute advice.

"FIVE MINUTES TIL AIRTIME!" a voice called from the ceiling.

"Don't worry, you'll get used to the lights," Walters resumed after the announcement. "Stay cool and don't let either one of these con men rattle you. You have truth and God on your side, and that is enough."

"Right," said Tom, a little out of breath.

"Don't worry, you'll do fine."

"Yes," said Amy. "We'll be fine."

Amy's panicked look belied her bravado. Walters felt for them. Who could be ready for something like this? Walters decided to play a little offense.

Straightening up, he stared down at the "journalist" and the "minister."

"You boys have any idea who I am?"

Stone and Jones exchanged blank looks.

Walters opened his mouth to speak, but was interrupted.

"Nicholas Walters," came a woman's voice from the shadows. "Multi-billionaire, business tycoon, and now a man wanted by the federal government."

Governor Rolfe strutted onto the set, focusing on Walters and ignoring Stone's and Jones's shocked expressions.

"What an odd match you are for this family of fugitives," Rolfe taunted.

"Mic her up," came the producer's voice over the intercom.

Smiling, Rolfe held Walters's gaze as she sat down and a mic was clipped on. Walters was not ruffled by the governor's composed response.

"I'm glad you're here, governor," Walters said.

"I was about to inform these two idiots," he said, motioning to Stone and Jones, "that, in addition to a number of successful businesses, I happen to have at my service a very large, very capable, very aggressive law firm. I have instructed my legal sharks — and they *are* sharks — to watch tonight's broadcast, and to monitor the three of you, tonight and in the future. If any one of you so much as tip-toes by a slanderous or libelous statement, my lawyers are gonna stick a lawsuit so far up your butt that *your* lawyers are gonna have to look down your throat to see what it says."

"Don't bluff, Nick," Rolfe countered, unshaken. "Mr. Smith here is a public figure, thanks to his appearance on GNBNC earlier this week. And by virtue appearing on this show tonight, Amy and the kid are public figures as well. All of them get less protection from slander and libel laws now."

"I'll bet Thomas Jefferson spins in his grave with you in the Capitol Building he designed, abusing the government he helped create," Walters replied. "You know as well as I do that Tom was trying to *stop* the media coverage, not encourage it. And that's also why the family is here tonight — they aren't, and don't want to be, public figures.

"But of course you don't understand that, because you've spent your entire adult life trying to *become* a public figure," Walters continued. "You chase publicity like a dog chases garbage trucks. But now you've caught the truck, and it's either gonna run you over or drag you down the street."

"It will do neither," Rolfe said. "Stick around. You'll see."

"Oh, I fully intend to."

"ONE MINUTE," the intercom announced.

Walters broke eye contact with Rolfe and leaned over, putting one hand on Tom's shoulder, the other on Amy's. "You two will do fine" he whispered. Then he planted a kiss on Billy's head. "So will you, little man."

"THIRTY SECONDS!" the intercom rang out.

Walters tousled Billy's hair, then stepped off the set, into the darkness behind the Smiths.

Tom gave Amy a smile. A feeling of composure swept over him. "We'll do fine," he mouthed, and squeezed her hand.

"Ten seconds!" called out the floor director. "Nine, eight, seven, six, five, four, three," and then switched to hand signals to count down to one. With a sweep of the floor director's finger in Stone's direction, and the blink of a red light, they were on the air.

EIGHTY-FOUR

"Good evening, and welcome to GNBNC and *ALL & Then Some!*" Stone spoke into a camera somewhere behind Amy. "I am Chip Stone, sitting in tonight for Alexander Langston LaMourgan, who has come down with a touch of the flu. LET'S DO THIS THANG!"

Everyone around the table jumped at the ferocity of Stone's latest attempt at a catch-phrase. Billy laughed, then burped.

"Tonight, we will talk, live in the studio, with the family of Billy Smith, and we will take your calls."

On a monitor in the control booth, and on televisions from Washington, D.C. to San Francisco to Beijing to London, the Smith family appeared, looking wide-eyed. Superimposed beneath was the toll-free dial-in number for the show.

"Also here tonight are two figures who've played prominent roles in this story — the Reverend Carter Ray Jones of the Jones International Ministry in Nashville, Tennessee, and Governor Mary Rolfe of Virginia."

The shot cut to Jones and Rolfe, a world map lit behind them. They simultaneously unleashed 10,000-watt, made-for-television smiles that vastly outshined the Arabian Peninsula floating in space between them.

"But for me, and for the billions of viewers watching tonight…"

Tom started at the word. *Billions? Could that be right?*

"… the most interesting guest on our program tonight is also the littlest —

Billy Smith."

A tight shot of Billy appeared on screen. The boy was gurgling happily, playing with his father's hand. Walters, in the shadows watching a monitor, couldn't help but smile. Cute kid.

"I suppose the first question should go to Billy," Stone said, "Since it was his words that began the week's events — events which have held the attention of the entire world. Billy, what brings you on the show tonight?"

There was a long pause, leading to a longer pause, as everyone at the desk and watching the show realized Stone was serious.

Really? Tom thought. On a monitor across the studio, Tom could see the camera was in tight on Billy, awaiting the toddler's response.

Tom could not know that Stone had once been talked into interviewing a parrot on live TV, having been convinced by the bird's publicity-seeking owner that the feathered animal could not only talk, but think and communicate with humans. It was only after the bird had pecked a gash into the anchor's scalp and pooped on his shoulder that the interview was shut down by the director, who had not been warned of the pending animal interview.

"Uh, he doesn't speak, really," Tom said.

"Oh. Is he shy?" Stone asked.

"No. He's *one*. He really hasn't started speaking yet, except for a few words, like mommy, daddy and truck."

Carter Ray Jones wasn't going to wait for Stone to be brought up to speed on human cognitive development, particularly since the reporter was so challenged in this area himself. There was money to be made here.

"Chip, one thing I've learned about you over the past week is that you are one heck of a joker," Jones said, not to save the dumb-ass reporter, but to pivot the discussion in a more profitable direction. "On a serious note, I'd like to say that I've learned a great deal about myself, about our nation and about God in the past few days, as this amazing story has unfolded."

Time to get down to business.

"At the Jones International Ministry in Nashville, Tennessee, where our 24-hour toll-free phone number is 999-GO SAVE 'M, we've followed the incredible saga of this blessed family, the Smith family."

The image on screen switched to the Smith family, two of whom were eyeing the big televangelist warily. Billy was sucking on four fingers and looking up at the ceiling.

"We've had our theology scholars working around the clock at the Jones International Ministry — phone number 999-GO SAVE 'M — looking for any precedent in human history for this week's events," continued Jones. In point of fact, the theological "scholars" had not been diverted for one second from their primary mission: digging up scripture verses that could be used — or twisted and then used — in the ministry's mission to separate believers from their money.

"Unbelievably, we haven't found a single instance of a baby being used by God to communicate to the world. More striking is the message: God's wish that we all live according to His word, and to support His work through tithing to God's ministries, such as the Jones International Ministry, phone number 999-GO SAVE 'M."

"Now hang on a minute," Tom cut in. "You know perfectly well that Billy, or God, or whoever, didn't say anything about giving money to your corrupt church!"

"Son," Jones said, with all the grandfatherly charm he could muster, "I understand how upset you are. Your family's been torn to bits by this miracle, and by the parasites and scavengers who've descended on you since then — scavengers like the media and politicians."

Jones spit out "media" and "politicians" as if they were rotten fruit.

"*And* you," Tom tried to say, only getting to 'and" before Jones cut him off.

"That's why I am committing to you, and to the billions watching tonight, that I will dedicate the stretched resources of the Jones International Ministry — phone number 999-GO SAVE 'M — to making sure your family is sheltered from the evil vultures of our degenerate society."

Rolfe, better than Tom at holding her own in televised mud-wrestling matches, zipped into the empty space between Jones's words.

"It just distresses me to see the destruction of this child by so many questionable characters," Rolfe injected. "From this televangelist to the media to the boy's father — a criminal excuse for a guardian if there ever were one. I have yet to see one — well maybe one — public figure who has shown himself, or herself, to be a true protector of the safety of this child."

Out of the corner of his eye, Tom saw his wife clench her fists on the desk top. Tom worried she'd take a swing at Rolfe.

For her part, Rolfe kept waving the red flag. She had only one route out of this mess, and it required paving over the parents of Billy Smith.

"Mrs. Smith, I see that you already are making fists," Rolfe said, aware of every subtle development around the desk. Rolfe leaned into her attack, eyes blazing, face furious. "Your and your husband's penchant for violence, and your willingness to put your interests before your child's, has me, and my family welfare chief, very concerned for the safety of your son."

So intent was Rolfe on tearing open Amy's and Tom's jugulars, she did not see the counterstrike coming from an unanticipated direction.

"NO!" Billy shouted at Rolfe.

Rolfe was shocked into rare silence. Billy did not let up.

"NO!" Billy said. "NO!"

Amy jumped in.

"He sees it! He knows what you are, and he's *one… year… old*! I know what you are too. I've known people like you all my life. People who only care about themselves, who'll say anything and hurt anyone just to get what they want. We're not dangerous. Billy's not dangerous. *You're* dangerous! You're… you're a *bad person*!"

"Bad pohson!" shouted Billy, pointing a spit-covered finger at Rolfe.

"Hey! He *can* talk!" Stone exclaimed.

Billy swung around and pointed at Stone. "*ASS-HO!*" he squealed happily.

"God?" Stone responded. "Are you in there?"

Amy and Tom stared at Stone. Billy blew a spit bubble and laughed.

"You just don't get it, do you?" Tom asked Stone. "*None* of you get it. *Of course* God is in there!"

"Really?" Jones said before he could stop himself.

Tom shook his head. "*Yes*, really! What kind of a minister are you? Wait, don't answer — I already know.

"God is what makes us different than the animals that we'd otherwise be

— although in your cases," Tom said, "He obviously didn't use his best stuff.

"Yes, God is in Billy. God is in me. God is in Amy and Nick. Believe it or not, God is even in you three criminals. He just can't get a word in sideways between your self-promoting bullshit!"

In the control booth, a sound technician reached for the "bleep" button to censor the offending word. Like most "live" talk shows, *ALL & Then Some!* operated on a several-second delay, in order to give the network time to cut out offensive language.

The producer, who also was the director since the last downsizing sliced her staff (again), called out.

"Don't bleep it! Let it go. This is why we're in this business."

"You and your profession are a perfect example," Tom continued, looking at Stone. "I've seen the news from the other side now, and I will never watch the news the same way again. It isn't about news. It isn't about the public's right to know. It isn't about anything except ratings."

"I love it," said the producer.

"A station in Richmond has a weather department called 'Storm Squad,'" Tom continued. "*Storm* Squad! In *Virginia*, where we've been in a *drought* for *three years*! How does that make sense? It doesn't. It's just about ratings.

"You come on at nine and say things like 'Is there a killer loose in your neighborhood? We'll tell you at 11.' Look, if there's a killer loose in my neighborhood, *tell me now!* Then, when I watch at 11, the answer is, 'No, there is no killer loose in your neighborhood.' So why are you scaring the crap out of us? Ratings, that's why.

"Then there are you politicians," Tom wheeled around on Rolfe. "You use hate and suspicion and anger to divide us against each other, just to keep yourselves in power. Three days ago, Governor Rolfe, you were ready to do anything — and I do mean *anything* — to get me to hand my family over to you, all so you could be president one day. Today, you seem just as ready to do anything you can to hang us, this time to *protect* what's left of your pathetic political career."

In a hotel room in Iowa, Mike Montegrande, turned to his campaign manager.

"Let's get some distance between us and her. And see if there's a game on."

Pulling his cell phone off his belt, the campaign manager speed-dialed the news desk at GNBNC with a scoop.

"The political parties and the politicians have taken this incredible legacy, this wonderful country, and you've hijacked it," continued Tom. "You're a bunch of one-person special interest groups, out for yourselves, abusing the second-greatest gift ever given man — the United States of America."

Tom turned to Jones. "But there's one more bunch of pinheads who've abused an even greater gift…"

Jones felt himself shrinking in his seat in anticipation of the onslaught. He didn't have to wait long.

"It's people like you, Jones," Tom said. "I'm not gonna call you reverend because you don't deserve it. I've got a couple of ministers at my church who actually work for God, who actually have earned some reverence. You haven't earned spit. God gave us this world and this life and you thank Him by abusing His name to line your own pockets. People come to you desperate for meaning in their lives and you just use them to get rich.

"I am so tired of the games you play, dividing people against each other and trying to find an enemy to rally against," continued Tom. "One day it's the Muslims — you call them all violence-loving terrorists. The next day it's the Jews.

"Then it's the women — you actually pick a fight about whether God is a man or a woman. Is this a serious point you're making? That *God* is a *man*?? Well, thanks for settling the question of whether God takes a piss standing up or sitting down. And as a bonus, we get some scriptural guidance on the whole toilet-seat-up-or-down issue!

"So you stir the pot, looking for any angle you can take to sell yourself as the spokesperson for God," Tom continued.

"People don't need a… a… *conduit* to hear God, to talk to God. And you don't need a little boy or even a miracle either. We have a direct line — we don't need some snake-oil salesman like Jones here to connect us to God for a price.

"God's voice is inside us, if we'll listen," said Tom, voice softening. "And it's all around us. He's all around us! You can hear God in people, you can hear Him in the rain, you can hear Him in the wind through the trees — *that* is God's voice. He is everywhere, talking to us all the time. We don't need signs and we don't need Billy and we especially don't need a piece of work like Carter Ray Jones to hear God."

Tom didn't know where this was coming from. He knew he believed what he was saying, but he hadn't really tried to put words around it since… until now. He looked into the darkness of the studio for a long moment.

"I know a lot of people don't know what to make of my son and what happened Sunday," Tom finally said, looking toward the red light on a camera. "My wife and I are looking for answers, just like you. I can tell you this, though: Our son is not The Second Coming, he is not God and he is not Satan. He is a wonderful, precious little boy with a big heart."

Exasperation washed over Tom's face.

"We didn't ask for this and, believe me, we would turn back the clock if we had a choice. And I can assure you, we aren't looking for any kind of payoff from what has happened. If we could go back to being nobodies and never hear another word about this again, it would be fine with us.

"But did God speak through Billy last Sunday?" he continued. "I can't prove it but, yeah, I think He did. But I also believe that what God said through Billy is nothing different than what we'd hear from God directly if we'd just listen close enough…

"'Love each other as I love you,' is what God said. Love each other as I love you. How much simpler could it be?"

EIGHTY-FIVE

An old warrior, now the leader of a people, mouthed the seven words he'd just heard: Love each other as I love you.

Love each other as I love you. It was a command, akin to the commands the old man gave every day — sometimes to gather information, sometimes to present recommendations, sometimes to carry out missions of death and destruction to protect his people.

But it also was a plea: the plea of a loved one, of a grieving parent, of an orphaned child, of a weary world.

Love each other as I love you.

It was a calling. It was clear, simple, self-evident.

Love each other as I love you. It was universal — a phrase that appeared, the leader knew, in one form or another in the texts of every significant religion on earth, no matter the sect, the nation, or the appearance of the believers.

The buzz of his intercom startled the man out of his reflections. He pressed a blinking button with a hand scarred by a lifetime of war and violence.

"Yes?"

"Sir, I am sorry to interrupt," said the assistant, the shock in his voice leaking through the speaker. Based on this tone, the leader braced for bad news. What this time? A bus and the dozens of souls in it destroyed? Innocent civilians, desperate for peace, gunned down walking the paths of their day-to-day lives? A rocket attack on civilian homes? The destruction of an apartment building and all within?

"Sir… it's…," stammered the assistant. "A call for you… from…"

The assistant said two words — the last two words the leader expected. The old man hesitated, then picked up the receiver and pressed the button connecting him to the waiting call.

"Hello," was as far as he was willing to go.

"Hello," came the reluctant reply.

On both sides of the line, a man heard the voice of his sworn enemy… the murderer of his people, of women and children and men…

"Are you watching?" the caller finally said.

The old leader looked at the television. "Yes."

"As am I."

A pause.

"Love each other as I love you," one man said.

"Yes," replied the other.

Another pause.

"It is simple, isn't it?" one said. "These are words that my God has spoken to my people. These are words that your God has delivered to your people too — is that not true?"

"He has."

"We have these words in common. Despite all our differences and our history and our claims upon it — we have these words in common."

"Yes. We do."

"Then… perhaps this is where we begin."

"Yes."

In dozens of capitals around the world, in ornamental edifices and primitive tents, similar conversations occurred between the bitterest of enemies.

Love each other as I love you.

At that moment, these seven words were the first in a multitude of unlikely conversations.

EIGHTY-SIX

Along a front stretching from Roanoke, Virginia, to Rehoboth Beach, Maryland, the warm air from the Gulf of Mexico was colliding with the cold air from the Ohio Valley. The result: the warmth was driven straight up, into colder and dryer layers of air.

On GNBNC, meanwhile, the ever-present news crawl at the bottom of the television made mention of a certain Southern governor. Even as the *ALL & Then Some!* show proceeded, Mary Rolfe, using her outstanding peripheral vision (developed through years of holding eye contact with constituents or donors while simultaneously scanning the room for someone more important she should be talking to), read the bulletin.

"CAMPAIGN SOURCES SAY MONTEGRANDE IS 'DISTANCING HIMSELF' FROM VA GOV. MARY ROLFE…"

Rolfe, still appearing attentive, immediately grasped the implication: she had no future in the Republican Party.

Intellectually, she knew she should stay cool. After all, the president was now in her corner, and if she could manage to paint the dad as abusive, she had a shot at a cabinet-level appointment, or perhaps an ambassadorship.

But… the *indignity* of being disowned on the national stage by her party's presumptive standard-bearer! After everything she had done for the GOP! She was their future! She was their savior! She was their one best shot of putting a woman in the White House!

A voice in Rolfe's head called out: *Relax! Play out the hand! You've got a long-term shot with the Democrats!*

In response, another voice — one Rolfe sometimes suspected others could hear — shouted down the plea for reason.

"Shut up! I will not be humiliated! *I will not be humiliated!!*"

The result of the clash of voices was as predictable as that from a warm front and a cold front colliding.

Slowly, imperceptibly, Rolfe began to rise to her feet. So gradually was her movement that Tom didn't even notice as he poured his heart out about God.

High above, the rising warm air was cooling, condensing into cumulonimbus clouds, some stretching tens of thousands of feet skyward.

At the *ALL & Then Some!* desk, Rolfe was now fully standing. Rolfe scanned the table, then reached across and snatched the giant, signature, old-timey *ALL & Then Some!* microphone in front of Chip Stone.

Having said his piece, Tom was looking, startled, at the politician holding the microphone. Amy, Jones and Stone were held captive by the sight as well. Finally Stone spoke up.

"Ah, governor?" Stone. "Is there… are you OK?"

The very first bolt of winter lightning that many residents of Washington had ever witnessed struck at that moment, arcing between the expanding thunderhead 30,000 feet above and a point on the ground near the capital city's center: the aluminum capstone topping the Washington Monument. The monument had weathered many strikes in the past, but this particular bolt was the most violent ever to touch the spire. The air around the tower instantly heated to 50,000 degrees Fahrenheit, melting the top of the capstone and sending out a blast of thunder that set off car alarms from the Mall to Chevy Chase.

Poor Chip Stone never saw it coming.

An accomplished softball player in high school and college,iss Rolfe had gripped the base of the absurdly large microphone with both hands and raised it high above and behind her head, her left arm cocked, elbow pointing straight back. Rolfe lifted her right foot two or three inches off the ground, then slid the foot forward slightly and back down to the ground.

Simultaneously, she drove forward off her left leg, rotating her hips with the torque and force of a catapult. Upper body following the hips, Rolfe whipped the microphone down and across her midsection, arms fully extended. Like the All Star she'd been, Rolfe broke her wrists at just the right moment, achieving maximum head velocity on the truncheon.

An enormous thunder blast shook the building, rippling the water in the coffee cups on the desk, just as the microphone's light metal casing exploded against the anchorman's skull. Fortunately for the newsman, the microphone was the newest and flimsiest piece on the set, and its disintegration absorbed most of the impact. However, the considerable remaining energy was borne completely by Chip Stone's head, and he flew back and out of his chair. His head struck the floor with a dull thump.

Tom yanked Billy away from the desk as bits of microphone flew like shrapnel.

"WHAT TH' HELL!?" Jones shouted.

Rolfe stood by the desk, shattered microphone stump hanging loosely in her right hand.

"*EEEEEEEEEEEEEYYYYYYYYAAAAAAAAAHHHHHHHHHH H!!!!!!!!!!!!!!!*"

The governor's eyes had a wild, even savage, gleam.

"This... *is... BULLSHIT!*" she bellowed.

Tom and Amy, crouched on the floor with Billy, awkwardly crab-walked away from the berserk executive branch official. Richard scrambled from the shadows, grabbed the Smiths and hustled them out of Governor Suddenly McCrazy's line of sight.

"Look, lady, get a-hold of yourse--" Jones shouted out, now ducking behind the desk.

"*SHUT UP! SHUT THE* HELL *UP!!*" and on 'hell' Rolfe grasped the lip of the desk with both hands and yank upward, like an Olympic weightlifter performing the clean-and-jerk.

The low-grade particle board desk was light, and gyrated wildly on a horizontal axis, flipping 420 degrees and throwing off pieces of cheap wood before crashing back to the set. One desk leg caught Jones across the nose, opening up a bloody gash.

"That's tears it," Jones muttered.

The televangelist turned his ample rear end to the audience, crawling away from Rolfe. It would only be later, reviewing the video, that the producer would notice the comic value of that particular shot. As for now, she was too busy making sure her crew caught every second of the unfolding... chaos.

"Camera Two! Zoom in on Rolfe! Camera Four! Pan right and try to get Jones's face! Camera One, stay on the kid! Cut to Camera Two!"

As Jones scrambled from the detonation site, a cameraman followed him with a shoulder camera. Jones, now on his feet, ran for the veil of darkness formed by the bright set lights, the cameraman on his heels. In the control booth, the image from that camera went dark.

"Camera Five, what the hell are you doing?!"

What the cameraman was doing was making $5,000 in cash in exchange for following Reverend Jones no matter where he went. Those were the instructions he'd received from Trip Stone, or whatever his name was. The reporter was probably dead now, but the money was already the cameraman's pocket, and the cameraman's word was his bond. He would follow the fat televangelist to Hell and back if he had to, and keep the camera rolling. That was the deal.

"Camera Five! Where are you going?!"

"What the hell is that noise?" the technician next to the producer shouted, and the producer listened.

It was breathing. Heavy, labored breathing.

It was Carter Ray Jones, hyperventilating into his wireless lavaliere microphone, clipped to his jacket lapel. And then... he spoke.

"Ladies (pant) and (pant) gentlemen."

"Should I cut his feed?" a technician asked, finger over the switch.

"No, let's go with it. Who knows what'll happen next. Keep the preacher's mic open, and give me a split screen — one side on Jones and the other on the set, in case Rolfe kills herself or anyone else."

Another jolt of thunder shook the building. The storm was intensifying.

On one side of the split screen, the shot switched between Rolfe knocking over set pieces and the Smith family huddling with Nick Walters. On the other half of the screen, Jones stood in a brightly light hallway, facing the camera. He was speaking between gasps.

"God (gag) spoke to me tonight (wheez)," Jones said. "(gasp) He told me to (cough cough)... to ask you, the people of His (cough cough hock hock) precious world to give of your hearts, give (pant, pant) of your souls, and most (hack) importantly, give of your wallet — through 999 GO SAVE 'M — OR, the Lord has told me, *He will take me from this world this very night!*"

"Oh for chrissakes!" the producer cursed. "Switch the audio to the set, and keep the split screen."

Not realizing he'd been silenced, Jones trotted down the hall and through a door marked "No Admittance," speaking and gesturing to the camera.

On Rolfe's side of the screen, the audio was now live, and just as odd.

"*Shit shit shit shit shit shit shit shit shit shit shit shit shit shit shit shit!*" Rolfe chanted as she dismantled the glowing backdrop to the *ALL & Then Some!* show bit by bit, using a desk leg to smash light bulbs a half-dozen at a time.

A couple more "shits" and we'll break South Park*'s record*, the producer thought.

"Cut to Camera One," she said.

The Smith family appeared on the screen, on the edge of the set lighting, a huge man standing between them and the governor. The family looked terrified.

"Put a boom mic over the family!" the producer barked. "Meanwhile, open up the preacher's mic!"

Jones was ascending a narrow staircase, heaving like a heifer in labor, drenched in sweat and coughing out what seemed to be an important point.

"...so the Lord (gasp) told me to go to the top of the GNBNC (oh lord, cough cough) building, to prepare myself for Him to take me up."

Jones stopped at a landing to lean over, hands on his knees. For a second it appeared Jones might vomit right there on worldwide television, but he managed to regain control, and began climbing again.

"And that ... is what... I'm doing..." Jones sputtered. "Unless... you can help me raise... $50 million... tonight by calling... 999 GO SAVE 'M."

On set, Rolfe now sported a slit skirt — not by design, but due to a nasty spill she took while charging a camera, swinging an *ALL & Then Some!* coffee mug. The normally well-dressed politician did not seem to notice the skirt issue, or any other detail, for that matter, of the receding rational world.

EIGHTY-SEVEN

"What the hell is going on here?"

"No idea. Who cares? It's a good distraction. You ready yet?"

"Almost. Can they see us here?"

"Naw. Between the crazy woman, the guy bleeding on the floor, and the bright lights, no one's looking over here. But hurry the hell up!"

"I'll be ready in a minute. Let me work!"

"All right! Just hurry…"

EIGHTY-EIGHT

"I am the Smith family's pastor," the old man said to the GNBNC lobby security guard.

"Yes, I'm sure you are," the guard said, not raising his head. "You can't go up."

A wall clock read 9:20 p.m. The show was nearly half over!

"Please, we must talk to the Smiths!" Waite said. "It's a matter of life and death."

"Uh huh, of course it is. No."

"Please, for the love of God!"

The security guard looked up into the old man's eyes. Fogherty met his gaze. Was... was that a glimmer of sympathy? Of understanding? Of belief?

"No."

Fogherty winced.

"Now, go away."

As Fogherty and Waite turned to leave, desperation rising, a shattering sound ripped through the lobby. As the crash of breaking glass faded, the roar of the protest crowd outside, mixed with the racket of a horrendous thunderstorm, grew louder and closer.

Protesters surged through the broken window, across sheets and shards of glass.

The security guard vaulted the desk and sprinted past the two reverends, headed toward the invaders. As he ran, he pulled a black pistol from his holster.

"*FREEZE! EVERYBODY FREEZE!*".

Demonstrating admirable ardor, the protesters ignored his commands and continued hopping through the shattered window. Not wanting to shoot anyone — yet — the guard holstered his weapon and began shoving protesters back through the opening.

"*C'mon!*" Waite whispered.

"*What?!*"

"C'mon, let's go!" Waite repeated.

"But the guard said no!"

"So did the Pharaoh, but that didn't stop Moses!" Waite hissed. "*Now move your ass, old man!*"

It was hard to tell who was more shocked by the outburst.

Waite stammered.

"I... I'm... I don't..."

A grin from Fogherty let Waite off the hook.

"All right, hot shit — I'm right behind you!"

Waite's mouth fell open.

"Didn't I ever tell you, boy?" Fogherty shouted over the noise. "I started as a U.S. Marine chaplain! Now *MOVE!*"

The two men dashed into the stairway as footsteps of security reinforcements echoed in a nearby hallway. Seconds later the preachers had cleared the melee and were climbing for the fourth floor where, according to a lobby sign, the studios for GNBNC were.

EIGHTY-NINE

This was without a doubt the wildest four minutes the producer had ever experienced, in or out of the television business. She was presiding over an unprecedented twin spectacle of a broadcast to several billion people. On one half of the split screen, the now 100%-certifiable governor of Virginia, wearing a torn skirt, half open blouse and high heels, was obliterating the *ALL & Then Some!* set; on the other half, a morbidly obese charlatan was (slowly) climbing six flights of stairs to the roof of the GNBNC building from where, he insisted, God would take him to Heaven unless the world threw $50 million into his electronic collection plate.

The control booth phone rang non-stop, but the producer wouldn't answer it. This was the most fun she'd had in 13 years in the news business, and she wasn't going to answer a call from Atlanta that might shut down the carnival.

"He's reached the top!" a technician shouted.

On screen, Jones stood at a closed door, trying to speak. His face shimmered with perspiration, and his shirt was stained from the front buttons to the center of his back. At some point during his climb, Jones had shed his expensive, white suit jacket.

The door behind Jones declared that only authorized personnel could proceed farther.

"The door's locked, right?" the producer asked anyone.

A technician, who'd once tried in vain to reach the roof on a fine spring day to smoke a joint, confirmed the assumption.

"So that's the end of the line for him, unless he drops dead of a heart attack. Which would also be the end of the line for him."

"What's he saying?"

The room quieted.

"If you will allow me a moment, I will use a key to open this door, and go out onto the roof, ready for the Lord to take me to my promised reward... Unless, of course, the world believes that the Reverend Carter Ray Jones International Ministry should continue our work of helping to protect and nurture Billy Smith's special family."

Jones fished in his pocket for the key and turned to the door, giving the world a full-screen shot of the wide, dark sweat stain down the center of the seat of his white pants.

Back on set, Governor Rolfe encountered the first serious resistance to her rampage — a security guard who'd watched the scene unfold on his television two floors up and dashed down to put an end to it.

The two opponents squared off across the shattered remains of Alexander Langston LaMourgan's desk, which Rolfe had been picking apart when she needed a new bludgeoning tool.

"Now, governor, I need you to calm down, just calm down," the guard soothed. "It's time to stop now, governor."

Rolfe stood in a half-crouch, legs flexed, shoulders square, arms high and ready.

"Really governor... it's over," the guard said, edging around the desk. Rolfe held her ground.

"Now, I'm gonna come around there, and we're gonna go sit down and rest for a minute, OK?"

When the guard was within five feet of the governor, Rolfe stumbled, then shuddered. Her eyes rolled up, then focused, then rolled up again, and she took a half stutter step to the left. Rolfe seemed about to collapse.

The guard stopped short.

"Governor?"

"Oh... dear..."

"Governor??"

"I feel…"

The governor didn't finish her sentence, but instead leaned forward, her hands on her knees.

"Are you OK, governor?"

"I feel… What's going on?"

Rolfe slowly straightened, looking wide-eyed at the disaster zone surrounding her. "Oh, my… gosh… What…? What on Earth happened?"

"Governor?"

"Y- yes. Who are you?"

"I'm security officer Darryl Pearlman, with GNBNC."

"What in heaven's name happened here?" Rolfe asked, surveying the wreckage, astounded.

"You don't remember?"

"No."

"Governor… you had some sort of seizure," Pearlman said, stepping forward…

…to within striking distance.

"HA!" Rolfe screamed as she drove her right foot hard and deep into the guard's groin.

Officer Pearlman dropped wordlessly to the floor. Rolfe watched him fall, then turned back to the set, where precious little remained to destroy.

Seeing a camera light blink on, Rolfe turned to face the viewing audience. For the hell of it, she decided to take a few others down with her.

"This is what I get! This is what I get!! I find out that Mike Montegrande is sleeping with his married campaign chairwoman. But I don't tell anyone, in exchange for a spot on the presidential ticket, and now he stabs me in the back!"

"Holy crap!" the producer exclaimed.

"Then the president promises me a cabinet appointment if I help him frame Tom Smith for murder. But what does that get me? Where's the president now?!" Rolfe shouted.

"Oh… my… God…" a technician mouthed.

"Oh my God!" shouted Montegrande, who'd turned back to GNBNC from a basketball game when Twitter exploded.

"Oh my God," muttered the president, sitting in his office.

"Bad pohson!" shouted Billy Smith, just off the set and 15 feet from the governor.

Rolfe turned toward the noise. Billy glared at her from his dad's arms. Amy *shhh*ed the child quietly, but it was too late. Rolfe had locked in.

Hiking up her torn skirt, Rolfe stepped over Chip Stone, still laying, bleeding, on the floor. Just as Rolfe lifted her back foot over Stone, the anchorman stirred, and squinted up at Rolfe.

"Nan-nan?"

Rolfe grinned. "Yeah. Nan-nan."

"Nan-nan!" Stone repeated. After Rolfe stepped past him, Stone rolled over onto his hands and knees, slowly making his way to his feet.

"*I've found the key!*"

It was Jones, still filling half the screen.

"Now I am going to step out onto the roof, and so help me God, if we cannot raise $50 million through my special, toll-free, holy hotline, 999-GO SAVE 'M, then may God take me!"

In the studio, and around the world, all eyes were on Jones hunched over the doorknob, repeatedly jamming the tip of the key into the metal around the key hole. Finally, by some miracle, he managed to stick it in.

With a triumphant look back at the camera, Jones turned the knob, swung open the door, and stepped out onto the roof. The storm's winds lifted Jones's gray hair toward the sky. The preacher stopped, and turned back toward the camera.

"NOW, AS GOD IS MY WITNESS--," he shouted over the wind…

And he was gone. There was never a question. The camera also never stood a chance. For that matter, neither did GNBNC's power system. Before the Reverend Carter Ray Jones could pause after the word "witness," a single, powerful lightning strike lit up his body with several million volts of electricity. His organs melted, his brain boiled in its own fluids, his shoes blew from his feet and off the top of the building. The heavy metal cross he wore over his shirt burned through the cotton fabric and branded the now dead preacher's chest. The instantaneous explosion of thunder knocked the solid roof door off one hinge, shattered the camera, and sent the cameraman tumbling down the stairs, unconscious but otherwise unhurt.

And it knocked out all power in the GNBNC building.

NINETY

The *ALL & Then Some!* set fell into darkness.

Everyone froze: Mary Rolfe in mid-stride toward the family; Chip Stone standing dazed next to the dismembered desk; the Smith family huddled together on the floor; Nick Walters standing close watch over his charges, with his chief of security positioned between the family and the governor; and, across the studio and in the shadows, a man with a rifle, deprived of light just as he lined up his shot on Billy Smith.

In the control booth, the producer told her crew to be ready to continue broadcasting when the emergency generator kicked in.

A second passed. Then another. And another. The emergency lights didn't come up.

Tom looked wildly around the pitch black studio. Where was Rolfe? What had happened to Jones? How badly was the security guard hurt? Why were the lights off? Weren't there any other police in the building? Tom felt a familiar rush of panic… but for the first time since his dad had died 31 years before, died right in front of Tom and his family in the living room — for the first time in all those years, Tom's powerful dread of death was justified. Death was near.

The crack of the rifle and a muzzle flash. Tom heard a muffled sound close by, then another shot rang out, and another, and Tom wasn't worried about muffled noises any more. With Billy in his arms, Tom grabbed fabric in front of him — was it Amy?

"*Get down!!*" Tom yelled as another gunshot split the darkness.

Tom pinned Billy to the cold tile, and waited for the next shot.

It didn't come. Instead, the emergency lighting around the set blinked on, and the bulbs' dim glow filled the room.

In the control booth, the producer quickly inventoried her monitors. All three cameras in the studio were functioning. The broadcast seemed to be continuing, albeit only on one half of the screen. The half previously documenting Reverend Carter Ray Jones's fundraising efforts now showed a blizzard of electronic snow.

"Cut from the roof camera!"

A long shot of the studio from Camera Three occupied the entire screen.

In the center, Rolfe stood defiant, either unafraid of the gunfire, incoherent or both. At her feet lay the crumpled security guard. On the edge of the set, the Smith family huddled together. On the opposite side of the screen, two men crouched, each holding something.

A high-pitched shriek filled the room, but not from anyone on camera. The producer tried to regain control of the broadcast.

In the Camera One shot, she could see Camera Two, with no cameraman. Camera Two's operator was flat on the floor, a coiled cord stretched from his headset to the camera.

"Camera One, pan left," the producer called, hoping to see what was going on. No response. The shrieking continued.

"Camera One? Pan left!" the producer repeated.

A muffled, very unhappy reply came back.

"Uh, somebody is shooting people down here," a voice said, low and quiet. "If you want the cameras moved, you better come down and do it yourself. I think me and the boys are gonna stay here on the floor."

"Holy shit," the producer said. "Get security on the phone."

"I've already got them," yelled a technician. "They're coming, but it will take a few minutes — all the lights in the building are out!"

The producer looked around the dimly but definitely lit set. "The emergency lights are on!" she yelled over the shrieking.

"Security says the emergency lights are not on anywhere except here," the technician responded. Looking for answers, he opened the control booth door, and found only more uncertainty. The room's faint emergency lighting leaked out into an unlit hallway.

"They're not on in the hall either!"

"So the only lights working are in the control booth and the studio?" the producer asked. "That doesn't make any sense! We don't have our own emergency generator."

As she tried to work out this impossible calculus, the source of the screaming appeared. Chip Stone stood up from behind the destroyed desk, clutching a dark stain on his shirt.

"I've been shot!!" Stone shouted through sobs. "Oh, God, please, no, don't let me die! *Don't let me die!!* I've been shot!"

Rolfe turned glassy-eyed toward Stone.

"Shut up you moron!" Rolfe shouted. "You're not shot! That's coffee!"

The producer could see the remains of a shattered coffee mug on the ground near Stone's feet.

"She's right!" she laughed. "It *is* coffee!"

Stone kept yelling, unpersuaded. "Oh God in Heaven above, please save me! I don't want to die! I don't want to die!!"

"I can't take this asshole anymore," the producer yelled. "Cut his mic!"

Immediately Stone's voice was reduced to a tinny background noise.

"Thanks," the producer said to the soundman.

"For what? I didn't do anything."

"You didn't just cut Stone's mic?"

"No."

"Then how…?"

In the studio, Tom struggled to make sense of the situation. Rolfe was still on her feet, like a freakish Frankenstinian experiment gone postal. Ten feet away, Richard lay on the floor, a large, tattered hole in his shirt, revealing a black vest with a deep indentation. He was breathing, but out cold. Nick Walters was nowhere to be seen.

Across the room, a dark-haired man with a rifle stood up from behind a wooden pallet and walked toward Tom and his family.

"No… *no*… NO…" Tom started in a whisper, then louder until he was shouting.

"NO!!!"

Tom stood and moved between the rifleman and his family. The man stopped, shrugged, and raised the rifle to his shoulder. Tom was looking right down the weapon's barrel.

This is it, Tom thought.

Focused on the gun, Tom caught movement out of the corner of his eye as a flash of a figure tore around a corner and across the room, toward the gunman. It was…

Reverend Waite?

The gunman reacted to the sound of running, but too late, and was struck full in the chest by a peace-loving (but very fit) preacher man.

The rifle spun away as they crashed to the floor. Not far behind came another running man, scooping up the rifle and pointing it at the two struggling men on the floor.

"No te muevas, amigo!" the man yelled.

It was…

Reverend Fogherty??

"Are we getting all this?" the shocked producer mumbled. The monitor showed an old man in a minister's outfit holding a rifle and yelling — in Spanish? — at two men wrestling on the floor… one who also appeared to be a minister.

"Uh…," a technician replied. "Yeah…"

"Let go of him and lay flat on the floor!" shouted Fogherty in American-accented Spanish. "Or I *will* shoot you!" In the leg, Fogherty added to himself.

The man fighting Waite stopped, then haltingly obeyed, all the while scanning the room.

"Now *you* freeze!" came another sharp voice, in broken English, on cue.

A man stepped from the shadows holding a pistol.

"Drop the rifle, old man," said the second gunman. His accent was thick, but his intentions were clear.

Fogherty recognized the monster who had confessed to killing — or trying to kill — the Smith family. He reluctantly put down the rifle.

The gunman looked around the room, and Chip Stone dropped to the floor like a rock, not shot for the second time tonight.

The man ignored Stone.

"Where's the kid?"

Amy reflexively pulled Billy close. The movement caught the gunman's attention.

"Ah," said the gunman, dark eyes revealing no emotion. Motioning with the pistol, he said, "Bring him to me."

Tom shook his head.

"Bring him to me!" the gunman repeated, louder.

Tom stood his ground.

"OK, then I'll come to him," the man said in a tone so cold that Tom shivered.

The man surveyed the space between him and the kid. A straight line to the family ran right by the still standing crazy woman. The gunman took one look at the disheveled, bloody, half-dressed figure and decided not to take any chances.

"Hey, lady!" he called out. "Move away."

Rolfe turned toward the man.

"Move away, señora!"

"Screw you!" Rolfe replied under her breath.

"Lady! I got a gun! Move your ass!"

"Shut the hell up," Rolfe said, squaring her shoulders to the gunman.

"Here's what I'm gonna do," the gunman said, losing patience. "I'm gonna take one step toward you, and if you don't *move* away, I'm gonna *blow* you away. You got that?"

"Here's what *I'm* gonna do," Rolfe responded. "I'm gonna take one step toward *you*, then another, and then another, and then I'm gonna take that gun, pull out the bullets, and jam one of those bullets through your heart using my bare hands. Comprende, señor?"

"Suit yourself," the gunman said, then swung the pistol up to chest height and pulled the trigger, sending a bullet into Rolfe's chest.

Amy pulled Billy's face close to her, so he wouldn't see what had happened. But what *had* happened?

The impact had knocked Rolfe back two steps — but she didn't fall.

Then she took one step forward. And another…

POW!

A second bullet ripped into the governor, just below her collarbone. This time she was spun around 180 degrees.

But, again, she didn't fall. In slow motion, Rolfe turned back to face her attacker, and took another two steps toward him. The gunman's jaw hung open, but his gun remained chest high. When Rolfe took a third step, closing to within five feet, the gunman stepped backward, stumbling over the base of a camera as he fired again, this time at Rolfe's head.

Blood sprayed from the side of Rolfe skull, spewing from a wide, fleshy gap where her left ear had been a split-second earlier. The glancing shot didn't slow Rolfe a bit, and before the gunman could comprehend that this woman had not fallen, much less died, she was in the gunman's face.

"I'm not having a very good day, friend," Rolfe growled. "Why should you?"

In a flash, Rolfe reached out, grabbed the man by the shirt and yanked him right up to her face. With a snarl she bit the attacker on the chin, ripping off a tablespoon of flesh in the process, then spit the chunk right back into the man's face. The gunman flipped out, falling away from Rolfe screaming in pain. He still had the gun, but didn't even seem aware of it as he pawed at his face with his other hand.

That gave Waite the opening he needed, and from a lineman's crouch he exploded up and into the wounded gunman's lower back, driving him forward, forward, forward until the man, arms flailing, crashed headfirst into a square steel support beam. The gunman's skull was the main point of high-energy contact with one of the corners of the I-beam, and he was knocked unconscious.

Fogherty scrambled for the rifle, just beating out the first gunman. Fogherty ordered the man back to the floor. But his command was drowned out by several large men breaking through the doors to the studio.

"FREEZE! EVERYBODY FREEZE!"

Five members of the GNBNC security detail stormed into the studio, guns drawn. Tom dropped to grab his family, finally sure they had been saved.

"I think I need to sit down," Rolfe murmured, before collapsing.

NINETY-ONE

It was an odd sensation, the squirting feeling inside his own chest. Yes, there was pain — a lot of pain. But alongside of the pain, the man could feel every beat of his heart, and with every beat he could feel a surge of fluid within him, and he knew. It was time.

"Tom…"

Beyond the pain, over the sensation of leaking within him, he could hear himself call out — raspy, gurgling, fading. The room was dark, and the man wondered if he were already dying, if his eyes were already failing.

"Tom!" he managed to half-bark.

"Nick?"

"Tom…"

"Nick! *Nick!*"

Tom ran over to Walters and knelt beside him, in a puddle of dark, thick liquid.

"Oh Jesus! Oh Jesus! You're OK! You're all right! You're going to be all right!"

Amy was beside Tom now. Billy sat, terrified, 15 feet away. Reverend Waite grabbed Billy and carried him to the far end of the set to protect him from the difficult situation.

"Let's get you an ambulance," Tom said, breathless. "Someone call an ambulance! *Call 911!*"

"They're on their way," a voice announced from the ceiling.

Tom didn't seem to hear. "Nick! Nick! Oh Jesus Nick!"

Amy's heart was breaking, for Nick and for her husband, but she was focused on Nick.

"OK, Mr. Walters…" she began.

"Call me Nick!" Walters said with a short laugh, followed by quick, short coughs. The wound in his chest emitted a tiny sucking sound with each cough. Walters tried to lift his head to look down at the source of the odd noise. Then his gaze returned to Amy, and his eyes crinkled some at the corners.

"Call me Nick," he managed to gasp, the corners of his mouth curled down in a grim smile, but a smile nonetheless.

Amy shook her head at the old man's guts. "OK Nick," she smiled back at him. "I'm going to take a look at this wound."

Walters nodded his head slightly, and looked up at the ceiling.

Amy gently pulled the matted, darkened sweater away from around the bullet hole, then turned her head away from Walters's face.

"Oh Lord…" Tom heard her whisper, and he realized Amy had turned from Nick so he couldn't hear what she said, and couldn't read her lips.

Opposite Tom, Richard knelt down beside Walters, having regained consciousness seconds before. He leaned in, examining the old man's bloody chest. Almost immediately Richard pulled back up, his face stony, revealing nothing. He looked at Amy and Tom. Richard knew Amy was an EMT in the Army, and her medical training was quite evident by the look in her face.

Amy saw her own diagnosis reflected in Richard's eyes.

"Richard…" Walters rasped.

"Quiet, Mr. Walters," Richard spoke, almost too low to hear. Walters heard.

"I'm sorry, Mr. Walters," Richard said, voice steady but sorrowful. "I'm sorry."

Richard had been shot in the chest, and the impact on the bullet-proof vest was so substantial it knocked the huge man out cold. Yet he obviously was blaming himself for Walters's wounding.

"I'm sorry, Mr. Walters," Richard repeated.

"It's OK, Richard," Walters said. "It's OK. It was time, Richard. It's OK."

Richard blinked once, his jaw muscles flexing.

"Richard…" Walters said. "Thank you."

"Of course, Mr. Walters," Richard said, smiling. Amy was amazed at Richard's composure, and the look in his eyes: warmth, and affection, but, still, unspeakable sadness.

"Let me get something under your head, Mr. Walters," Richard said. Walters nodded slightly.

Tom locked eyes with Walters. "You're OK. You're going to be OK. Don't die. Please don't die! Please don't die!!"

"Tom…, Tom…" Walters said

"You can't die. You can't die!"

"Tom…"

"You can't!" Tom's voice cracked, and he took a quick breath. "Not again…"

"Tom, it's OK," Walters managed to get out.

"It's *not* OK! It's *not* OK!" Tom almost shouted. "Where's Billy? WHERE'S BILLY??

"Tom, no," Amy said, trying to grab her husband by the shoulders.

"Where's Billy?!" Tom was shouting, looking wildly around. "Bring him here. Billy, heal Nick!! Heal him!! *Heal him goddamnit!*"

Startled by his father's shouting, Billy began to cry. Amy rushed to her son and gathered him in her arms.

"Heal him," Tom whispered, his shoulders dropping, beginning to shake, as he leaned back over Walters.

One of the cameramen had returned to his station and was zooming in on the scene around Walters, but only those in the control booth noticed. There, on the monitors, was a tight shot of the tragedy unfolding.

A tear fell from above onto Walters's dry face, dripping down his cheek.

Tom's felt a hand on his cheek — a rough hand. It was Walters.

"Tom, listen," Walters said, and Tom paused, taking a breath, trying to listen.

"Son, don't shout at your little boy," Walters said gently, firmly. "Even if he *were* God, you don't have to yell."

Tom grabbed Walters's hand.

"God can hear you, without yelling," Walters said. "He can hear the whisper of your heart. He knows you're upset. I know you're upset. You're losing me, just like you lost your father."

"No!" Tom whispered, and he pulled another sorrowful breath.

"But it's time for me to go now," said Walters. "This is part of life. It's the price we pay for getting to live."

Walters looked deep into the young man's eyes.

"Maybe you and your family are who I was meant to help, where I would make a difference. I think you were, and I thank you for that," he said. "I was never there for my children, and I should have been. You and your family gave me a second chance, and brought more meaning to my life than any job ever could.

"Don't curse God — thank Him for giving you this life, even this moment," Walters said. "I'm praying right now that I'll get to spend eternity in those few loving moments that I *did* have with my children, before I left them for my business.

"Tom," implored Walters, color fading. "I'm at peace. So please, be at peace. Be at peace with this."

Reverend Fogherty had crept to Tom's side, and knelt and put his arm around Tom's shoulders.

"Be at peace, Tom," Walters gasped out. "I love you, son."

As Walters's eyes closed, Tom's opened up. He sank his face into Reverend Fogherty's shoulder, and wept.

NINETY-TWO

March 1 was warm, warmer even than relatively temperate Commonwealth of Virginia was used to. In the mountains near Charlottesville, the snow that covered much of the ground during February had melted away, and on this pre-spring day, song birds flitted from tree to tree, chirping and gathering materials to construct their summer homes.

Tom and Amy sat on the patio outside the French doors of Nick Walters's dining room, warming themselves and watching their son romp in the reborn greenness of the lawn.

After Walters had died that terrible night in Washington, the Smith family had moved temporarily, and reluctantly, into the Walters's estate. Tom and Amy had resisted the idea — they felt like squatters — but Walters's chief of security and the businessman's attorney had insisted. It was what Nick would have wanted, they said, and finally Tom and Amy had relented — but only for a little while. As soon as the world had calmed down about Billy and all that had happened that unbelievable week, they planned to move the family back into their home on Crystaldale Lane in West End Manor. But Tom and Amy dreaded that their world would never return to normal. If they couldn't move back to their home, what could they do?

Reverend Waite stepped through the doors from the dining room, sipping from a coffee mug and smiling at the sight of Billy playing in the grass. Richard had asked Fogherty to spend some time with the family, to help them deal with the traumatic week. Fogherty had demurred, and instead asked Waite to take the lead on this assignment.

After watching Billy for a moment or two, Reverend Waite turned to Tom and Amy.

"They're ready for you," he said.

Tom and Amy shared a look of apprehension, then rose and walked into the house, and over to the door of the richly appointed study in the front of the home.

A deep breath, and Tom opened the door and walked in with Amy. Several people in the room rose, and the first to reach them, hand extended, was a man whose face emanated the essence of Nick Walters.

"Hi Tom, Amy," the man said, smiling. "I am John Walters, Nick's son."

Tom felt a rush of sadness for the man.

"I am so sorry for your loss."

"And I for yours," Walters responded. "I know you were close to my dad."

In turn, the rest of the room introduced themselves: Nick's other son, Daniel, Nick's daughter Madison, and their spouses all stepped forward. A beautiful, older woman introduced herself as Nick's former wife, then introduced her husband.

Nick Walters's attorney gently suggested that they all sit down.

"We're here today to read the last will and testament of Nicholas Walters."

"Can I say one thing?" Tom interrupted. The lawyer nodded.

"We really don't belong here. This is a family matter, and as much as we did love Nick and appreciate everything he did for us, we are not family. I'm sure this is a tough time for you, and we have no business being here."

"To the contrary," the attorney said. "Nick's will specifies that you both be here."

"And moreover, you belong here because you *are* family," John spoke up.

"Each of us," he said, motioning to his siblings, "lost a father years ago, when dad was so engrossed with his companies. He was never the dad we needed.

"But you made it possible for us to have our dad back. You gave him the chance to be the man he always knew he should have been, and you gave us the chance, through your ordeal and through the broadcast that night, to see into our dad's eyes and into his heart and to see how much he regretted our lost relationships. It was the apology that we, in our anger and hurt, never allowed him to make. For each of us, it was a healing moment."

The others in the room nodded in agreement.

"As sad as it was to lose dad, it was a moment of redemption, for him and for us, when you held his hand as he died, when you pulled from him the exact words that we needed to hear. You brought us together again, as a family. Your presence here today is not just appropriate, it feels very natural to us all."

Again the others nodded.

Tom opened his mouth, but could not get out words. Amy provided the words for her husband.

"Thank you."

"You are also here as part of the proceedings today," the attorney said. "I will read the exact language of the will momentarily, but I can give you the essence of it right now."

"Nick, as you know, generated a tremendous amount of wealth during his life," the attorney continued. "More than two billion dollars, in fact. It was Nick's wish that this wealth be distributed equally among his children…"

Amy and Tom both responded with confused smiles. The attorney smiled back but did not slow down to explain. Instead, the lawyer reached into an accordion folder in front of him and pulled out what looked like four small black key chains, the kind that can unlock a car door with the push of a button. John Walters laughed out loud when he saw the devices.

"Congratulations!" he said to Tom.

Tom looked even more confused in response.

"Dad sent one of those to all of us a while back," John said. "We don't know which security service it is connected to, but it must be top shelf. The one time I had to use it, I was overwhelmed by security people within five minutes. In the note he sent with it, Dad said it's some kind of family security plan he'd bought into."

A light went on in Tom's brain — *the security service!* The same that warned them of the impending commando attack that morning, and the same that had alerted Richard that fighter jets were moving in to intercept the helicopter.

"Nick wanted me to give you these security remotes," said the attorney. "You are now covered by the same security service that protects Nick's family."

Tom and Amy realized that their world had just flipped. Their family might now actually have a chance at, if not a normal life, then at least a life of relative safety from the thousands of still obsessed crazies.

"Thank you," Tom said to the family. It didn't seem enough, but he wasn't sure what else to say.

John Walters grinned in reply. "Of course," he said. With a glance, Walters invited the attorney to continue.

This one is a chip off the old block, Tom thought with admiration at the younger Walters's composure and grace.

"To Nick's three natural children, he asked me to express his deepest apologies," said the attorney, continuing the process. "He knew very well that he could not buy your love. He noted that he'd tried that years ago without success. But with nothing else to give, he asked that you each be granted one-quarter shares of his fortune — approximately $480 million each."

Tom smiled again. He was glad to see this turn of good fortune for Nick's kids. They seemed like good people.

"And to you, Tom and Amy," the attorney continued. "Nick also bequeaths the sum of approximately $480 million dollars, along with this estate."

Tom and Amy were dumbstruck. Finally, Tom's thoughts gained traction. "This can't be right. This isn't right. We aren't Nick's children. We have no right to any part of his inheritance. We cannot accept it."

"That is a noble sentiment," John said, smiling. "It speaks well for you and helps explain why dad came to be so fond of you both."

"We," John continued, again speaking for his siblings, who nodded in agreement, "are very satisfied with your presence in this room and in dad's will. You gave us a gift, and gave dad a gift, that we never would've had. You belong here, and that inheritance is rightly yours."

"If I may add to that," said the attorney. "Please allow me to read a passage from Nick's will, where he addresses you and Amy directly: 'Money can't buy happiness,' he said. 'Lord knows, I'm a poster child for the truth in that. But it can sometimes buy some space, and within that space maybe you can build a somewhat normal life for your family.'"

Tom couldn't stop himself. Amy was fighting it too, but neither could hold back the tears. For three weeks, they'd not only been grieving the loss of their friend, but the loss of their lives, as they had begun to understand that nothing would ever again be "normal."

Now they had a chance to build a real life, or at least to create around Billy the feel of a real life, while the rest of the world forgot about The Miracle at St. Thomas's.

"I... don't... know what to say," Tom murmured.

John smiled. "Say a prayer."

"Yeah," said Tom. "Yeah."

"We will," said Amy.

EPILOGUE

Following her serious wounding on international television, Governor Mary Rolfe took an extended, open-ended medical leave from her job (ironically, under a medical leave act that she had introduced as a state senator six years before), and checked herself into Freeman Psychiatric Pavilion in Richmond, Virginia. According to an FBI missing person investigation, after Mary Rolfe was released 18 months later, she bought a one-way ticket to St. Barts in the Caribbean. She has not been heard from since.

But she was *seen* since. Governor Rolfe's rampage on *ALL & Then Some!* was almost immediately pirated, remixed with audio from the event into a goofy rap song and became a viral sensation.

Governor Rolfe was replaced by Democrat Lt. Governor Jim Moron ("it's pronounced *mo-ROW-an*"), who immediately leaked to the press that he was positioning for a run for the presidency in five years. Sadly for acting-Governor Moron, he lost the intervening gubernatorial election and went back to selling used cars. The winner of that election, Republican Jack Cruuck ("it's pronounced *cru-WOK*") immediately announced that he was a candidate for the Republican presidential nomination, at which point his chief of staff, Scott Butler, resigned.

The Jones International Ministry and Christ Almighty Family Theme Park folded in the wake of Carter Ray Jones's sudden death — not because Jones had died, but because a raid by the FBI, the Bureau of Alcohol, Tobacco and

Firearms, the Securities and Exchange Commission, and the Nashville Sheriff's Department revealed that the ministry's accounting firm had falsified earnings reports. Turns out the ministry did not gross $1 billion annually after all.

Chip Stone landed a job anchoring *Inside Edition*. Deborah Norville, formerly anchor on *Inside Edition*, wound up on *The View*. Whoopi Goldberg, formerly of *The View*, went to GNBNC, where she took over the *ALL & Then Some!* show. Alexander Langston LaMourgan retired to Driggs, Idaho, where he became a potato farmer.

Lewis Plinkdunk, the recently promoted assistant to the director for *ALL & Then Some!*, accepted a post as assistant deputy press secretary in the office of the president after the election. After serving 3 1/2 years in that capacity, Plinkdunk returned to the news business, accepting a position as the assistant associate producer for *Good Morning USA*.

Stonewall Jackson, former press secretary to Governor Rolfe, became chief spokesperson for the Society for the Prevention of Cruelty to Animals.

The two assassins were deported to Venezuela, and were back in the U.S. within 48 hours.

The president of the United States denied that any deal had ever been made with Governor Rolfe. GOP presidential candidate Mike Montegrande similarly denied any deals with the governor. Montegrande went on to say that, given the long list of women who had claimed affairs with the president, it wouldn't be surprising if the president had slept with Governor Rolfe. The president responded that if Montegrande wanted to play that game, he would be happy to release "a list I have in my pocket" of women that Montegrande had liaised with. From there, the campaign turned *really* dirty, and both candidates surpassed 90% in their negative ratings. At a crucial point in the campaign, the president was caught downloading child pornography and, on the same day, a whistleblower leaked certain Montegrande business records that showed he was a tax cheat, stiffed small business owners he worked with, fooled around on his wife while she was giving birth, and once intentionally ran over a puppy in the middle of Fifth Avenue. Despite the new allegations, both candidates' staunchest supporters remained committed, saying, essentially: "he may be a philanderer / child-porn user / tax cheat / scumbag / puppy killer, but he's right on the issues."

The presidential campaign reached new lows in sleaze, even for an American election, and in late October, Ralph Nader entered the race as a third-party write-in candidate. Voter turn-out plummeted to a historic low: just 35%. Ralph Nader won a plurality of the vote and the Electoral College. President Nader's vice-president, Michael Moore, wasted no time claiming an international group of business leaders are ruling the world and *may* have connections to the Knights Templar. Voters welcomed the hijinks of Vice-President Moore and his boss — like the business cabal claim — viewing the wacky proclamations as the first step toward putting politics (if not government) back in its rightful place as harmless entertainment. Eventually Vice-President Moore came to be known as "Crazy Uncle Mike."

Just four weeks after the event at St. Thomas's, a food fight of a public debate broke out between Jack Munroe, owner of GNBNC, and Mike Titan, owner of 39% of the radio stations in the country and 32% of the television stations. The issue: FCC broadcast station ownership limits and affiliate rights. Munroe was trying to keep Titan from acquiring more stations, citing "the right to free speech guaranteed in the Fourth Amendment." Titan was trying to force Munroe to take GNBNC public, since it was "un-American" for one person to own so dominant a network as GNBNC. Each side claimed possession of leaked memos from the other's camp that contained damning information. The media couldn't resist so media-centered a story, and soon there were reporters covering the reporters who were covering the reporters who were covering the spat between media moguls. As the battle between the two uber-egos became more personal, each slung allegations about the other's business ethics and accounting standards, which then led to charges regarding the other's marital fidelity, sexual orientation and use of hair-growth and/or hair replacement techniques. The pitched public pissing match pushed every other story off the front pages, including that of the miracle kid of St. Thomas's, and many of those formerly hot stories never reignited.

Oddly, if anyone had had access to both camps, they would have realized that the initial set of leaked documents had come from neither Munroe's nor Titan's people, but instead from a post office in New Jersey in an unmarked envelope. Also odd, at least to Tom Smith, was the fact that the head of his family's security detail, an imposing and wily security pro named Richard, was able to predict each turn in the media mogul news story before it hit the airwaves.

ABOUT THE AUTHOR

Writer and humorist Chuck Hansen has worked as press secretary for a member of Congress, speechwriter for a Virginia governor, communications director for a Virginia Secretary of Transportation, executive speechwriter and communications professional with four Fortune 500 companies, and humor columnist for a number of magazines and newspapers. Prior to finding his direction in life, Chuck worked as a bouncer in a Caribbean saloon, blackjack dealer, private detective, copier salesman, donut maker, daycare teacher, and waiter (for 2 hours). Chuck and his wife, Stacy, have two adult children, Daniel and Madison, and live in Midlothian, Virginia.

69261466R00183

Made in the USA
Columbia, SC
14 August 2019